Praise for t

EXI

"The intensity Hamilton generates here is almost too much—like a wailing siren growing steadily louder at the same time its pitch climbs ever higher—but readers will be utterly powerless to close the book. Noir is all about characters attempting to find options for themselves where none exist. The brilliance of this thoroughly uncompromising novel lies in the way Hamilton, with the legerdemain of a master conjurer, turns despair to hope and back again, finally blending the two into their own unique nightmare world. Stunning." —*Booklist* (starred review)

"A compelling trek across very dark terrain putting Nick Mason through increasingly pulse-pounding paces with so much nonstop suspense, I read the book in two sittings." —*The Huffington Post*

"*The Second Life of Nick Mason* rocketed Steve Hamilton to literary stardom, all the reasons for which are on clear display in that book's sequel, *Exit Strategy*. . . . The book's brisk prose wondrously sets the tone, starting with, 'You kill one person, it changes you. You kill five . . . it's not about changing anymore.' Think Don Winslow at his coolest, as Hamilton turns up the heat in a bold, bracing, and brilliant thriller." —*Providence Journal*

"Moves so quickly you instantly find yourself sucked into its slipstream and pulled along like a water-skier behind a low-flying rocket careening toward the finale." —*New York Journal of Books*

"A page-turning thriller." —*Chicago News*

"Another knockout performance . . . Hamilton has carefully crafted an atmospheric, edgy thriller with strong characters and a swiftly escalating tension level. . . . Easily one of the best crime novels of the year—even though it surely will be facing strong competition." —*Lansing State Journal*

"If you enjoy thrillers drenched in moral ambiguity and propelled by nonstop action, you should check out this series." —*Dayton Daily News*

"One of our favorite authors, Steve Hamilton, continues the gritty, action-packed saga of Nick Mason in his newest book, *Exit Strategy*. . . . If you have weekend plans, clear them. This is the kind of book that demands to be read in one sitting. . . . The pacing is stunning, cinematic in its precision." —*Harbor Light News*

"How does Nick resolve this second life he is now forced to live? The manner in which he does so is revealed in this fascinating novel by Steve Hamilton, and the suspenseful way he accomplishes it is typical of what we have come to expect from this author, in this newest page-turner. . . . Expect the unexpected from this wonderful author. . . . Highly recommended." —*Midwest Book Review*

"A fiery, muscular narrative that travels at relentless speed, *Exit Strategy* is a page-turner." —*Seattle Review of Books*

THE SECOND LIFE OF NICK MASON

"So good, it legitimately stands shoulder to padded paranoid shoulder with the classics of the crime noir genre. . . . There are so many terrific elements in this novel—Nick's haunted character, a plot that never darts in the direction you expect it to, and a truly ingenious climax—that I could be here till Labor Day singing its praises." —Maureen Corrigan, NPR's *Fresh Air*

"A suspenseful, fast-paced crime novel with the same heart, well-drawn characters and muscular prose that fans of [Hamilton's] popular Alex McKnight series and his fine stand-alone novels such as *The Lock Artist* have come to expect." —Associated Press

"A fine premise, a vibrant setting, a charismatic antihero . . . It's a tight, gripping book about a man hell-bent on reinventing himself against long odds." —*The New York Times*

EXIT STRATEGY

A NICK MASON NOVEL

STEVE HAMILTON

G. P. PUTNAM'S SONS   NEW YORK

G. P. PUTNAM'S SONS
Publishers Since 1838
An imprint of Penguin Random House LLC
375 Hudson Street
New York, New York 10014

Copyright © 2017 by Cold Day Productions, LLC

The Library of Congress has catalogued the G. P. Putnam's Sons hardcover edition as follows:

Names: Hamilton, Steve, author.
Title: Exit strategy : a Nick Mason novel / Steve Hamilton.
Description: New York : G. P. Putnam's Sons, 2017.
Identifiers: LCCN 2017003034 (print) | LCCN 2017007932 (ebook) | ISBN 9780399574382 (hardback) | ISBN 9780399574399 (epub)
Subjects: LCSH: Ex-convicts—Fiction. | Organized crime—Fiction. | BISAC: FICTION / Crime. | FICTION / Suspense. | GSAFD: Suspense fiction.
Classification: LCC PS3558.A44363 E95 2017 (print) | LCC PS3558.A44363 (ebook) | DDC 813/.54—dc23
LC record available at https://lccn.loc.gov/2017003034

First G. P. Putnam's Sons hardcover edition / May 2017
First G. P. Putnam's Sons international edition / May 2017
First G. P. Putnam's Sons premium edition / April 2018
G. P. Putnam's Sons premium edition ISBN: 9780399574405

Printed in the United States of America
1   3   5   7   9   10   8   6   4   2

TO JULIA
AGAIN AND ALWAYS

EXIT STRATEGY

1

YOU KILL ONE PERSON, IT CHANGES YOU.

You kill five . . . it's not about changing anymore.

It's who you are.

Quintero knew this. He'd seen it in other men. Had seen it in himself. He saw it now as he watched Nick Mason prepare, remembering the day he picked him up at the gates of the federal prison in Terre Haute.

Remembering Mason's first job, in the motel room. The look on his face afterward—blank, bloodless—when he brought the Mustang to the chop shop.

When he said he'd never do it again.

Until the next phone call.

That was the unwritten contract Nick Mason had signed. Twenty years of his life back in exchange for his service to Darius Cole. On call twenty-four hours a day, seven days a week. To do whatever was asked of him.

No matter what it was.

*   *   *

MASON STRIPPED OFF HIS SHIRT to reveal the lean, hard muscles of a middleweight and pale white skin with no tattoos.

Even after five and a half years inside, he had come out without one drop of jailhouse ink on his body. Cole had made sure of it. Mason strapped on the soft-armor tactical vest, thick enough to stop anything up to a .44 Magnum, then he pulled on the black turtleneck over that. With the black pants, the black rubber-soled shoes, it was the uniform of a professional. He took the black balaclava, formed it into a skullcap, and put it on over his close-cut hair. He pulled down the mask, adjusted it across his eyes, took one look in the mirror. Satisfied, he rolled it back up.

Quintero took the black canvas bag from his shoulder and put it down on the table. Mason unzipped the bag and looked inside.

"Everything you'll need is in there," Quintero said. "You have to remember, these are high-end guys. Top shape, know how to use their firearms."

"How many of them?"

"Between ten and twelve," he said. "Not enough to stop you."

Mason shook his head as he tried on the scuba gloves.

"What's the most important thing I told you?" Quintero asked.

"Stay off the twenty-first floor," Mason said. "At exactly ten o'clock, it's going to blow."

"Once that happens, you'll be able to walk right out of there."

Mason nodded.

"Tell me the plan again," Quintero said. "Step by step."

"The delivery truck," Mason said. "It enters the parking garage at exactly nine thirty-five p.m. . . ."

NICK MASON WATCHED THE TRUCK turn into the parking garage from Columbus Drive. It stopped at the large metal door while the driver waited for the man at the window to slide the door open. This gave Mason twenty seconds to climb under the truck, grab on to the exhaust system brackets, and lift his body's weight from the concrete, the canvas bag looped tight to his back. The scuba gloves were thin and flexible, giving him a good grip and protecting every surface, even the underside of this truck, from fingerprints.

The truck rolled a hundred yards until it came to a stop, and the door slid shut behind it. When the truck was turned off, Mason lowered himself to the ground and stayed there, the canvas bag next to him.

It was 9:37 p.m., most of the business offices on the ground floor closed, the dinner rush at the restaurants over. Mason waited for the driver to get out of the truck, then followed a dozen yards behind him. He was inside the building.

The Aqua. Eighty-two stories high, one of the most distinctive buildings in downtown Chicago, on the north side of the Loop, with undulating balconies that wrap around the building on all four sides like rippling water. Inside, the theme continues through all of the decor, from the blue-and-green color scheme to the saltwater fish tank in the lobby.

Mason moved quickly, without rushing, knowing exactly where to find the freight elevator. The target was on the forty-third floor, so he hit the button for 42, then used the fireman's override to take him all the way to his floor without stopping.

When he got to the forty-second floor, Mason stepped out of the elevator into the empty hallway. He spotted a room service tray on the floor outside one of the rooms, picked that up, and emptied it of all of the items except for the silver plate cover. Then he went to the stairwell at the end of the hallway and took the stairs up to forty-three.

Mason cracked open the stairwell door and scanned the hallway. The marshal was sitting in a chair outside the door, seven or eight doors down. Young, maybe thirty. Stocky. He looked more bored than vigilant. Mason opened up his canvas bag, took out the Mossberg 500 shotgun. Pistol grip model, with the shorter barrel. Six-shell capacity. It was loaded with what the manufacturer artfully called a crowd control munition, silicone plugs that they said would cause "nonlethal but incapacitative trauma" upon impact.

Incapacitative trauma.

In other words, it would only make you *wish* you were dead.

"*You need to get over this,*" Quintero said to him. "*Killing one man and leaving everybody else alive.*"

Mason didn't answer. He loaded the plugs into the shotgun.

"*That gun in your hands, you think it cares who's on the other end?*"

Mason looked up at him.

"*You gotta be the same way,*" Quintero said. "*Before this bullshit gets you killed.*"

Mason took the H&K USP semiautomatic from the bag and put it in his belt. The cartridge held fifteen nine-millimeter rounds, with a sixteenth already chambered. Finally, he took out the stun baton and hooked it to his belt. Eighteen inches long, three pounds of reinforced aluminum, with a "police force level" rating of twelve million volts that would shut down a man's entire neuromuscular system. One more piece of insurance.

Mason dropped the empty canvas bag to the floor, put a pair of low-profile plugs into his ears, then took one final moment to breathe, to focus on what was about to happen, because once it started it would all flow quickly, one movement after another, without a single beat of hesitation.

He opened the stairwell door and moved down the hallway. The room service tray hid the semiautomatic in his belt—positioned at eleven o'clock for a right-handed cross draw—and also hid the baton and most of the shotgun.

The marshal stood up and said, "Hey! You can't be here!"

That moment of indecision as the marshal reached for his radio. Mason dropped the tray and leveled the shotgun at the man's chest, had just enough time to see the young man's eyes go wide as he pulled the trigger and sent the silicone plug into his abdomen, just below the tactical vest.

The marshal went down, curled up in a ball. He wouldn't be getting back up, not without a lot of help and some pain medication. Mason pulled the balaclava down over his face as he approached him. The man looked even younger up close—a kid who had no business being stationed here alone. Mason reached into the man's jacket and removed the Glock from his holster, along with his radio. Then he took out the pen from his own pocket—the tip had been replaced by a DC adapter and the barrel contained a circuit board that would read the 32-bit hotel code and repeat it back to the card reader in less than a second.

He knew the clock was ticking now. Somebody had heard that shot, was already calling down to the front desk.

"The marshal inside the room is the leader of the team. He's

an iron man. Eight hours straight, he doesn't leave his client's side. Not to sleep, not to eat, not to use the fucking bathroom— unless he actually drags the man in there with him.

"He takes this shit personally, and he can shoot. They got one of his target sheets hanging up at the range. So don't fuck around."

Mason plugged the pen into the charging port on the bottom of the door's locking mechanism and the light flashed green. He pushed the door, ready to kick it all the way open when it caught against the security latch, but the door swung free.

Mason stepped inside, staying close to the wall. He didn't see any movement in the room. The only light was the nighttime ambient glow coming from the window. He took a few more steps into the room, his right finger on the shotgun trigger. As he looked into the small kitchen, then the bedroom and the bathroom, the truth became obvious:

There was nobody here.

No marshal. No target.

The room was a decoy.

"How do we know the accountant will be there? If he's in WITSEC—"

"We have a marshal on the inside. McLaren has been moved up to Chicago for a pretrial deposition."

Ken McLaren, once Darius Cole's chief accountant. A former IRS agent, a genius at moving money overseas, "re-domiciling it" by investing in businesses that all looked legal on paper, then bringing the money back, avoiding any taxes.

For almost a decade, he made Cole a shitload of money.

Then McLaren's son got picked up on the University of Chicago campus with a dealer-weight bag of ecstasy pills, and they held that over McLaren's head until he agreed to testify against Cole.

"You're setting up for the retrial," Mason said.

"You don't need to worry about that. All you need to worry about is—"

"I know. I hit him, then I leave."

"Don't even think about the second thing until you've done the first."

Mason went back out to the hallway and grabbed the marshal, still curled up in a fetal position and holding his abdomen. He cried out in pain as Mason dragged him into the room and closed the door.

"Where is he?"

The marshal didn't respond. Mason put the barrel of the shotgun against the man's temple.

"Strike one . . . Where is he?"

"Fuck you," the marshal said.

Mason moved the barrel from the man's temple to his leg, pulled the trigger, and sent the silicone plug at sonic speed into the thigh muscle. The man recoiled from the shock of it, and then a half second later the trauma arranged itself into one coherent message to his brain and he started screaming.

Mason gave the man a few seconds to wear himself out. Then he put the barrel back to the man's temple.

"Strike two . . . Where is he?"

"Up," the man said, sputtering and trying to catch his breath.

"Up where?"

"Ten floors. Fifty-three."

"Which room?"

"I don't know."

Mason put the barrel against the man's temple again. "5307."

Mason took the handcuffs from the man's belt, hooked one to the man's right wrist, and dragged him a few feet over to the bar top, where there was an old-fashioned brass footrail near floor level. He hooked the free cuff to the rail, then he took the phone off the bar and threw it in the kitchen sink. As he bent down to take the man's cell phone, he put his mouth close to his ear.

"If he's not there, I'll make you wish I had killed you."

Mason picked up the room service tray on his way out, went back to the stairwell, and climbed ten floors to fifty-three. He cracked open the hallway door.

The hallway was empty.

No man out front, one more way to keep the room a secret.

Mason moved quickly down to 5307, took out the pen, and keyed the lock. He was surprised once again when the door didn't catch on the latch, barely had time to process how the marshal had set him up for this, when the door behind him swung open.

"Freeze!"

Mason turned just in time to face the gun blast and feel the impact against his chest, the bullet halted by the vest but the force spreading out through his body like he'd been hit by a sack of cement. He pulled the trigger of the shotgun as he fell backward, but the shot was high. The marshal was already stepping forward, lining up for his second shot, when Mason fired again. This time, he hit the man in the groin and he went down, landing on Mason's legs.

Mason pushed the man off him. This man was older, with graying hair and a worn face—had probably been a marshal for thirty years at least. Sworn to protect his clients with his life. He clutched at his groin with both hands, his eyes closed tight, sucking in air with rapid breaths through clenched teeth. Mason took the man's Glock and his radio and then dragged him into the apartment across the hall.

The place was barely furnished. Couch, television, coffee table, lots of empty space and nowhere to hide. He went into the kitchen. Then the bedroom, looked under the bed, in the empty closet. He went into the bathroom and slid open the shower curtain.

Where the hell is McLaren?

Mason came back into the main room, stood there for a moment, remembered where he was, what made the Aqua the Aqua: the balconies on every floor, all the way to the top. He went to the curtain and pulled it open.

The accountant was outside, pressing up against the far corner of the iron railing. He wasn't the man Mason had expected—not a pencil-pushing scarecrow but a man who obviously spent time at the gym, even if the biceps that strained against his dress shirt were purely for show. Mason slid the door open, felt the cold rush of air against his face. He could hear the traffic on Columbus, fifty-three stories below. A siren wailed in the distance, probably already on the way to this building, while a million lights from the city glittered all around them. Under any other circumstances, it would have been a beautiful place to be.

The accountant stood up straight and looked him in the eye as Mason took the semiautomatic from his belt.

The time for nonlethal force was over.

As Mason raised the semiautomatic, he saw something in McLaren's eyes, turned a beat too late, and felt the impact on his right forearm. The gun clattered to the balcony floor and was kicked away as Mason swung around to face the recovered marshal. *I should have made sure he was out,* the words ringing in his head even as he faced a bigger problem, as the marshal lined up Mason and hit him across the jaw. Mason came back up, swung his foot right into the man's groin, and put him down again.

He was reaching for the baton on his belt when the accountant tackled him from behind, the momentum carrying them back into the room. Mason, the accountant's arms still locked around him, landed flush on the coffee table and flattened it. Mason twisted around and grabbed for the man's neck, but the accountant had fifty pounds on him, and he started swinging wildly at Mason's head. He felt McLaren's wedding ring scrape one of his cheeks, felt another blow next to his eye, and then as the man tried to aim a fist into his ribs, he let out a cry of pain as his hand crumpled against the tactical vest. Mason, still clutching the metal baton, laid it against the side of the accountant's head.

Mason rolled them both over just in time to see the marshal pick up the shotgun from the floor. Mason grabbed it and twisted it away, breaking at least one of the marshal's fingers as the gun went off, feeling the heat through his gloves as the television screen exploded. Mason hit the button on his baton and jabbed it right into the man's neck, sending twelve million volts into his body. The marshal was frozen in place until Mason took the baton away and hit him in the head with it, sending him to the floor for the last time.

Mason picked himself up, found all of his weapons, and wiped the blood from his cheek.

"Make sure he knows," Quintero said to him. "Make sure he knows who sent you."

"You think there's going to be any doubt in his mind?"

"I'll pay you," McLaren said. He was slowly getting to his feet, one hand pressed against the side of his head where Mason had hit him. "Whatever Cole's paying you, I'll double it."

"It's not always about money," Mason said as he raised the semiautomatic again.

This was the one step Mason didn't have to plan for. Didn't *want* to plan for, or think about, in any way. He knew this moment would come, knew that everything else would fade to gray, that the target would stand before him and he would pull the trigger, everything reduced to pure technique: concentrate on the front sight, let the target become nothing but a blur. One more breath, then a smooth pull.

"Please," the accountant said. And Mason pulled the trigger three times.

Chest, chest, head.

The body hit the floor.

Mason looked at his watch. It was 9:57 p.m. The decoy room had cost him valuable time.

He had three minutes to get out before Quintero's bomb went off.

2

MASON LEFT THE DEAD ACCOUNTANT IN A POOL OF blood, stepped over the body of the unconscious marshal, and opened the door. Hearing footsteps and voices to his left, Mason went right.

He opened the stairwell door and started going down, still carrying the shotgun, the semiautomatic tucked back into his belt. The balaclava was still pulled down over his face, until he pushed it up clear of his mouth so he could breathe as he pounded his way down one set of stairs after another.

He made it down ten floors. Then twenty. The numbers went by in a blur, as he looked at his watch and saw that he had less than two minutes left. He was on the landing of the twenty-seventh floor, pausing for one second to grab another breath.

He heard the squawk of a radio on the other side of the hallway door, froze for one beat and was about to continue going downward, but then the door opened and he found himself suddenly face-to-masked-face with one of the marshals. The man quickly recovered from his shock and yelled, "Freeze!"

Mason shot the first marshal below the vest line. The silicone plug folded the man in half and made him drop his gun. Mason threw himself behind the cover of the door, racked the shotgun, and in one smooth motion emerged to take down the second marshal. He pulled himself back behind the door again, racked the shotgun one more time, and recognized the subtle, hollow feel of an empty weapon.

Fuck. All six rounds gone.

Staying behind the door, Mason let the third marshal come closer until he could see the barrel of his Glock. He slammed the door on the man's arms, pulled the Glock away and hit him across the face with it. Wrapping him up, Mason pressed his forearm against the man's throat, the other arm to the back of his neck, and locked everything together. Ten seconds of steady pressure on the carotid artery, cutting off the blood supply. Then he let the marshal slide to the floor.

He checked his watch.

One minute.

He heard the voices above him again. More footsteps. He kept going down the stairs, one flight after the other. Until he heard another voice yelling and, a half second later, a gun blast and the metallic sound of a slug ricocheting off the rail inches from his hand. He threw himself against the wall and took the semiautomatic from his belt. He didn't have time to think about lethal force versus nonlethal force versus anything else in the world. He pictured what would happen next if he hesitated: the marshals cornering him, ordering him to drop his weapon, taking him away in handcuffs, just the first step in a process he'd already been through once before. Only this time he'd end up in a prison cell for the rest of his life.

Whatever he had to do, he was not going to let that happen.

There were voices below him now, echoing the voices above, which were getting louder. He threw open the door and ran down the hallway. He had no choices left.

He was fifty feet down the hallway when he realized where he was.

The twenty-first floor.

"How the hell am I supposed to get out?" Mason had asked Quintero. *"These weapons aren't exactly quiet."*

"The twenty-first floor is being renovated, so it'll be empty at night. There are explosives in one of the rooms, and they'll go off at exactly ten o'clock. Exactly. Make sure you have your watch right."

"What if I'm on that floor?"

"There's eighty-two fucking floors in that place, Mason. You only got one to avoid. Just be on the move at ten o'clock and you'll get out."

He didn't bother checking his watch. He knew he had seconds left.

"Drop the weapon!"

Mason turned and fired the semiautomatic just to give himself cover. But then he felt another impact, this time high on his right shoulder, the pain so much different from the shot that had hit him in the vest. This pain was sharp instead of dull and concentrated in one white-hot pinpoint.

I'm hit. The words rang hollow and far away in Mason's mind. Not urgent, just information. A problem that he didn't have the time to solve yet. He fired again and saw the marshal retreat behind the door, turned just in time to see another marshal coming from the opposite direction.

"Get on the ground! Get on the ground!"

Mason fired at the doorknob closest to him, kicked open the door, and ran through the empty room. He barely registered the bare drywall and paint cans, shooting out the back window as he ran, shattering it into a million pebbles of glass just before he went through to the balcony and over the edge of the railing.

The next moment was nothing but heat, light, and sound, obliterating everything else. The force of the explosion chased him, as sudden and immediate as a giant animal pursuing him into the cold night air. He grabbed at the railing with one hand, already feeling it slipping from him, the street twenty-one stories below waiting to receive his falling body.

A second wave hit even harder than the first, and he had to let go. He felt himself falling, reaching out with nothing more than pure instinct until another iron railing slammed against his left arm and he wrapped his arm around it. He was one floor below the explosion now, the cold like a dive into the ocean, but as he grasped the rail he felt his fingers slipping again. Hanging there, trying to pull himself over, he could hear the fire raging on the floor above him. Another window blew out. The sirens wailed in the distance. He looked down and saw the flashing blue lights on the police cars twenty floors below him.

It all felt so far away, everything but the pain in his right shoulder and the four inches of cold metal he could feel through the glove on his left hand, the last anchor keeping him from falling.

Mason gathered himself and tried to raise his right arm. Nothing. The arm was dead.

He could feel the blood trailing down his arm. His right glove was wet, blood dripping from his fingertips. His left hand was growing more numb by the second. His grip was weakening. He could hold on for one more minute. Maybe two.

After everything he had been through, to die this way . . .

He thought of his daughter, pictured her face in his mind, pictured her running across the soccer field. Said her name out loud—"*Adriana*"—in defiance of the howling wind that swirled about him. He tried one more time to swing his right arm up to the rail.

Got it.

He had the iron railing under his armpits now, and as his feet scrambled against the edge of the balcony he found purchase and pushed himself up over the top. He collapsed on the balcony, lying on his back and taking long breaths of air. There were more sirens down on the street, the police cars' wails mixing with the firetrucks' honking bass notes. In one second, the Aqua had become the center of the world. As Mason rolled to his feet, he touched his right shoulder with his left hand. He couldn't feel blood through his glove, but as he pulled it away he saw shiny bright red.

He tried the window. This one was unlocked. He went through another apartment, stopping to rummage through a laundry hamper until he found a red shirt. It was short-sleeved and three sizes too big for him, but he slipped it over his black shirt, the entire right side of which was now soaked in blood. He stopped for one more moment, felt the room spinning and had to reach out to steady himself against the wall. Then he went out the door and into the chaos of the hallway. The fire alarm was blaring wildly, hazard lights strobing on either side of him. A dozen people were moving toward the stairwell. Mason joined them, folding the balaclava into a skullcap again. Wondering if there was any chance he could blend into the crowd.

There were at least a hundred more people in the stairwell. Every age, every race, but all with one thing in common: the blind panic of something *real*. They could all feel it. This was *not* a fire drill. Somewhere a few floors above them, these people were stumbling onto the inca-pacitated marshals, probably causing a new round of panic on top of everything else. But down here on the twentieth floor, it was a simple issue of survival, of getting down the stairs and then out onto the street.

Mason kept up with the throng until he had to stop again for a moment and brace himself against the wall. When an older woman touched his arm and asked if he was all right, he looked away from her and kept moving. The crowd kept growing, as more people streamed off each floor into the stairwell like tributaries into a river, until reaching the ground level and emptying into the lobby.

"There's an exit directly in front of that doorway." Quintero's instructions coming back to him now. *"Fifty feet and you're out."*

Mason hung back, looking through the doorway at the main entrance. A half dozen marshals stood by, not stopping anyone but carefully scanning the face of everyone leaving the building. He saw the marshals stop a man around Mason's age and size, check him over, then finally let him go.

"If there's a problem, you have another exit to your right. A hundred feet."

He looked in that direction, saw another group of marshals watching the other exit.

"Your third choice is the tunnel. But you go down there, you're out of options."

Mason looked toward the glass doors leading down to the underground pedestrian walkway, the rat's maze of tunnels that ran beneath most of the Loop. There was one local cop at the entrance directing people away, back toward the main doors.

"Use the tunnel only if you have no other choice."

As Mason edged his way out into the lobby, he stayed

against the wall until he saw the cop talking to a middle-aged couple. He slipped the balaclava back over his face and moved quickly to the entrance. The cop was turning just as Mason got there and barely got his hands up before Mason hit him with a left cross. Mason stepped over him, swung open the glass door, and went down the stairs to the tunnel.

"Go north. Then west. There are exits on Water Street, Columbus, Stetson."

Mason's shoulder was on fire now, and he could hear someone coming down the stairs after him.

"After that, stay left at every intersection. If things get really fucked, find the abandoned tunnel just before Michigan Avenue."

He was trying hard to keep the map of the tunnels clear in his mind, but his head kept spinning and the map with it.

More voices, pounding footsteps, echoing loudly against the tile walls. Everything looked blue in the harsh artificial lights, cops seemingly everywhere in the maze, as Mason started running, his heart pumping and more blood soaking into his shirt.

I'm lost. I have no fucking idea where I'm—
There!

He saw plywood boards covering the entrance to what had once been a freight train tunnel. There was a door cut into the plywood, kept shut with a padlock. He shot at the lock and missed it the first time, focused his eyes and shot again. Then he pushed the door open and made his way down through the darkness. There was water dripping, rats moving somewhere close to him, the smell of dust from another era. He reached for the stun baton so he could use the flashlight on the end, but it was long gone.

He staggered and tripped his way across the old railroad tracks until he saw a dim light shining up ahead. A city block away, but it looked like a distant star in the sky. The creak of wood behind him, more voices, a thin beam from a flashlight, searching for him.

Mason picked himself up from the ground one more time, saw the light growing brighter, and finally found the wooden stairs leading upward. He made it to the top and put his right shoulder to the wood without thinking about what he was doing, almost passing out as a wave of pain and nausea swept through him. He pushed the door open, the sudden glare from a streetlight almost blinding him.

It was all a blur after that. He made his way down the street, turning away from the sirens and the blinking lights as they went by. He found his car somehow, through muscle memory and sheer guts. Got behind the wheel, turned the ignition, missed one car after another by inches as he pulled out into traffic.

And then he made his biggest mistake of the night.

He headed north.

3

WHEN LAUREN OPENED HER DOOR, SHE SAW BLOOD.

She tried to catch Nick as he collapsed across the doorway. He hit the floor hard. The dog, locked in another room, started barking.

"Oh my God! What happened?"

He didn't answer. She felt his soaking wet shirt, saw the drops of blood spilling onto her hardwood floor. In one of his pockets, a cell phone was ringing. Lauren shut the door behind Nick and pulled him into the apartment, back against the wall. He let out a moan as she started to remove his shirt.

"Who did this to you?"

She stopped when she saw the black tactical vest.

The surprise lasted for only a moment, then that feeling turned into something else. She'd always known this day would come. When he'd leave, he couldn't tell her where he'd go, what he'd do . . . All she knew was that he hated doing it. And now, whatever he'd done tonight, it was going to kill him. He was going to die right here on her floor.

"It's not so bad. You're okay," she said. It felt like both a lie and a prayer.

She undid the vest's Velcro straps, slowly pulling it from his body. He let out another moan, and she saw the wound to his shoulder. A jagged hole in his flesh just above his collarbone, close to his neck. The blood flowed again, streaming down his chest. Lauren gasped, nausea and panic nearly overwhelming her. She willed them away. Running to the kitchen for towels and the portable phone, she slipped on the blood-wet floor but didn't fall. When she returned, she pressed the towels against the wound with one hand. With the other hand, she dialed.

Mason reached up and slapped the phone out of her hand. It skidded across the floor.

"No," he said. His voice was ragged, like he couldn't catch his breath. "No calls."

"You're bleeding to death."

"No nine-one-one! Just let me—"

"Are you crazy?"

Mason grabbed her wrist.

"Nick, please . . ." She tried to pull away.

Mason held on. He was losing consciousness.

His cell phone rang again. This time, Lauren slipped it out of his pocket and read the screen.

PRIVATE NUMBER.

"Don't answer that!" He slurred the words, his eyes fluttering shut.

Not *ever* touching his phone: it was one of the things she had promised him. That, and she'd never ask where he'd been or what he'd done.

"I have to answer," she said, pulling out of his grasp. "You'll die if I don't. I'm not going to let that happen."

*   *   *

MASON FLOATED THROUGH an ocean of darkness. Beyond light, beyond sound. As he slowly came toward the surface, he heard words being spoken somewhere in the distance. Words that didn't yet mean anything.

My name is Lauren. Nick's been shot. He needs help. He won't let me call nine-one-one. What do I do?

Mason turned away from the surface and dove back down into the darkness. He stayed there for a minute, or an hour, or a day, until he felt himself rising again. There were sounds—a knock on the door, the muffled bark of a dog, a woman yelling—drawing him toward the surface. Then he broke the surface and saw a face looking down at him.

Quintero was kneeling before him on the floor, a brown plastic bottle in his hand. As he poured the peroxide onto the wound, pain racked Mason's body again, every muscle clenching so hard it was like a seizure.

"What . . . are you . . . doing? . . . How . . . did I . . . get here?" Mason said, eyes unfocused.

"I don't know, man. But you fucked up."

Quintero poured some of the clear liquid into a metal mixing bowl. The gold chains around his neck were swaying with every movement, the muscles flexing and animating the world of tattoos on both arms.

"Lauren," Mason said as it came back to him.

"I'm here."

Her voice came from somewhere behind him. He strained to see her, but Quintero put one hand on Mason's chest to steady him.

Why'd I come here? Mason asked himself. *Because this place is my refuge. From that first night she brought me here, this became the one place I could come and at least pretend that nothing else in my life could find me here.*

And now I've destroyed it.

"Come here. Hold this," Quintero said to Lauren, waving a gauze pad at her. "Press it to his shoulder."

She didn't move.

"He's going to bleed out if you don't help me," he said, louder but still calm.

Mason could see it in Lauren's eyes: she knew this man. He was her nightmare. The man who followed Nick. Gave him orders. The obstacle that stood between Nick and her having a life.

She didn't move.

"It's okay," Mason told her. "You can help him."

He focused on her face, her lips, her brown eyes, now filled with fear and worry. It had been her short brown hair that had first caught his eye the minute he walked into the pet shop to buy Max, the way it shouted *youth* and *independence*. A carefree life. But it was her honesty, her basic goodness, that ultimately drew him in, all those things about her that seemed to represent what he couldn't have for himself.

Quintero held the cotton gauze up to her. "Take it. Press it to his shoulder."

She took the gauze but did not kneel, her eyes focusing on the bulge showing through the back of Quintero's untucked shirt. Mason could see the thought forming in her mind. She didn't know guns. Hated them. But . . .

"Just do what he tells you," Mason said. *And don't try anything stupid.*

The spell was broken, any thought of going for Quintero's gun gone. She got down on her knees and pressed the gauze to the wound, the pure white cotton turning instantly red and wet in her hand.

"Harder," Quintero said.

Mason looked out the window at the darkness and the lone streetlight that burned high above the pavement. A blue light flickered, moving across the wall. A police cruiser passing by on the street below. Following the light, he reconstructed his drive here, from the Aqua to this apartment building, just around the corner from Wrigley Field.

"My car," Mason said. "It's probably blown."

Quintero shook his head at him. "You were supposed to bring it to the shop."

Mason wasn't going to argue the point. Nudging Lauren's hand away, he tried to look at the wound, but it was too close to his neck to see.

Lauren threw the blood-soaked gauze onto the floor. Quintero looked over to her, his expression cold and menacing. "Grab more cotton and get back down here."

"I'll be fine," Mason said to Lauren. "Just keep calm. He knows what he's doing."

Quintero poured more of the peroxide into the metal bowl. After that, he dropped in a pair of tweezers and an X-Acto knife.

"You." He pointed to Lauren. "Forget the bandages. Get me your sewing needles. Thread, too. *Strong* thread."

That did it. Lauren stood up. "This is bullshit. I'm calling nine-one-one."

She pulled Nick's cell phone out of her pocket, but before she could dial the first digit, Quintero was on his feet.

"Look at me," Quintero said, pointing at his own eyes. "You can help or you can let him die on your floor. That's up to you. But the one thing you're *not* going to do is call an ambulance. Understand?"

Lauren nodded, but the phone was still in her hand. *Three digits,* she thought. *She could dial them with her thumb.* 9-1—

Someone snapped his fingers. When Lauren looked up, Quintero had a gun on her. Her breath caught in her throat.

He snapped again. Held out his free hand. "The phone."

"Give it to him," Mason said, trying to prop himself up.

Lauren handed Quintero the phone.

"Needle and thread. Now."

"Nick . . ." She was looking at him, fighting back tears, refusing to give in to them.

"Get him the thread," Mason said. "It'll be okay."

She shook her head and left the room. When she left, Quintero helped Mason back into a sitting position and took the tweezers out of the peroxide.

"What happened today?" he asked Mason.

"I got the target. Had some trouble getting out."

"You shouldn't have come here."

"Don't worry about her." Mason didn't even want to say her name aloud in front of this man. "Just get me out of here."

"You can't move yet."

Quintero spread open the sides of Mason's wound, poked the tweezers around inside the shoulder. The pain had Mason diving back down into the darkness. Quintero pressed his hand against the back of the shoulder.

"No exit wound. The bullet's still in there. Vest must've stopped it."

"So take it out."

"No shit. You think this is the first time I've done this? Just shut up and stay still."

Quintero dipped the tweezers in the bowl again. "This is gonna hurt like a bitch."

Mason clamped his eyes shut and waited. He felt the touch of cold metal and then the same electric jolt of pain, doubled now, then tripled. A welding iron cutting through his nerve endings, sending showers of sparks in every direction.

"Stay still," Quintero said in a calm whisper.

Mason was beyond hearing him. He kept his eyes

closed, counting the seconds, until the pain suddenly eased and he could take a breath. He heard the slug ping into the bowl and opened his eyes.

"Forty caliber," Quintero said.

"I need a better vest."

"Or don't get shot."

"The target wasn't in the right room," Mason said, the anger replacing the worst of the pain. "Your source had bad intel."

"And you dealt with it," Quintero said, picking up the X-Acto knife.

"What are you doing?"

"Got to clean the edges so I can sew you up."

Mason squeezed his eyes shut, felt the same surge of electricity shoot through him again as Quintero scraped and cut.

Lauren came back into the room, carrying a spool of thread and a selection of needles. She held them out to Quintero. "Here."

He took one of the needles. Made a face. "This the best you got?"

"I sew ripped jeans, not bullet wounds."

He ignored that and snapped off two feet of thread from the spool.

"You're not going to want to watch this," Quintero said.

"I'm not leaving," she said.

Quintero shook his head, reached into his shirt pocket, and pulled out a fold-up pair of reading glasses. They sat low on his nose. A strange moment of stillness as he carefully threaded the needle, this former gangbanger with the green-and-white La Raza tattoo on his arm and three rings in his ears, guiding the thread through the eye of the needle with the skill of a seamstress.

Mason closed his eyes one last time as he felt the needle piercing his flesh. He tried and failed not to picture Quintero going down through all the layers of his skin, crossing the open wound, and up through the skin on the opposite side. Straight, then diagonal to come back, then straight again. He felt the pull as Quintero tightened the thread, the fresh sting as he paused to wipe away the blood and douse the wound with peroxide.

"I need your help again," Quintero said to Lauren as he began to pack the wound with bandages. "Rip that tape into foot-long pieces."

"I'm sorry," Mason said, looking past Quintero at her. *Sorry had never sounded so inadequate.*

Mason thought he saw a thousand things in Lauren's expression. He hoped forgiveness was one of them.

When Quintero was done securing the last piece of tape, he lifted Mason to his feet. He threw Mason's left arm over his shoulder. "Now we go."

"Wait," Lauren said, putting herself between them and the door. "Go where?"

"Someplace safer."

"Safer for who?" she asked.

"For all of us." He looked at Mason. "Let's move."

Lauren closed the door behind them and surveyed the bloody mess that was her front hallway. She collapsed to her knees, wrapping her arms tightly around herself. The rush of adrenaline was gone now, leaving her weak. But that's not what started her sobbing. It was the thought that even if Nick Mason lived through this . . .

She might never see him again.

QUINTERO LED MASON into the hallway and down the stairs. He gave the street a quick scan, opened the apartment building's door, and walked Mason to his black Escalade parked half a block away.

"My car . . ." Mason said.

"Already taken care of."

Quintero pulled out into traffic. The SUV stopped at a light, as a police car crossed silently through the intersection, blue light flashing.

"You really fucked up," Quintero said, easing the Escalade away from the intersection. "This is gonna come back on all of us."

"What do you mean," Mason said, "*all of us?*"

"You know the rules. Everyone's in play."

After everything else he had been through that night, Mason needed a moment to let that sink in.

"Your job was to take out the accountant," Quintero said. "Mine was to drive to Elmhurst. Wait to hear from you . . . Or not."

Mason sat straight up in the car seat. Elmhurst meant two things:

His ex-wife, Gina.

His daughter, Adriana.

It was a threat Mason had heard before: you fail, they die. A simple equation. But tonight, a bullet dug out of his shoulder, his blood all over Lauren's apartment, the threat felt more real somehow. Tonight, he had come inches away from losing more than just a few pints of blood.

He steps out of this vehicle, Mason said to himself, the entire scene coming to him at once. *He walks up to the front door. It's locked, but that barely slows him down. One foot against the door, just next to the dead bolt. By the time everyone wakes up, he's already up the stairs. Maybe Brad has a gun, maybe he doesn't. It doesn't matter. As much as he wants to protect his wife and stepdaughter, he has no idea how. Not against a man like Quintero.*

He takes the first bullet in the forehead.

Gina is screaming. In another room, down the hallway,

a room Mason has never even seen before, his daughter Adriana is sitting up in her bed.

Is she crying? Does she try to hide? Try to run?

Mason stopped the movie in his head before it could go another frame.

"Don't you ever threaten my family again," Mason said. "Ever!"

"Don't give me a reason," Quintero said, keeping his eyes straight ahead, "and I won't have to."

From the moment Mason had walked out of that prison, he'd been thinking about what it would take to break free from this second life he'd found himself in.

He'd been watching. And waiting.

But on this night, as Quintero drove him down the dark streets of Chicago's North Side, Mason knew that the watching and waiting was over.

I am going to burn you down, he thought. *You. Darius Cole. Everyone else who works for him.*

I am going to burn you all down.

4

LESS THAN FIVE HOURS AFTER BEING AWAKENED BY A phone call in the middle of the night, U.S. Marshal Bruce Harper stood seven hundred miles away from home, looking at the greatest failure of his life.

Harper wasn't just a twenty-seven-year veteran of the United States Marshals Service, the USMS—he'd spent the last ten years as the Assistant Director in charge of the Witness Security Program, or WITSEC as they called it in Arlington, overseeing hundreds of deputy marshals in ninety-four districts across the country. Earlier in his career, Harper had worked directly for Gerald Shur, the original founder of WITSEC, and still talked to him at least once a week. He was already dreading the next call with Gerald because in almost fifty years of the Program's existence, over eighteen thousand WITSEC clients had been protected and no client—at least no client who followed the Program's rules—had ever been killed.

Until now.

Their first murdered witness.

And it happened on Harper's watch.

As he walked through the firebombed hallway of the Aqua's twenty-first floor, the scence like something out of a war zone—the walls blackened and three doors in a row blown out and lying haphazardly on the floor—he tried to piece it all together.

Harper went into the room where the incendiary devices had been placed. A dozen paint cans had been smuggled in, all sealed tightly, with diesel fuel inside. The marshals were cooperating with the FBI on the investigation, and Harper had been told that they'd already found the security feed showing two painting contractors bringing up the cans. They were chasing down the list of approved contractors working on this floor, compiling a list of all employees, but Harper didn't hold out much hope.

Whoever had brought them up here, the cans were stacked with great care to go off in a rapid chain reaction, with one central fuse activated by a digital timer. Harper went to the balcony where the window had been blown out, twenty-one stories above the streets of Chicago. The morning traffic on the Loop was heavy now. Everyone going to work, already forgetting about last night's big news from downtown . . .

This is not my city, he said to himself. He'd never lived here, never worked here, had never spent more than a day at a time here—although he had a strong feeling that was about to change.

How did this happen?

It was the first question he had asked when the phone call came, had been asking himself ever since. But now that he was here to see it in person, that question was replaced by another:

How did none of my deputy marshals die?

He had enough injuries to fill a ward: four deputy

marshals with severe burns—they were all mostly sheltered by the fireproof doors when the explosion went off on the floor—another three found incapacitated on the stairwell, two with abdominal trauma and a third found unconscious, apparently choked out. The young deputy marshal on the forty-third floor, the one who'd been stationed at the decoy door, was another abdominal case, with separate muscle trauma in his left thigh. He was young enough, he'd probably be walking again in a couple of weeks.

"The shooter was wearing a black mask," the deputy marshal had told him. Harper had stopped at the hospital first to interview him before coming here. *"Brown eyes, mid-thirties maybe. And he was a Southsider."*

"How do you know that?"

"I've lived here my whole life. I know a Southsider when I hear one."

That left the deputy marshal who was stationed in the room itself: Greg Davis, a man with almost as many years in the Service as Harper. Harper would have trusted him to guard his own kids, along with his retirement fund, but Davis had been shot with another of the six silicone plugs recovered in the building. He had also been both shocked and hit in the head by the stun baton they found in the hallway, not far from the Mossberg 500 shotgun.

This guy had no problem killing McLaren, Harper said to himself, looking at the fire-blackened HK USP nine-millimeter semiautomatic they had found. *But he went to a hell of a lot of trouble not to kill anyone else. Even if that meant carrying extra weapons.*

What kind of man does that?

Harper was dying to catch him, so he could ask him that question in person. And he *would* catch the man. It was only a matter of time.

He went up to the fifty-third floor, where the marshals had kept one of two secret apartments. This apartment wasn't even known to most marshals in the local district office. Unless you were actively guarding a high-value client here, you had no reason to know it existed.

He walked into the main room of the apartment. There were barely any furnishings beyond the immediate functional needs of the client who'd stay here for a night or two, maybe a week at the most. A small kitchen and a table to have meals on. Television hooked up to basic cable. A couch and coffee table, now reduced to scrap wood. Deputy Marshal Davis had been found on the floor nearby, unconscious. On the other side of the room, next to the now destroyed television, they had found Ken McLaren. He'd been shot three times—twice in the chest, once in the head—with the semiautomatic.

Harper had walked past a dozen other men, all doing their jobs, when he'd first arrived. Feds, fire investigators, more marshals from the Northern Illinois District of the USMS. But now he stood alone in the room, a moment of stillness in the chaos of this day, looking down at the exact spot on the floor from which the body had been taken away. A splatter of blood arced across the wall. The carpet was stained where the blood had soaked through. As he turned, he was startled to see a man standing in the room with him. He was a few inches shorter than Harper, a few years younger. Dark coloring, watchful eyes. A coiled energy, even as he stood still. He wasn't a deputy marshal, or one of the FBI agents Harper had met on the way in, but the scuffed dress shoes and the dark blue sports jacket that needed a good pressing screamed law enforcement. Unless he's a first-rate undercover, a cop only looks like one thing: a cop.

Harper looked the man in the eye. "This better be important, Officer . . ."

The man took out his star. "*Detective* Frank Sandoval. Area Central Homicide."

"If you're here to gloat over the Feds fucking up, you've had your look. The door's behind you."

"I left a message for you two days ago. You should have returned my call."

"What are you talking about?"

"I was trying to pull your coat."

"About what?"

"About *this*," Sandoval said, flaking off a piece of wallboard. "This clock was already ticking as soon as Darius Cole got his retrial. I'm surprised it took this long."

"Bullshit. How could you know that?"

"If you took my call, you'd have your answer."

Harper took a beat to calm himself. "Mr. McLaren was in the Program for almost twenty years. During that whole time, he had never had any contact with any past associates or—"

"Yeah, I know how it works. Leave your whole life behind, start a new life in a new place, nobody will ever find you, right?"

"Not if you follow the rules." Harper had read every word in McLaren's file that morning while he was sitting on the plane. This man who once worked as a forensic accountant for the IRS, who would later help Darius Cole move millions of dollars in dirty money back and forth between the U.S. and a dozen other countries without paying any taxes. This same man who was relocated from Chicago to Asheville, North Carolina, after testifying against Cole in the original trial. He was given a one-bedroom apartment and a job at a strip mall doing walk-in tax returns for people who couldn't wait to get their two-hundred-dollar refunds, with a federal probation officer looking over his shoulder to make sure that was the most creative thing McLaren ever did with other people's money.

"You got your rules, Cole has his," Sandoval said. "It didn't matter where you stored your witness. He was as good as dead."

Harper's whole life had been dedicated to the Program, to the belief that *any* witness can be protected. From *anyone* other than maybe God Himself. *You do what you're told, you'll be safe.* He'd been telling that to witnesses and their families for decades and he'd always believed it. Because it was always true.

Always.

But now McLaren's body was proof that there's no such thing as *always* and that everything he'd based his career on was a lie. Today, Bruce Harper was standing in the middle of the Program's first failure, the proof of that still soaked into the carpet beneath his feet.

"If you have all the answers," Harper said, "share them with the whole class. Darius Cole is at Terre Haute, one of the most secure facilities in the country."

"He could have reached out from the fucking moon."

Harper shook his head. "He's not the first criminal with contacts on the outside. How did he find out where we were keeping McLaren? That doesn't happen, Detective. *Ever.*"

"That's something you're going to have to find out for yourself," Sandoval said. "All I know is, if you've got one marshal with a weakness, Cole has already found him."

Harper's mind was already racing through the possibilities. Already making a list of every marshal, deputy marshal, administrator, *anyone* who might have had access to this information.

It wasn't a long list.

Unless the leak was here. In Chicago.

He hated to even think it, but it was unavoidable: *If you had to pick one city to find the one compromised marshal in the country, which city would you honestly choose?*

"So what about the shooter?" Harper said. "You got a name for me or are you just here to say, 'I told you so'?"

"I can give you a name. Or I can do even better, take you to his house."

Harper looked at him. "Are you serious, Detective? Because I'm really not up for any more—"

"I know you're already having a bad day," Sandoval said. "But when you see where this guy lives, you're gonna lose your breakfast."

5

THE BURNER CELL PHONE THAT DARIUS COLE WOULD USE to call Nick Mason that morning had already changed hands five times on its way to his prison cell.

It had started its journey in a carton of cigarettes that was dropped into the northwest corner of the yard by a remote-controlled four-blade drone after a one-mile flight from its launch vehicle parked on the banks of the Wabash River. The carton contained six ounces of loosely packed marijuana—that was the throwaway payload, strictly for show. The CO stationed on the night shift perimeter post retrieved the carton and removed the marijuana, weighed it and carefully logged it in, before handing it over to the contraband team. He held back the cell phone, the ten hundred-dollar bills, and the dozen fentanyl patches that were also hidden inside the carton, placing the phone, the patches, and five of the bills beneath the seat of his patrol vehicle. The remaining bills he put in his pocket.

The day shift CO in charge of maintaining the patrol vehicles removed the other five bills from beneath the seat and put those in *his* pocket. Then he put the cell phone and the fentanyl patches in a plain manila envelope and dropped it in the big white mail crate.

A few minutes later, an inmate trustee sorted that mail onto his cart, placing the manila envelope beneath the other mail headed to the Special Housing Unit. But before leaving the mail room, he opened the envelope and removed two of the fentanyl patches. He reached down and placed one on the inside of each thigh. The patches would deliver a continuous seventy-two-hour double dose of synthetic opiate bliss. More than ample payment for making one extra delivery.

The trustee was feeling just about perfect by the time he got to the Special Housing Unit. That's where most of Terre Haute's high-profile inmates were kept, and some of those had "special needs" that were addressed there: larger cells, natural light, and better food than the rest of the inmates ate—hell, better than the guards ate.

The grateful inmate who received the unmarked envelope removed the remaining fentanyl patches, and then, as the final step of the journey, walked the phone over to the private cell of Darius Cole. Cole had no use for the patches, of course. He didn't need any kind of chemical high to escape this prison, at least in his mind. The cell phone was the inmate's payment to Cole in exchange for Cole's permission to sell the fentanyl to other inmates in SHU.

Cole had been using cell phones at USP Terre Haute ever since he arrived in 2005. But when the President signed the Cell Phone Contraband Act of 2010, some bureaucrat made it his singular mission in life to decrease the number of cell phones in the prison. As in any open market anywhere, the only thing this succeeded in doing was driving up the price. From stocks on Wall Street to drugs on the street, the principle was the same. If you make it hard to get, you don't stop it. You just make it more profitable.

When another bureaucrat decided to move the focus back to the flow of illegal drugs, the cell phone market was suddenly flooded. Cole figured half the men in his Special Housing Unit had them that year. Even if you didn't, you could still buy phone time for a dollar a minute. Then a gang member incarcerated in Baltimore got caught ordering a hit from his cell and suddenly the market was tight again. He couldn't even rely on one of the guards he kept in his back pocket to bring one in from the outside.

Cole inspected the new phone, made sure it got reception, made sure it was compatible with at least one of the chargers he already had in his cell. Then he dismissed the inmate and dialed ten digits from memory.

THREE HUNDRED MILES NORTH, Diana Rivelli looked down at the man who lived in her town house, wondering if he was still alive. She had found him when she had come home from work after midnight—he was lying on the couch, his shirt off and bandages wrapped around his neck and right shoulder. Whatever had happened to him, his breathing was shallow, and there was a thin spot of blood coming through the white fabric.

He was still here when she had woken up this morning, hadn't moved an inch. Diana had sat watching him for almost two hours, waiting to see if he would wake up, wondering if there was anything she could do for him. Not for the first time, she asked herself how he had ended up here, this stranger who slept on the other side of the house, who answered his cell phone and then disappeared without a word.

Diana was dressed for work, already late, and wondering if the staff at Antonia's would be ready for the lunch rush. But Mason still hadn't moved. She put one hand on his neck, felt his pulse, kept her hand pressed against his skin for one beat longer, feeling the warmth of his body.

I don't want to know what happened to him, she told herself. It was a rule she followed, one of many that kept her life in order: *Never ask where Mason goes. Never ask what he does.*

From somewhere underneath him, she heard his cell phone ringing. Mason stirred, and before he could open his eyes, Diana was already gone.

AS SOON AS MASON lifted his head, he felt the stitches pull at the skin of his shoulder. He winced in pain and grabbed for the phone, hit the button, and put the phone to his ear. "What do you want, Quintero?"

"Were you as sloppy last night as you are on the phone right now?" Cole asked. "Using a name? And the wrong name at that?"

The instantly recognizable voice jolted Mason upright. He was in the living room, on the couch, had never even made it to his bed. It was just after nine. He'd slept maybe seven hours.

"What happened last night?" Cole asked. It was only the second time he'd ever called Mason directly. "I don't like what I'm hearing."

Mason got to his feet slowly, head spinning. He went into the bathroom with the phone still pressed to his ear. He looked at his taped-up shoulder and the multicolored streaks that ran right up his neck.

"Are you listening to me?"

"I'm right here."

Mason left the bathroom, went to the refrigerator, and

opened it. He was dying for orange juice, settled on a bottle of Goose Island Ale.

"I hit the target," Mason said. "Then I got out. As soon as I heal up, I'll be—"

"You're not focusing on the problem you created."

"You mean getting shot?" Mason said. "That problem?"

"The fuck you want, a Purple Heart?" Cole asked. "I've been shot four times."

Mason closed the double-door refrigerator and opened the beer. The town house was quiet, like most mornings. His roommate Diana must have already left for the restaurant, preparing for the lunch rush. He couldn't even remember the last time he had talked to her.

"I did what you told me to do," Mason said. "Why are you calling?"

He walked out of the kitchen to the deck and stood at the railing as the video camera watched him, the red light blinking. A constant reminder of where he was, even if Mason rarely thought about it anymore. The surface of the pool was rippled by a soft wind coming off the lake.

"I called you," Cole said, "to let you know what had to happen next."

That's the moment Mason should have known something was about to go wrong. But he was distracted as he looked down at the street.

Just below the town house ran Lincoln Park West, then the park itself with its zoo and botanical gardens. Beyond that was Lake Michigan, glittering in the morning sunlight. A perfect, five-million-dollar scene, but today Mason saw only one thing:

A black sedan parked on the street.

"I've had enough women in my life," Cole said. "Only one or two I really cared about."

Mason saw the window roll down. A face looked up at him. No attempt to hide.

The man who had sent him to Terre Haute, who five years later had sat across from him in Diana's restaurant and promised that he'd send him back. Who had taken the flash drive with information about the corrupt SIS crew from him, had used it to bring down the entire task force, and had still promised him that nothing would ever change between them.

Detective Frank Sandoval.

"You got to put business first. Way it's got to be."

Sandoval nodded his head. He was talking to someone else in the car, an older man with the hard face of a veteran. Both of them looked up at him through the windshield.

Mason raised his beer bottle to Sandoval in mock salute.

"Are you there?"

"Yes." He put the bottle down and turned away from the railing.

"I didn't ask you to do this yourself."

Mason stopped dead. "What are you talking about?"

"I'm talking about a loose end. I can't have it."

Everything else faded into the background. There was nothing but the sound of one man's voice coming to him through the air from a prison cell in another state.

"She's got nothing to do with this," Mason said. "She's not going to—"

"You went to her apartment. You bled all over her floor, and today she's reading about what happened downtown."

Mason tightened his grip on the phone. "Listen to me. She knows I have another life . . ."

"If that's true, then we already had a problem."

"She doesn't know anything else," Mason said. "There's no reason to—"

"This is on you," Cole said. "You caused this when you went over there. Remember that."

Mason heard a click and then nothing but dead air. He quickly dialed Lauren's number. It rang a few times, then went to voicemail.

"Get away from wherever you are," Mason said. "Right now. Go someplace safe. And call me."

Mason wondered if she'd even live to hear the message or if she was already dead. He struggled into some clothes, gritting his teeth as he worked the shirt over his shoulder. Running down to the garage, he opened the door and saw . . .

Nothing.

Fuck.

Mason had left his car at Lauren's place the night before and, as Quintero had promised, it was long gone by now, at the chop shop, cut into pieces.

He went out to the street. *I'll make Sandoval take me to her,* he thought. *I don't care what he says.*

But the parking spot was empty, and he barely caught a glimpse of the black sedan as it disappeared around the corner. He scanned the street for another moving car.

Nothing.

Mason started running, feeling the sharp pain in his shoulder with every step. The pet shop was over a mile away.

Please be there, he thought. *Be in that shop, standing behind the counter. You didn't answer your phone because you were busy with a customer.*

He ran down Lincoln Park West and rounded the corner. Another two blocks and he saw the pet shop. His head was spinning as he got to the door and pushed it open.

There was a woman behind the counter. But it wasn't Lauren.

"Can I help you?"

"Where is she? Where's Lauren?"

"Not here today. She asked me to—"

Mason went back outside. He saw a taxi coming down the street, ran out, and nearly got himself run over by a car coming the other way. He ignored the honking, stopped the cab, got in the back. Gave the driver the address, pulled out his cell phone.

"Hurry," he told the driver as he waited for the call to go through. "Don't stop for anything."

The call went to voicemail again. He ended the call and tried Quintero. The phone kept ringing. No voicemail.

Fuck. He's there right now.

He dialed one more number. The restaurant. He asked for Diana, told the man it was an emergency.

"I need you to go somewhere," he said to her as soon as she got on the line.

"Nick, I'm working."

"It's important. I'm going to give you an address."

He gave her the number on Addison Street, told her to get there as soon as she could. Then he hung up and tried Lauren again. Voicemail.

He pictured Quintero in her apartment. Just like last night, only now he was alone with her.

I did this, Mason said to himself. *I brought this into her life. And now her life is over.*

"Go faster," Mason told the cabdriver. "I'll pay you anything. Just get me there."

The driver threw up his hands. He was stuck at a light with nowhere to go. Mason started calculating how long it would take him to run there, assuming he didn't pass out. But then the light changed and the cab moved again. They found some open space on Clark Street, made a good run until it was time to cut in on Addison. As soon as the car stopped again for a light, Mason threw some money over the seat and was out of the car before the wheels stopped moving.

Mason ran the last four blocks down Addison, crossing the intersections in front of cars that barely missed him.

When he got to the building, he saw the black Escalade parked out front.

I'm too late.

He used his key to open the front door, went up the steps two at a time. The door to her apartment was ajar and he could hear Max barking from somewhere inside. He pushed the door open and was hit by the smell of bleach. He looked down at the hardwood floor in the hallway, realized she must have been up half the night cleaning up his blood.

The dog kept barking. He looked around the corner. The living room was empty.

Where are they?

When he went into the bedroom, he saw Quintero sitting on Lauren's bed. Mason froze, and the two men locked eyes for a long moment. The dog barked again, breaking the spell. He was next door in the spare room Lauren used as an office.

"You don't want to be here," Quintero said.

"I'm not letting you do this," Mason said. It was an obscenity that this man was here in the room, touching her bed.

"That's not how this is going to work, Mason. You *know* what I have to do."

Mason heard a noise in the bathroom, realized it was the shower being turned off. Quintero had been sitting here, waiting for her.

"I don't kill women in the shower," Quintero said, as if reading Mason's mind.

"You're not killing anyone today."

As Quintero stood up, he picked up the gun that had been lying on the bed behind him out of view. It was a black Sig semiautomatic with a suppressor screwed into the barrel.

"It's already done," Quintero said, pointing the barrel at Mason's chest. "Don't make this worse."

"Go ahead," Mason said. "Kill me, too. Then you can tell Cole you'll be taking over my job."

The door to the bathroom opened. Quintero looked away for an instant, just long enough for Mason to grab the barrel of the gun and pull. The gun went off, the sound dampened by the suppressor, and the slug going right through the soft wood of the closet door. As Quintero pulled back, Mason went with him, heard Lauren's scream as he rolled all the way over the bed, onto the floor. Quintero shoved his fingers into Mason's bullet wound, making him cry out in pain. But he didn't let go of the gun.

The two men remained locked together, the gun held at an impasse between them. Mason knew he didn't have the strength to hold on. Not today. Quintero's face was above him, the face that represented everything in his life that he had no control over, and now as he felt his hands slipping from the gun he wondered if this face would be the last thing he'd ever see.

But then another face came into view. Lauren, standing above and behind them. She had on a white robe and was holding something, a silver pole, which she wielded like a sword. Lauren raised the pole above her head, then brought it down hard on Quintero's back. The man's eyes went wide, and the breath left his body, as Lauren swung the pole again, this time hitting him square in the back of the head.

Mason grabbed the gun from him, was about to turn it, when the pole swung one more time and hit him in the shoulder. He almost blacked out then, almost dropped the gun and lost everything, but he held on and waited for his vision to clear.

"Stop," he said to Lauren. "It's okay, I've got him."

He kept the barrel of the suppressor pointed at Quintero as he slowly got up. When Quintero moved, he jabbed it in the man's stomach.

"I will kill you if I have to," Mason said to him, letting himself imagine what would happen if he pulled the trigger. The problems he would solve. But then the other problems that would replace them.

"Nick . . ." Lauren said. She was hyperventilating, barely able to speak. "Why is he here again?"

He looked over at her for just a moment, long enough to see her leaning against the dresser. She was still holding the silver towel bar, now bent, in her left hand. Her face was drained of color. No longer a warrior, she was back to being the woman from the pet shop again.

"Pack some clothes," Mason said to her. "Anything of any value to you."

"What are you talking about?" Lauren said, fighting to catch her breath. "Where are we going?"

"Just do it. Right now."

"You're killing everyone you love," Quintero said, still sitting on the floor. He put one hand on the back of his head, then checked his fingers for blood. "Her. Your wife, your kid . . ."

"But you won't be here to see it," Mason said.

Mason kept his eyes on Quintero as he heard Lauren moving behind him, opening drawers and taking out clothes. She went into the bathroom to change. That's when Mason finally spoke again.

"Here's the official version," he said to Quintero. "You came here. You took her away. You killed her and you disposed of the body. Nobody will ever find it. Do you understand me?"

"You're asking me to lie to Cole."

"I'm not asking."

He watched Quintero work that over in his head. Watched him do the math.

"If she shows up somewhere . . ."

"She won't," Mason said. "I'll make sure of it."

Quintero shook his head. "You're going to fuck both of us."

Lauren came back into the bedroom. "Where are we going, Nick?"

"I don't have time to argue," Mason said. "Pack your bag right now. And get the carrier for Max. He's going with you."

"Nick, I'm not—"

"Pack your bag," Mason said, letting a hard edge come into his voice. He didn't turn to see the effect.

"I'm not going anywhere without you."

"Pack. Your. Bag. Now."

She swallowed hard but didn't move.

"Look at him." Mason nodded at Quintero. "Why do you think he came here?"

"I'm not giving up on us," she said. "Just because some—"

"Are you listening to me or not?" he said, the anger and the menace in his voice sounding alien to his own ears. But this was the way it had to be. The time had come to burn the bridge, and the road on both sides.

"Nick . . ." She looked lost now, still holding the towel bar. Quintero sat quietly and watched them.

"I'm saving your life," Mason said. "You're leaving."

"What about us?"

"There is no us," he said. "Not anymore."

He hated to say it, hated everything that was happening, almost as much as he hated the thought of a bullet in her head, because he was stupid enough to believe they could have had something—a life, a future—together.

Tears ran down her cheeks. He looked away, the gun still pointed at Quintero, while Lauren packed. A few minutes later, he heard the door buzzer.

"That's Diana," Mason said. "Go let her in."

He heard her going down the stairs, then a pair of footsteps coming back up.

"What the hell is going on?" Diana said, stepping into the room and seeing Mason sitting on the bed with Quintero on the floor.

Mason didn't have to see Diana's face. He knew how much she despised Quintero. How much she feared him.

"Take Lauren to the airport," Mason said. "Stop at the restaurant first. There's an envelope with ten thousand dollars in it taped under your desk. Give that to her. And when you drop her off, just leave. She'll pick a flight and she'll go. Neither of us will ever know where. Do you understand?"

"No," Lauren said. "First you cut my heart out, now—"

"Diana," Mason said, ignoring Lauren, "do you understand?"

A long silence before Diana finally spoke. "Yes."

"I'm not going anywhere," Lauren said.

"Don't move," Mason said to Quintero. Then he stood up and went to Lauren. Her eyes were still red. She wiped her face and looked up at him.

"You can't do this to me," she said. "We've been working so hard to be together."

"It was a mistake."

"Listen to me," she said. "I'm not stupid. I already knew something like this was coming, okay? I already made my peace with it a long time ago. So I don't care what you say. I'm not going to just—"

"I killed a man last night," Mason said.

Lauren stopped short, like she'd just been slapped in the face.

"I went into that building downtown," he said, "the one that was on fire. I found the man I was looking for and I killed him."

She kept looking up at him without saying a word.

"Last time, I killed a cop with a shotgun. I blew his body apart. Diana was there. She can tell you it's true. Before that, I killed a man with a knife, cut his throat and watched him die while I was still holding him."

The tears ran down both of her cheeks again.

"Wake up, Lauren. I kill people. That's my life. You stay, you die, too."

She shook her head, still unable to say a word.

"Diana's going to take you now. Don't come back here. Ever."

She stood there for a long time until Diana took her by the arm and led her out of the room. Mason watched her put together the rest of her things, close up her suitcase, and open up the spare room door to let Max out. She put a leash on him but he strained against it when he saw Mason in the bedroom. He got to within three feet of him before Lauren pulled Max back.

Diana was struggling with the big dog carrier in one hand, the suitcase in the other. Lauren stopped to look Mason in the eye one last time. She opened her mouth as if to say one last thing. But no words came out. Both women left.

Mason sat down on the edge of the bed. Quintero stayed on the floor. He didn't speak.

"You're going to take me to your shop," Mason finally said. "I need a new car."

LAUREN LOOKED OVER at the woman driving. Diana Rivelli. She had been the stranger Lauren found living with Nick Mason. With the dark hair and the dark eyes and the ageless beauty that she didn't even seem to be aware of. She was just as much a stranger now, just as much a mystery, even after Lauren had found a way into Mason's life.

I have to go, Lauren thought. *I have to leave the only place I've ever known.*

Why does Diana get to stay?

"Was that all true?" Lauren said, wiping her face again. "The things Nick said, about what he does?"

"We all do what we have to do," Diana said, keeping her eyes on the road.

"And I have to go."

"You *get* to go. Which makes you the lucky one."

"How am I lucky, Diana? My whole life is over."

"Your life is still yours. I'd trade places with you in a second. The man who owns Nick's life . . . he owns mine, too."

"People can't own other people."

"Tell that to the man who owns me," Diana said. "I may live in a nice cage, but I'm still a slave."

"I don't understand any of this," Lauren said.

"You just didn't want to see it," Diana said. "But you had to have some idea. What did you think he was doing when he had to leave you? Delivering flowers?"

Lauren didn't answer. They rode on in silence until they reached O'Hare.

"Where am I supposed to go?" Lauren said. "Back home to my parents?"

"No, don't go there. Go somewhere nobody can find you. At least for now."

Lauren looked at her, shaking her head in disbelief.

They drove up to the terminal. The dog sat in the backseat, looking out the window. Lauren got out with her suitcase. An agent came over and helped her with the dog carrier. Max strained at the leash for a moment, then gave up and sat down on the pavement.

"Promise me you'll take care of him," Lauren said, pausing at the door and waiting.

"I have enough to do just taking care of myself."

Diana just looked at her. A car behind hers started to honk.

"Promise me," Lauren said again.

Diana nodded. Lauren closed the door and walked away.

She had no idea where she was going. Or what she'd do when she got there.

The only thing she knew for sure was that she'd never come back.

6

BRUCE HARPER WOULD REMEMBER NICK MASON'S FACE,
as he'd looked down at them from his luxury town
house, for the rest of his life.

Never mind ruining the WITSEC Program's perfect
record, embarrassing four thousand U.S. marshals and
deputy marshals all over the country, putting a black
mark on Harper's twenty-seven-year career. None of that
really mattered.

What mattered was the fact that, if Detective Sandoval
was right, Nick Mason had killed a witness Harper was
sworn to protect, injuring nine of Harper's men in the
process.

And Harper couldn't do anything about it.

At least not yet.

He was sitting across the desk from Rachel Greenwood, an AUSA—Assistant United States Attorney—for
the Northern District of Illinois. Mid-forties, attractive

in an all-business kind of way, hair pulled back tight, rimless glasses. Harper was meeting her for the first time, trying to take her measure. He glanced at the framed photograph on her desk, which might have been taken when she was a few years younger, with a husband who had the smile and the haircut of an attorney, probably in private practice. Two teenage kids, a boy and a girl. The whole family wearing white shirts and smiling for the camera on a bright happy day that was nothing like today.

Harper had already checked in at the U.S. Marshals' office on the twenty-fourth floor, next to the U.S. District Court. They had told him an AUSA was hot to see someone immediately, so Harper had come down here to the fourth floor himself. He wasn't going to send anyone else to fall on the sword. He would answer for the Service's failure.

As he rode down the elevator, he thought about how many agencies were represented in this one city block on Dearborn Street—the DEA, the IRS, two U.S. senators, the Post Office—one of the greatest concentrations of federal power outside Washington, D.C. The last time Harper had come here, it had struck him how easy it would be for another Timothy McVeigh to hit the federal government—just roll a rental van filled with a fertilizer bomb down Dearborn Street.

But now he only had one thing on his mind.

"I appreciate you making the time to come down here," Greenwood said from the other side of her desk. "I'm honored. The Assistant Director of WITSEC himself."

Her words were dripping with civility, even if this was the one day that being in charge of WITSEC was anything but a badge of honor. She knew it. And she knew that *he* knew it.

"It's not a good day," he said. "I've got nine deputy marshals in the hospital."

"Plus one dead witness."

"That's on me. I take full responsibility."

"What does your taking responsibility do for me, Mr. Assistant Director?"

Harper was getting the picture. Greenwood didn't want a pound of flesh. She wanted answers.

"Nick Mason," he said.

"Is that name supposed to mean something to me?"

"He works for Darius Cole."

He knew that would stop her, because Darius Cole was the most important person in AUSA Greenwood's life right now. It was Greenwood who helped send Cole to prison for life in the first place, after offering deals to both of the witnesses who eventually testified against him. Harper wasn't surprised, now that he was sitting in her office. He'd met AUSAs all over the country—some of them were overmatched by the job, some were bright and ambitious but clearly on their way to something else. And some were born to represent the United States in court, even if that meant carrying too many cases, working too many late-night hours, for not enough pay and no recognition at all. Some of the best, Harper knew, were women. They had a special talent for putting together a case, for closing the deal, for turning co-defendants into cooperating witnesses by slipping right by a man's defenses, appealing to him on a primal level that goes all the way back to the cradle: *I'm on your side. I want to protect you.*

She'd been second chair at the original trial and now she was lead on the upcoming retrial. Which made her life this morning almost as fucked up as Harper's.

"Mason was doing time with Cole at Terre Haute," Harper said. "Cole got him out."

"I remember this now. There were problems with the original testimony. The detective came forward and admitted that he—"

"It was a lie," Harper said. "Cole orchestrated everything. He wanted Mason on the outside, to work for him."

"Work for him as in killing witnesses?"

"Among other things."

She took a beat to process that. "How do you know this?" she finally asked.

"The homicide detective who put him away. Frank Sandoval, partner of that detective who admitted to planting the evidence. He drove me by Mason's town house an hour ago. He's going to help me nail him. Or I'm going to help him. Frankly, I don't care who gets the credit on this one."

"Can Sandoval connect Mason to last night?"

"If he could, we'd be putting Mason in handcuffs right now."

She wrote down the name on her legal pad. "Nick Mason," she said. "Local guy?"

"Sandoval says he comes from a place called Canaryville."

She let out a breath and shook her head. "Figures."

"Colorful part of town, I take it?"

"My grandfather was a cop in this city back in the Prohibition days. He met all the big gangsters. Al Capone, Bugs Moran. Used to tell me stories about them when I was a little girl. But the worst of the bunch, he said, was a man named Gene Geary. The most ruthless killer he ever met."

"Let me guess," Harper said. "Canaryville."

"That's where all the stockyards were," she said. "My grandfather said you could walk down the street and smell death in the air."

Some things never change, Harper thought. He wasn't

going to say it out loud, not to a woman whose life was dedicated to trying to change them.

"It was a mistake to bring McLaren here for the deposition," Greenwood said. The subtext hung in the air: *It was a mistake to assume the Service would be able to protect him.*

"It shouldn't have been a mistake," Harper said. "None of this should have happened."

"But it was and it did," she said, then moved on. "Just one man did this?" More subtext: *One man against how many again?*

"We believe so, yes."

"How did he find out where you were keeping McLaren?"

"We don't know that yet."

She shook her head. "We were doing okay right up until then."

"What are you—"

She held her palms up to stop him. "Come on. You've already suggested that Cole compromised a detective to get Mason out of prison. You know and I know he got to someone in the Marshals Service."

Harper took another moment. He tried to remember what his late wife had told him about counting to three before answering a tough question.

He didn't even get to *one*.

"No," he said, "that's not possible. Not in my office."

"Yet apparently it *is*."

Harper didn't want to say it: *The leak must have been local. The one and only time the Service is compromised and of course it was someone from the city that turned corruption into an art form.*

"Look," Harper said, making himself take a breath, "we're on the same side here."

"Not if you're more interested in covering the Service's ass, we're not. I'm just trying to make sure I have at least one witness left when we get to this retrial."

"How the hell did Cole get this retrial, anyway? I thought that would be almost impossible."

"It should have been," Greenwood said. "But Cole did something pretty goddamned brilliant. If you remember that original trial, we filed for an anonymous jury . . ."

"Like Nicky Barnes's trial."

"Barnes was the first, yes. But there are two things about anonymous juries . . . One, they sometimes backfire. Like John Gotti's first trial . . ."

"The hung jury."

"With the foreman who had connections to the family. If that jury hadn't been anonymous, the connection would have been exposed and he would have been thrown out. But the second problem is where Cole makes his case for retrial . . . Because the Appeals Courts already have a standing prejudice against anonymous juries based on the built-in presumption of guilt. So they end up setting these ridiculous fairness standards for the deliberations. Very tough to meet. It's a weakness nobody ever exploited before. Not even Gotti in all those motions for retrial he filed."

"I don't understand," Harper said. "That trial was twelve years ago. How could Cole—"

"Out of nowhere," Greenwood said, "twelve years later, one of the original anonymous jurors supposedly finds Cole's attorney and tells him they deliberated improperly. They went over details of the case in the hotel, talked about how Cole must have been guilty if they were being locked away in a secret location. It was the one bomb that couldn't be ignored."

Harper looked at her, exasperated. "You don't believe this shit . . ."

"I didn't hear the motion," Greenwood said. "The Seventh Circuit Court of Appeals did."

"So, step one," Harper said, "get the retrial. Step two—"

"Start killing the key witnesses."

Harper thought about it for a beat. "And now we've only got one left."

Isaiah Wallace. Darius Cole's childhood friend and most trusted confidant. The man most responsible for putting Cole away. And the man we most need if we're going to keep him there.

Assuming we can keep him alive.

A thought that before last night would have been little more than a joke.

"We actually had a third potential witness for the original trial," Greenwood said. "Don't know if you knew that."

"I didn't."

"We never tried to flip him. He could have tied Cole to several homicides, but . . ." She shook her head as her voice trailed off.

"Wouldn't have made a good witness?"

"My boss at the time told me not to go after him unless I had to. He disappeared a few years later, ended up in New York, got popped not that long ago. Doing life at Dannemora, if I remember. So I really want to make sure that Mr. Wallace is—"

"We're moving Wallace to a WITSEC black site," Harper said. "He'll be absolutely untouchable. In the meantime, you can help me put Mason away. If we need a wiretap request or have to authorize overtime . . ."

A fact of life in modern law enforcement: if the U.S. Attorney doesn't want to go after a suspect, you can't charge him with a federal crime.

"I'll be happy to help you," Greenwood said. "But in

return, I'll need to meet with Mr. Wallace to prepare him for the retrial."

"I'm sorry but no."

She tilted her head at him. "Did you just say no?"

"I can set up a video feed," Harper said. "If we can get the judge to agree to it, we'll have Wallace testify that way, too."

"Not good enough."

"It will have to suffice."

"I need to see him in person. He's the key to my remaining case and I need to be absolutely certain that he's ready."

"Do you want me to protect this man or not?" Harper asked. "His own mother's not going to be able to see him in person. Not until the retrial is over."

"I am the U.S. Attorney prosecuting Darius Cole, not Isaiah Wallace's mother."

"Sorry."

"'Sorry' doesn't work for me. My job was already hard enough, Marshal. I'd be taking McLaren's pretrial deposition right now if . . ."

If the entire U.S. Marshals Service hadn't failed him.

Harper shrugged, unwilling to give in.

Greenwood stood up, came around the desk, and sat on the front edge of it, looming over Harper.

"You really want an interagency pissing contest, Marshal?" Greenwood asked. "If you think you'll win just because I have to sit to pee . . ."

She leaned over and lifted her phone out of its cradle.

"What do you think?"

"I'll see what I can arrange," Harper said. "If you don't mind flying to his location."

"I'll go anywhere," she said, giving him a tight smile. "I'll even wear a blindfold on the way."

"Mason won't get to him," Harper said. "Nobody will. I promise."

"I know you've had a tough twenty-four hours," she said, giving him another smile. "I'll let you go now."

As he shook her hand, he was glad he'd never have to face her in a courtroom.

7

IT WAS A BAD DAY TO BE NICK MASON.

The woman he had been trying to build a life with had been a minute away from becoming a statistic. A bullet through her head, in her own bedroom. One of a thousand unsolved cases in Chicago worth a few inches in the morning paper. Now she was gone, along with the dog that had brought them together.

And his neck and shoulder still hurt like hell.

He was driving the new car he'd been given after Quintero had taken the Pontiac GTO and had his men obliterate it in the chop shop. The replacement, another in a seemingly endless line of cars from Darius Cole's collection, was a 2004 Jaguar XK8. It was the first car Mason had seen that wasn't a classic muscle car—but it was jet black, like all of Cole's other cars, and when Mason thought about the year, it made sense: this had once been Cole's personal car, bought new right before he went to prison.

Mason pulled out from the shop, in the afternoon

shadows cast by the Cook County Jail, blew through two red lights and gunned it down California Avenue, feeling the power in the engine but with no idea where he was going.

Until he knew where he *had* to go. And the one person he had to see. The one person who could remind him why he was here. Why he had signed this contract and accepted these terms for a second life.

MASON DROVE CAUTIOUSLY through the West Side, eyes in his mirrors as much as on the road ahead. Even without clocking a tail, he would speed through red lights, pull into dark driveways, double back again. Trying to leave the violence and threat that was his second life at the city line before entering Elmhurst. A suburb of maple trees and fresh-cut lawns. Soccer fields and a restored movie theater on Main Street. A world apart.

Mason's daughter had been four years old when he went away, nine when he came back. He still hadn't seen the bedroom she had all to herself on the second floor of that house in Elmhurst. He pictured it in his head: soccer ribbons and trophies on her shelves, stuffed animals on her bed, posters on her walls.

He'd stood at the front door of the house. One time. Three steps into the hallway was as far as he'd come into her new world.

Some nights he would drive by, look up at her darkened window, imagine her sleeping on the other side of the glass. During the soccer season, he would come to her games whenever he could, stand off to the side and watch her running after the ball. She was fast, built lean and tall like her mother. Then the soccer season ended and it felt like his daughter was taken away from him again, disappearing into the routine of the school year and weekends away with her mother and her stepfather. And Mason was back to driving by their house just to make sure they were safe.

Today, he needed more than arm's length.

Mason rolled down North Avenue, knowing school would be out soon. He saw her elementary school just off Saint Charles Road, a building of glass and brick surrounded by acres of perfect green grass. A long line of cars streamed around a loop in the front of the building. All of these parents picking up their children, taking their normal lives for granted. They had no idea what Mason would have given just to be one of them.

Mason parked the car in a side lot and walked back to the fenced-in playground. Some of the parents were getting out of their cars now, coming over and calling out to their kids. Mason stood and watched the scene, oddly reminded of the busy days out on the prison yard when it was just as bright and sunny and there were just as many voices in the air all at once.

Then within one second the whole world went quiet and receded into the background as Mason caught sight of her.

Adriana.

Her hair was longer now but still lightened from the sun, just as her mother's hair would be well into the fall. Her cheeks were red as she chased after someone. She darted in and out of the crowd of children until she finally caught a boy by the shirttail and stopped him. He turned to face her, pushed her away, and sent her to the ground. Mason stopped breathing and remembered having the same reaction when she was knocked down on the soccer field—but now it seemed like his reaction was even more automatic, Mason already leaning forward, ready to move, ready to protect his girl, with no thought as to what that would mean.

Mason had always lived with violence. It was impossible to avoid growing up on the streets of Canaryville. But now . . .

Mason *was* the violence.

He let out his breath as Adriana got back to her feet, laughing. The boy ran away and his daughter kept chasing. He watched her, looking back toward the front of the school, waiting to see Gina appear. Unless it was Brad picking her up, but in the middle of the afternoon he was probably at work. Doing his normal job in an office building downtown.

No, it'll be Gina. It'll be good to see her, too.

As much as it hurt him, he still wanted to see her face, wanted to remember the best part of his life.

He kept watching and waiting, standing by the school yard fence, until it occurred to him that nobody was doing anything about it. No uniformed security guards had come up to him to ask him if he belonged here. In fact, Mason could see no guards on the premises at all.

Someone could walk over to her right now, Mason thought. *Anyone. Just grab her and pick her up, bring her back to his vehicle and take her away.*

Who would stop him?

Mason turned and scanned the vehicles that were lined up in the front driveway or parked in the side lot as if already searching out the one man who would do this. He saw a black vehicle, focused on it. A pickup truck. He found another. A Nissan SUV.

Then he saw it. The black Escalade. With the tinted windows.

Quintero's words from the night before echoed in his head: *Your job was to take out the accountant. Mine was to drive to Elmhurst. Wait to hear from you . . . Or not.*

Mason felt a raw, burning panic in his throat. He had sent Lauren away forever, just a matter of hours ago. It was something he had to do, to protect her.

And yet, here was his daughter. Still here in Chicago. Still in danger.

"Hello . . ."

Adriana's voice cut through everything else in his head, but he heard her struggling for what to call him.

"Call me Nick. Would that be okay?"

"Nick? Okay."

He looked down and saw Adriana standing against the fence. She was peering up at him, squinting in the afternoon sunlight.

Mason went to the fence and got down on one knee. He took one more quick look behind him, then turned to his daughter. "Hey, sweetie," he said, his heart pounding out of his chest.

"Why are you here?"

"I wanted to see your school."

"This is it," she said, making a grand gesture to everything behind her. "And that's my teacher right over there. Mrs. Martin."

She nodded toward the woman standing next to the side door of the school. The woman was watching Adriana carefully, *watching Mason*, this stranger kneeling at the playground fence.

Go walk over to that Escalade, he thought, *if you want to see the real danger.*

"I miss seeing you play soccer," Mason said. "You're really good."

"I like softball better," she said. "I'm going to play in the spring."

"You could play both." He imagined himself sitting in the bleachers in April and May, another chance to see her every week.

"I can hit the ball *really hard*," she said. "Mom says I get that from you."

"She talks about me?" He tried not to sound surprised.

"Sometimes."

They spent another few minutes together talking about nothing. Mason asked her about the boy she'd been horsing around with. She asked him a few questions about his life and he had to lie to her. He hated to do it. He had no choice.

A man's voice came from over Mason's shoulder. "Is this your daughter?"

As Mason stood up, he was already working out what this meant, Quintero out of the vehicle, this close to his daughter.

When he turned, it wasn't Quintero, though Mason was no happier to find himself staring into the intensely dark eyes of Detective Frank Sandoval.

"Your Jaguar over there?" Sandoval nodded toward the parking lot. "Change of pace for you."

Mason didn't answer him. Rule number three: *When in doubt, keep your mouth shut.*

"Hard to keep track of your cars."

Mason let that go, turned back to his daughter.

"We gotta talk, Mason."

Mason shook his head.

"Who are you?" Adriana asked, looking back and forth between the two men on the other side of the fence.

"I'm a friend of your father's," Sandoval said, bending over to address her. "You must be Adriana. I've heard a lot about you."

"You're not his friend," Adriana said, squinting up at his face. "You're a policeman."

Sandoval smiled. "How do you know that?"

She patted her right hip, then pointed. "I can see your gun."

Sandoval buttoned his jacket. "You got a sharp kid," he said to Mason.

"And you're interrupting."

"Didn't mean to butt in," Sandoval said. "Just wanted to ask you something. About what you gave me . . ."

He didn't need to be any more specific. Mason had only ever given him one thing—the flash drive off a dealer's laptop, with enough information to bring down the whole SIS task force. He'd given it to Sandoval not because he wanted to help his career but because he knew Sandoval was the only cop clean enough, and stubborn enough, not to bury it.

"What about it?" Mason said.

"Did you tell anyone else?"

"If you got other cops looking at you, that's got nothing to do with me."

Sandoval looked at him for a long moment, nodded, and turned to leave. Turned back. Smiled.

"You talk to your girl, but we're not done." He pointed at his car. He waved to Adriana. "Nice meeting you."

She didn't wave back.

Sandoval shook his head and returned to his sedan. Mason watched him get behind the wheel, noting that the detective was alone now. Whoever had been in the car with him that morning was gone.

"We're going to Denver," Adriana said.

Mason got back down on one knee. "When?"

"Soon! Mom says we might live there."

Mason had to hide his surprise again. This time, it was a lot harder.

"What about school?" Mason said. "And soccer? And—"

"They have all that out there," Adriana said. "But I don't want to leave, anyway. I want to stay here!"

I want you to stay here, too. But Mason couldn't say it out loud.

"Adriana!" It was Gina's voice, tinted with alarm. Her expression a mixture of worry and anger.

Mason saw her coming toward them, moving a notch too quickly for a woman just casually picking up her daughter from school. She had the expensive haircut of an Elmhurst woman, the clothes, the diamond earrings—but he could still see the Canaryville girl he had fallen in love with. The girl he had given up everything for—his careers stealing cars, then taking down drug dealers, then doing commercial break-ins. He gave it all up for her, rebuilt a house on Forty-seventh Street, rebuilt his entire life. And even when he made the biggest mistake of his life and ended up losing it all . . .

He was doing it for Gina and Adriana.

At least, that's what he told himself.

Gina was on the other side of the fence from Mason, and whether she meant it or not, the simple geometry of the situation said something important to him: *We're on this side, you're on the other. This metal fence keeps us safe from you, with or without the razor wire on top.*

"I was just driving by," Mason said. "I wanted to see where Adriana goes to school."

"Can he come over today?" Adriana asked her mother. "I want to show him my new bike."

"Today's not good," Gina said to her. "We have to pack, remember?"

"What's this about going to Denver?" Mason asked.

"It's Brad . . ." she said, then hesitated. "He got a really nice job offer."

"It's a long way from Chicago."

The idea of his daughter living a thousand miles away . . . He didn't want to show her how much it hurt him. He didn't want to get in a fight with her. Not here. Not in front of his daughter.

"We haven't decided yet, Nick. We were going to call you and let you know."

It sure as hell sounds decided to me, Mason thought.

"Can you come with us?" Adriana asked.

Gina gave Nick a subtle shake of her head. Mason went back down to one knee.

"I can't come," he said. "But when you get back . . ."

He struggled to find the words.

"I want to come visit you," she said. "I want to see where you live!"

Mason looked up at Gina.

"We'll talk about it," Gina said to her. "We should go now."

"I know what *We'll talk about it* means," Adriana said. "It means *We won't talk about it*."

Mason didn't want to play Adriana against her mother, but he wanted to have this time with her. While he still had the chance, Mason wanted to have just *one day*.

He watched his ex-wife thinking it over. The inner war between the woman he'd married, who knew what Adriana meant to Mason, and the Mama Bear, who'd kill a dozen men and lay down her own life to protect her.

When she looked through the fence at him, for one quick moment all of the years and everything that had happened between them fell away and she was Gina Sullivan Mason from Canaryville. A woman who could see how much her daughter's father wanted to spend time with her.

"Maybe we can do that," she finally said. "As soon as we get back, okay? Now, we have to get going."

Adriana jumped up and down and waved to Mason as she went off with her mother. Mason wanted to hug her so badly, but the fence stood between them and he didn't want to press his luck with a big production of going around it. In the end, he settled for a promise that Gina would call him as soon as they got back from Denver.

Mason watched Adriana get into the minivan, waving at her again just before the door closed and the vehicle rolled away. Standing there, his gaze following the van, he tried making sense of it.

Even on a day that should be a good one, a day in which I get to see my daughter . . . I find out that she'll be moving a thousand miles away.

He didn't feel like dealing with Sandoval now. But thinking he could ignore the cop, hoping that he'd just go away, wouldn't work. He'd tried that. It was like a fly banging against a window, convinced that the *next* time the glass wouldn't be there.

Mason leaned against the driver's-side door of the sedan.

"What'd you really want?"

Sandoval took a long look at Mason. He pointed to the white tape peeking out over Nick's shirt collar. "What's that about?"

"Cut myself shaving."

"Adriana's a beautiful girl. Sharp."

"There a point to this?" Mason said, losing patience.

"I used to think you were sharp, too. Now I'm not so sure."

"You're going to hurt my feelings."

Sandoval smiled. "You've been living a charmed life, Mason. Your luck almost ran out at the Aqua. But that's not why I'm here."

Nick said nothing, waited for him to continue.

"I want Cole."

Mason ignored that and said, "We're done."

He took a few steps toward the Jag.

"I'm trying to save your life here, Mason. Maybe your girl's life, too."

Mason stopped, turned, and went back.

"You have something to say, say it."

"I already told you once," Sandoval said. "I'd trade a dozen of you to get to your boss."

"What's this got to do with my daughter?"

"That guy you killed at the Aqua. McLaren. He wasn't some scumbag drug dealer or dirty cop. Your boss has you hunting federally protected witnesses now."

Mason forced himself not to react.

"McLaren was Darius Cole's accountant and one of two star witnesses against him at trial," Sandoval said.

Mason looked away. He wanted to be behind the wheel of his car, driving away fast.

"You don't care about your own life," Sandoval said. "Your choice. But think about your girl and your ex."

"What's the point, Sandoval?"

"You think your life sucks now? What's it going to be like if Darius Cole is back on the street? You know what happens to Cole's loose ends. Soon as he gets out, you're just as dangerous to him as McLaren was. Hell, even more so."

Hard truths, no matter whose mouths they come out of, have a certain ring to them. But somewhere inside, Mason knew all this before the cop had said a word.

Sandoval kept at it. "You think the guy who comes to clean up after you is going to use nonlethal loads on innocent bystanders? No, Mason. The only question is, does he do you or your family first?"

Mason had heard enough. He turned and walked away from Sandoval's sedan, heat rising just beneath his skin. Across the lot, he saw the sunlight reflected against the tinted windows of the Escalade. Then the vehicle pulled out of the lot.

For one horrible second, he thought it was catching up to Gina's minivan, but as it pulled out onto the street, it turned and went in the opposite direction.

Mason got into his own car and left. It took him two minutes to clock a new car on his tail. He'd always suspected that someone else might be tailing him, at least some of the time. Because even a man like Quintero couldn't follow him 24-7.

Another member of Cole's organization, Mason said to himself. *Someone I haven't met yet. Maybe the man Sandoval was talking about. The man they'll send to tie up Darius Cole's loose end.*

He was tempted to jam on the brakes at the next busy intersection, get out of the car, and go introduce himself. But then he had a better idea.

He took out his cell phone and called the one man who could help him turn this day around.

8

"SANDOVAL IS A PROBLEM."

Quintero sat behind the tinted glass of his vehicle, holding his cell phone to his ear and watching Detective Sandoval approach Mason at the school yard fence. Mason's body language gave away the tension he must have been feeling, as he stood up stiffly and faced the man, with his own daughter just a few feet away.

"No names," Cole said.

"We're encrypted, right?"

"No names," Cole said again. "And we got more important issues than the cop."

"Like what?"

"Our second target will be moving soon."

"Where?" Quintero said.

"When I know, I'll tell you. Just be ready."

Quintero kept an eye on Sandoval as he headed back

to his car. Now Mason's ex-wife was there behind the daughter. It was a regular family reunion.

"That thing I asked you to do with the woman," Cole said, "you take care of it?"

Quintero took the phone away from his ear for a moment. He had been working for Darius Cole for eighteen years and not once had he ever lied to the man. Because Quintero was not a liar, first of all. And, second, if you were ever going to choose your first man to lie to, it wouldn't be Darius Cole.

But the truth would be worse: telling Cole that he hadn't followed an order, hadn't killed Mason's girlfriend and disposed of the body.

"Are you there?" Cole asked. "Did you take care of it or not?"

"It's taken care of."

Quintero swallowed hard, imagined Cole deciding whether or not to believe him.

"What about our third target?" Quintero said, changing subjects. "There's someone in New York I can reach out to."

"That issue is already being resolved. Today."

"Solving your problems is *my* job."

"The man's eight hundred miles away."

"I told you, I have a contact on the inside."

"I think I probably have a few more," Cole said. "Your job is to solve the problems I *tell* you to solve. Not to worry about anything else."

Quintero looked at Mason one more time, and the two other people who one day might *become* a problem Cole told him to solve.

"Get your head on straight," Cole said, reading his employee from a prison cell three hundred miles to the south. "Take care of your business and I'll take care of the rest."

*   *   *

THE REST OF THAT DAY'S business was about to take place, eight hundred miles to the east, just as Cole was ending the call. A Department of Corrections bus was heading down the three-lane girder bridge that connected the borough of Queens to Rikers Island, rattling down the thin metal strip, while airplanes roared in across the water to the LaGuardia runway on the far banks of the East River.

A man named Sean Burke was sitting in the front row, the only one of the seventy-one passengers who had a bench seat to himself. The CO on the other side of the grate kept a constant eye on him as if waiting for him to do something interesting. But there was a bored, almost half-asleep look on Burke's pale, freckled face, and surrounded by a few dozen other men who resembled interior linemen or heavyweight contenders, you'd never suspect that Sean Burke was the most dangerous man on the bus.

Burke was born in 1977 in a town called Crossmaglen in occupied Northern Ireland. When he was five years old, he watched his father get dragged from their home in retaliation for a sniper attack against British soldiers. His father died in prison soon afterward, and Burke vowed to take his place in the ongoing fight. He didn't care about a united Ireland or any other principle the IRA was fighting for. His first, overwhelming motivation was pure revenge. In the years that followed, when Burke proved himself to be a fearless and vicious killer, the killing itself became all that he knew.

Just after the 1999 cease-fire, Burke was about to be arrested by the Royal Ulster Constabulary. He fled the country for Chicago, where a cousin owned a corner bar in the heavily Irish South Side neighborhood of Beverly. When he overstayed his visa, Burke went underground, working cash jobs and ultimately proving himself as fearless and as vicious as he had in Northern Ireland—and just as invaluable to organizations that trafficked in violence.

Burke never did look anything like a violent man. Not then, and not now as he rode the bus back to Rikers after his transfer hearing. With his slight build, red hair, freckled face, and disinterested demeanor, he was a man begging to be underestimated. But his cut muscles rippled and pulsed beneath his jail fatigues. Without an ounce of fat, every inch of him, body and soul, was devoted to one thing: destruction. Burke was a lion masquerading as a house cat.

Underestimating him was the mistake his cellmate had made up at Dannemora. Burke was three years into his life sentence when the new man in the top bunk laughed off the warnings and tried to take Burke's blanket on a cold Upstate New York night. The instantaneous results bought Burke a new set of charges, a resentencing, and a transfer to the New York supermax at Southport. He had three more days to spend here at Rikers, where they'd been keeping him in the Central Punitive Segregation Unit, a five-story gray tower of solitary nine-by-eight cells, home for five hundred of the most dangerous prisoners on the island. No television, no phone, a tiny slit high on the wall the only excuse for a window. One hour of rec per day, meaning a walk in shackles to stand alone in a small courtyard, staring up at the airplanes flying overhead.

Burke had always been a fan of Johnny Cash, the worn cassette tapes his only physical connection to his father, their sound his only memory of better times. He played Cash's songs in his head now, a running sound track for his days at Dannemora, the volume turned up even louder here at Rikers. "Folsom Prison Blues" was his favorite, and now he knew more than ever how a man could listen to a train going by and think about the people inside just like Burke thought about the people on those jets coming in and out of LaGuardia.

But Burke sure as hell wasn't going to hang his head and cry.

When the bus pulled up to the CPSU tower, Burke stood up and shuffled off with the rest of the prisoners. Each man was wearing handcuffs and leg-irons. They were led into the processing area and then loaded onto the elevator a half dozen at a time, with one CO to watch over them as they were taken up to their floor. There were no buttons to push on this elevator—it was all controlled remotely.

When Burke was put into the elevator with five other men, all headed toward the fifth floor, the doors slid shut and the elevator jerked upward.

"What'choo doing in the Bing, white boy?"

It was one of three large black men who said this to Burke, using CPSU's unofficial title. He'd heard this tower called the Bing by several of the COs—as far as he could tell, *bing* was the sound of a man losing his mind after twenty-three hours a day in a solitary cell.

Burke looked up at the man's face, then at the even larger white man standing next to him. "Ya gonna let him talk to me that way?"

The big white man looked down at him and laughed. Mocking Burke's brogue, he repeated the line back to him. *Yee ganna let heem tawk to me dat why?* He laughed some more, and said in a heavy New York accent, "Let me guess, you're a fucking Red Sox fan, too."

Burke looked the man in the eye. "I hate all American sports," he said. "And I've never even been to Boston, you ignorant piece of shite."

The man smiled even wider and that's when Burke

knew something was seriously fucked. Under any normal circumstances, this would be a challenge. But here, right now . . .

Burke took a quick look around the rest of the elevator, finally noticing the one thing that should have caught his eye immediately: no CO, just the five large men— three black, one Latino, and his new white friend—and Burke. All of them wearing handcuffs and leg-irons.

The elevator ground to a halt between floors.

"Looks like we're stuck," the white man said.

It's a setup, Burke said to himself. *But they made a mistake: they kept us all shackled.*

Now it's not even a fair fight.

Burke didn't hesitate. If he was the kind of man who waited for the enemy to make the first move, he would have been buried in a Crossmaglen graveyard years ago.

He reached up and circled his forearms around the white man's neck, using the man's height to give himself the first advantage. The man was strong and resisted going down, exactly what Burke had counted on. Using the big man's resistance for leverage, Burke swung his shackled feet around and kicked the black man at the back of the elevator car in the throat. The man went down, gasping for air and clutching at his throat.

Everything slowed down for Burke now that the fight was on. Still using the white man to push off, Burke slammed his feet into the testicles of one of the other black men. The white man's resistance waning, he lost his balance, taking Burke down with him. Using the falling man's momentum, Burke thrust his legs on the Latino's left knee. Something cracked and the Latino toppled sideways, grabbing his leg and screaming Spanish curses.

Burke caught himself just before hitting the floor, going down to his knees and keeping the handcuffs tight against the white man's neck. The last man in the eleva-

tor, the third black, was already swinging one of his
chained legs toward Burke. It was a labored, slow movement that Burke had no trouble anticipating. He yanked
the white man's head in front of him like a shield to take
the blow. The white's nose snapped as the black's shoe
found its mark. That would turn on the white man's tear
ducts, Burke knew, moving him down to the bottom of
the list.

The only one left standing, the third black man, was
about to swing one of his shackled feet again. He still
hadn't learned his lesson. Burke ducked it easily and
swept the man's other leg out from underneath him. He
thumped hard against the elevator floor, the wind going
out of him in a single rush. Burke brought his elbow
down, and down again, on the man's throat.

The man he'd kicked in the groin was back in the
game. He swung at Burke with both hands clasped together, connecting with the side of Burke's head. The
man swung again and Burke ducked, then drove his
shoulder up into the man and pinned him. He pulled at
the man's already-damaged groin with both hands, lifting
and tearing. The man collapsed, vomiting and writhing in
pain.

Quick count: two dead. Three men still moving, but
not for long. Burke turned and faced the Latino with the
wrecked knee. Burke opened his hands as wide as they
could go and drove the man's head back against the wall,
the thin part of his skull hitting hard enough to knock
him out. Working systematically, Burke choked the life
out of him and then the third black man by squeezing
their necks until their tracheas collapsed and their throats
filled with blood. That left Burke with one other man still
alive in the in the midst of the vomit and carnage.

Burke knelt down next to the white man, his face
smeared with mucus and blood from his broken nose.

"Who arranged this party, boyo?"

"Fuck you," the man said, spitting blood into Burke's face.

Burke calmly wiped the blood away, then grabbed the man's right hand and bent his little finger until it snapped. The man screamed.

Fingers were such convenient things in a situation like this. So simple to break yet so many nerve endings connected to the brain.

"I didn't hear you," Burke said. "Who was it?"

He moved to the next finger, bending it backward until it snapped. The man screamed again.

"I don't think it was one of the Gambinos," Burke said. "They wouldn't hire a whole fucking United Nations to do this."

He broke the third finger.

"No," the man screamed, shaking his head. "No, no . . ."

"I didn't think so."

He broke another finger. Now all four fingers of the man's right hand were bent back at unnatural angles. Burke took all of the fingers in one hand, squeezing them together, as he took the thumb with his other hand. The man screamed even louder.

"I think I know who it is," Burke said, "but, all the same, I'd like to hear you say his name."

When Burke had first come to Chicago, he'd ended up working for an aging local gangster on the South Side until the man drew the attention of an emerging crime figure, a man who was moving to consolidate all of his financial operations in the entire city. The old man refused to cooperate and a representative was sent to have a conversation with him. Burke intervened and killed the representative, and then the next two men who came afterward. The man who sent them had already demonstrated a certain wisdom about when to make friends rather than enemies or when to make *employees*. He'd just bought out the services of a La Raza gang member named Quintero and now decided to do the same with Burke. Instead of going to war with this kid, he would hire him. Burke's first job: kill the gangster he was protecting.

Burke continued to work for his new boss, receiving his assignments through Quintero, and ultimately killing more men than he could count—until he was finally given an order he didn't feel like obeying. After shadowing a rival dealer for two days straight, living on nothing but coffee and cigarettes, Quintero called him at the last minute and told him to back off. Burke killed the man anyway just so two days of his life wouldn't have been totally wasted. When Quintero reminded him of the price for disobedience, Burke said, *"You know where to find me."* Cole sent a half dozen men. Burke sent them all back. Dead.

Burke left Chicago soon after that and ended up in New York, finding work with a newly revived version of the Westies, the infamous Hell's Kitchen gang sponsored and protected by the Gambino crime family. But it was a new generation of criminals born and bred in New York, and even though they all had Irish last names, Burke found no common ground with them. They were more interested in buying clothes and getting laid, and when Burke killed a Gambino lieutenant for calling him a mick for the hundredth time, not only did they fail to protect him, they handed him over to the police. For the first time in his life, Burke was sent to prison.

And now, three years later, he waited to hear the name of the one and only man who could have reached him in a fortified tower on an island in the East River.

"Cole," the man said between screams. "It was Cole, it was Cole."

"There you go," Burke said, bending the man's thumb back and tearing the joint away from the palm just for the hell of it. The man fell backward, fainting from pain.

Burke stood up, brushing himself off as well as he could with both hands still cuffed together. Then he stood with one foot on either side of the man's head, pressing the leg-irons into his neck.

The elevator came to life with a jerk and started moving upward again. Burke listened impassively to the gurgling sounds coming from the white man's throat, until they stopped. When the elevator got to the fifth floor, Burke stepped over the body of the now-dead man into the arms of a dozen screws, all waiting for him with clubs and pepper spray.

"Now *this* is a proper party," he said, nodding with approval. "Feels just like home."

As the guards worked him over, and the pepper spray closed his eyes and throat, Burke kept asking himself the same two questions:

After all this time, why is Cole coming after me again?
And what am I going to do about it?

MASON IGNORED THE BURNING SENSATION in his healing right shoulder as he aimed the sniper rifle. He put all of his focus on the crosshairs, on his breathing, until he pulled the trigger and the butt of the rifle kicked against that same shoulder. He had to close his eyes for several seconds, dealing with the pain, acknowledging it, accepting it. He opened his eyes and took off the ear protectors.

"Low. Low. Low. Every shot's been low," Eddie said.

"No," Mason said, putting the rifle down on the bench. "Exactly where I'm aiming."

They were shooting at an outdoor range in Joliet, a few miles outside Chicago. There were closer ranges, but it was Eddie's suggestion to come here, and Mason liked the fact that you could clearly see the range from the parking lot. When he pulled his Jag into the lot, the gray sedan that had been following him all the way down here from Adriana's school was nowhere to be seen. But the next time he looked up, Mason noticed Quintero's black Escalade parked in a back corner of the lot. Mason wasn't particularly worried. All Quintero would see was Mason practicing his shooting skills, getting some tips from his old friend who happened to be an ex–army sniper. No reason for him to question that.

"Look at my target," Eddie said, nodding to his *bottle*—the center mass plus the head. "If the target had been human, he would have taken every round straight through the sternum.

"Now look at yours," he said, pointing to the shots along the beltline on Mason's target. "What are you try-ing to do, pick his fucking pocket?"

Mason didn't answer, because that's exactly what Ma-son was trying to do. It's what he'd done at the Aqua. It's what he meant to keep doing. It would've been hard to explain to Eddie, because even though Mason killed peo-ple, complete strangers, he lived by a code: *No innocent victims.*

But Eddie wasn't finished.

"Every yard you add to a shot amplifies all the factors affecting it. Wind, drop, all of it. Center mass, Nick. Cen-ter mass. Whenever you try to pull off one of those Holly-wood shots, you put your own life at risk."

Eddie was sounding like Quintero, Mason thought. *And I've got a hole in my shoulder that proves them both right.*

Mason knew Eddie was trying to protect him. Eddie Callahan, who was built like a tank, had been Mason's best friend ever since they were kids running around

Canaryville. Eddie was the one kid in the group who had a real set of parents, and they sent him away to the army when he was twenty-two years old. He came back a year later, identified as a natural-born sniper but drummed out when he couldn't put up with asshole sergeants telling him what to do every minute. With a good rifle, a good scope, and a minute to dial it all in, he could still hit anything under a thousand yards.

Today, they were just shooting holes through paper with rifles and a couple of semiautomatic pistols that Eddie had brought with him. The irony wasn't lost on Mason: he didn't even own a gun, because whenever he used one, he left it at the scene. If he wanted to practice, he had to borrow guns from Eddie.

When they were done shooting, Eddie slipped a Browning 1911 into Mason's hand.

"You're taking this home with you."

"Don't need it. When I get a job, I get the hardware, too."

"This isn't for a job," Eddie said. "This is for you."

Mason held the pistol in his hand, thought about what Eddie was saying to him.

He's right. I may need this.

"I appreciate you coming down here," Mason said. "What did you tell your wife?"

"I told her I was going shooting," Eddie said as he closed his gun case. "She knows it's how I unwind."

"Did you tell her I'd be here?"

Eddie hesitated, and fought off a half smile.

"Yeah," Mason said, "didn't think so."

Eddie lived in a little house in Bridgeport now. As South Side neighborhoods go, it was one step up from Canaryville. He had a small business in his garage repairing computers, twin three-year-old boys, and a wife, Sandra—*Don't call me Sandy*—who made no secret about how she felt about Eddie's old friend Nick Mason. The fact that Mason took the fall for the harbor job and Eddie did zero days in federal prison didn't seem to factor into the equation.

"Listen," Mason said, "I'll tell you why we're really here."

"I was wondering when you'd get to it."

"I need your help again," Mason said, taking a quick look at the parking lot to check on Quintero. "I'm willing to pay you."

"I know what you did for me, Nick. You don't have to pay me."

"I have a safe-deposit box at First Chicago on Western," Mason said. "There's ten thousand dollars cash in there on the first of every month."

"Who puts it there?"

"That's the first thing I want you to find out. Tomorrow's the drop day. I need you to watch the bank, figure out who's leaving the money, follow them wherever they go."

"How will I know who to follow?"

"Use your instincts," Mason said. "This person is a member of Darius Cole's operation. I don't even know what color they'll be. But a pro's a pro."

"A pro doing a job. I'll keep my eyes open."

"Take pictures," Mason said. "Wherever you follow them. Write down the addresses. I need to start collecting information."

"No problem," Eddie said. "These are the people you work for now?"

Mason nodded. "We're doing counter-intel on the entire organization. Everybody we can identify. That money they give me every month, we're going to start using it against them. I'm also paying you with it."

"I told you, Nick, you don't have to—"

"This is going to be a full-time job, Eddie. You're going to have to explain this to your wife."

Eddie took a moment to think it over. "Or just don't tell her anything."

"You work in your garage. How the hell are you going to explain being out all the time?"

"I'll tell her I got a new job. Fixing computers at different locations all over the city."

"Next thing," Mason said. "Don't look right now, but there's a black Escalade in the back corner of the parking lot. I want you to follow it when I leave. Find out where the driver lives."

"Done."

"Last thing," Mason said. "Next time I go on a job . . ."

"Yeah?"

"I'll call you," Mason said. "I want you to go out to Elmhurst and keep an eye on Gina's house. If I don't call you back by a certain time, that means I'm dead. Which means you've got to do one final thing for me."

Eddie nodded his head slowly as he waited for it.

"You find that black Escalade," Mason said. "You go up to the window. And you put a bullet in the driver's head."

9

DETECTIVE FRANK SANDOVAL WAS ALONE. AGAIN.

He was on his way out of Homan Square, the redbrick monolith that took up one whole city block between Fillmore Street and a set of railroad tracks. Once an abandoned Sears warehouse, now it belonged to the Chicago Police Department. It was home to the Evidence and Recovered Property Section, which is why Sandoval was there dropping off the bag of clothing he'd recovered from the house on Sixteenth Street.

Homan, as most cops called it, was also home to the Organized Crime Bureau, the ballistics lab, and the SWAT unit. It had also been home, at one time, to the Special Investigations Section, or SIS, an elite task force of rock star cops who'd been given a blank check to take guns and drugs off the streets using any means necessary.

A month earlier, Sandoval would have had to make his way through a crowd of people gathered around the Homan Square gates. Protesters with signs reading *Stop Po-*

lice Terror and *No Gitmo in Chicago* after the newspapers broke the story that thousands of suspects had been detained here over the past decade, denied access to attorneys and never allowed to make contact with their families. Some of them, according to the papers, physically tortured—like this was some sort of Third World dictatorship.

As he drove through the gates, Sandoval didn't have to wonder where the protesters had gone. They had moved on to other parts of the city, even to the sidewalk in front of the mayor's house, to protest the police shooting of yet one more unarmed black man. Sandoval didn't wear a uniform anymore, but whenever he identified himself as a member of the Chicago Police Department, he could feel the unspoken words hanging in the air: *You are the enemy.*

It was a city that had paid out over a half billion dollars to the families of victims shot by the police. A city where most cops on the beat didn't see much reason to do more than the minimum anymore: answer the 911 calls, but don't make proactive stops, don't put yourself in a situation where you can lose your job. Or your life.

Sandoval parked and went inside. The evidence window was on the first floor. At one time SIS had the top-floor offices overlooking the whole city. Those were empty now after Sandoval had turned in the information that put SIS out of business. And seven of its members in prison.

Sandoval's identity as the man who brought down SIS had never been officially revealed. No medals, no photos in the paper of him shaking hands with the mayor. He wondered how long that anonymity would last, was already starting to get that icy feeling down his back that other cops were watching him. That's why he had asked Mason about it—the only other man who knew about where that information had come from. Because cops walk a tightrope. You ask any officer what he thinks of dirty cops and he'll tell you they should fry. But you turn in brother cops, no matter how dirty, no matter how much blood on their hands, and you're a rat. And for a lot of cops, a rat is worse than anyone the rat turns in.

As Sandoval walked down the hallway, there was something eating at him, something he'd missed that day, but he couldn't identify it. He ran through everything he'd done so far: going to the Aqua, meeting Marshal Harper, his conversation with Mason at the school. Then, finally, his real job.

There'd been plans for him to transfer to days, but there was still something about the second shift that appealed to him. Even if it had sped up the end of his marriage, and even if it made it almost impossible to see his kids during the school week, Sandoval was secretly happy when the transfer got put on hold. His mornings were free for him to keep tabs on Nick Mason. Then he'd go to work and the sun would go down in the middle of his shift or it would be down already if it was the dead of winter. The city waking up a second time with a brand-new energy, the last of the sunlight reflecting off the glass buildings, the streetlights beginning to glow on the bridges over the river.

This was his Chicago. A city that would see over four thousand shootings that year alone. And over seven hundred murders—more than Los Angeles and New York combined.

The most beautiful, fucked-up, heartbreaking city in the world.

He watched the gloved evidence technician going through Derrick Moss's clothing. Moss was the main suspect in the brutal rape and murder of a teenage girl, but when Sandoval went to serve the warrant, Derrick was nowhere to be found. He was gone, but he'd left behind the clothing he'd worn the night before. Pants: blue denim. Shirt: white tee. Socks: white athletic. Shoes: white Air Jordans, brand-new.

"They always find money for the Jordans, huh?"

The tech smiled at him, waiting for acknowledgment of his social commentary. Sandoval just looked at him. And then it hit him:

The shoes.

He wasn't wearing them because he was still in the house.

Sandoval hurried back outside to his car, called his new partner as he drove back to Sixteenth Street. Tony Alonso, a twenty-year veteran detective who dressed better, looked better, talked smoother than anyone else at Area Central. Sandoval wasn't convinced he was half as good a detective as he thought he was. Or even a quarter as good. But right now, Sandoval needed his partner.

He pulled up in front of the house again, one story on a city lot barely big enough to hold it. Got back on the radio, called for Alonso. Heard nothing back but silence. He called for the dispatcher and asked for backup, gave her the address.

There's a back door leading into the alley, he thought, reconstructing the interior of the house in his mind. An alley behind it running parallel to the street, like a thousand others all over the city.

He saw the front door open for one moment. A young face looked out at him. Then the door slammed shut.

God damn it.

Sandoval drew his Glock 27 as he crossed the street. He was years past the days when he wore a radio on his belt and a mic on his shoulder. He could only hope that someone else was on the way as he hit the narrow passageway between the Moss house and the house next door, climbed over two garbage cans, and kept going. When he got back to the alley, he looked east, saw nothing, looked west, caught a brief glimpse of someone turning a corner.

Let him go. You don't do this by yourself. The voice of reason in the back of his mind. He ignored it and kept running.

When he got to the end of the alley, he found a small group of men standing together. All of them were black. None of them was Derrick Moss.

"Which way?" Sandoval asked them.

They stood silently, watching him. The old rule in Chicago, reinforced by recent events and made more emphatic than ever: *You don't give anything to a cop. Ever.* Even as he brushed past them, they did not move aside.

Sandoval crossed the street to a small church that stood on the corner. He took out his cell phone and dialed his partner's number.

"Where are you?" he asked as soon as the call was answered.

"There's another unit on the street. I'll be right behind them."

"I'm at the church at Fifteenth and Austin. Suspect is inside."

Now you wait, Sandoval thought. He circled the church, watching for the man in case he decided to run again. As he came under an open second-story window, he heard an older man's voice. He couldn't make out the words, but the voice was tightened by fear.

Sandoval looked up and down the street, swore to himself, and went to the back door. It was unlocked. He pulled it open.

He was in a storage area, barely illuminated by the late-afternoon sunlight streaming through a single high window. He saw chairs and audio equipment. Another door on the far side. He moved across the room, put his ear to the door, and heard the same man's voice on the other side.

"You don't have to do this," the older man said in a careful, measured way. Most likely, the pastor of this church. "Let me help you."

Sandoval pushed open the door a fraction of an inch. He saw the back of a lectern and wooden benches where the choir would sit during the service. The voice was louder, but he still couldn't see who was speaking.

"Don't do this, Derrick. You got a chance to make this turn out different."

He knows him. He's reasoning with him.

Sandoval pushed the door open all the way and stepped into the sanctuary. He led with his Glock, held it with both hands, moving it in perfect sync with his sight line. Left to right: empty pews, an aisle, more empty pews. *Where are they?* He swung the gun all the way to his right and saw them. An older man, in a black shirt with a clerical collar, and a younger man, sitting at the edge of the front pew.

Derrick Moss.

"Show me your hands!" Sandoval yelled.

Moss leapt to his feet and ran along the wall toward the back of the sanctuary. Sandoval kept the gun trained on him as he moved down the center aisle to cut him off.

"Get on the floor, Derrick! Get on the floor!"

Moss hit the rear door hard and flew back. It was locked.

"Get on the floor now!"

The next few seconds lasted an eternity as the young man turned to face him, his eyes wide open, his hand moving to his back pocket.

"Derrick!"

Two visions of the future popped into the detective's

head: Sandoval's two kids watching a black box being lowered into the ground, policemen in uniform firing off their guns in salute. Or a different black box, lowered into a different plot of ground on the other side of the city, while the streets burned over yet another black man shot down by the police, this time in a church.

In a church.

Derrick's right hand came away from the back pocket. As Sandoval's finger slowly squeezed the trigger, Moss's mother's words from earlier that day rang in his head: *He doesn't carry a gun, please don't let them shoot my boy.* And something in that face, the empty look of despair and fear . . .

"It's just a phone!" Moss said. "It's just a phone!"

He dropped the cell phone to the floor and got down on his knees. Sandoval let out his breath and moved forward, pressing the man's chest against the floor and putting cuffs on his wrists. He stayed on his knees, one hand pressed on the back of the young man lying next to him. He felt own his heart pounding in his chest.

You were dead, he said to himself. *If that was a gun, you were dead.*

Sandoval didn't move for several more seconds as the pastor moved closer to sit in the last pew and Derrick Moss kept his forehead pressed against the floor.

Finally, Sandoval heard the sounds of footsteps in the hallway outside, the door being pushed roughly open, wood splintering as the lock gave way. A half dozen men in uniform burst into the room, guns drawn. Another terrifying second as Sandoval looked up into the dark tunnel of another cop's gun.

"Secure!" Sandoval said. The cop lowered his weapon. Two other cops picked up Moss and led him out of the room. Another two attended to the pastor, asking him questions and offering to send for an ambulance. Nobody said a word to Sandoval.

Not one word.

He went outside, took a breath of cold air, saw Alonso coming up the steps. It looked like he'd stopped to get his suit pressed on the way here, with another stop for a shoeshine while he got his hair cut.

"What the fuck took you so long?" Sandoval said, all his adrenaline finding its release. "Do you know what could have happened in there?"

"Yeah, I know," Alonso said, stepping close to Sandoval and looking him in the eye. "You should be careful going in alone. That supercop shit's gonna get you killed someday."

"The fuck you talking about?"

Alonso was already shaking his head and turning away from him. Sandoval grabbed him by the lapels of his jacket.

"Hey, I'm talking to you."

"We don't need any cowboys on this crew," Alonso said.

"What's that supposed to mean?"

"It means what it means," Alonso said, looking him in the eye. "We're not safe if you don't have our backs. And you're not safe if we don't have yours."

Alonso turned away again. This time, Sandoval didn't stop him.

He knows, Sandoval said to himself. *Which means* everyone *knows.*

There's twelve thousand cops in Chicago. SIS was a disgrace to every other cop who ever served this city. So some cops will shake my hand. Some will buy me a drink. Some will ignore me. Some will wonder if I'm watching them a little too closely.

But the only ones I'll think twice about are the ones who want to put a bullet in my back.

As he watched Tony Alonso getting into his car, he noticed for the first time just how nicely he kept it polished. To go along with the tailored suit and the perfect haircut.

How many cops had been on their way to becoming SIS rock stars themselves, counting the days until they got that call from Homan Square?

A FEW HOURS LATER, after the sun had gone down and his shift was over, Frank Sandoval sat on the front porch of his dead parents' house in Avondale. The house where he had grown up and had dreamed of someday becoming a cop like his old man. The house where he'd later move back in after his marriage ended, like a man going back in time.

He had a bottle of Dewar's on the little table next to the wooden chair and he was drinking alone.

When he went inside, he lay down on the bed and stared at the ceiling, waiting for sleep to come. He could still feel it in his bones, that moment of truth when he could have either killed a man or died himself . . .

And with the rat label hung on him for bringing down SIS, he wasn't sure there wouldn't be payback waiting for him down the next blind alley or around the next dark corner. Even so, on this night his only thoughts were of another man. The man who, less than five miles away, was sitting on the deck of a Lincoln Park town house, looking out at Lake Michigan. The man who would always live inside Frank Sandoval's head as long as he was free: Nick Mason.

*   *   *

ON THE OTHER SIDE OF TOWN, Eddie sat in his Jeep, watching a house in a neighborhood they called La Villita. The Little Village.

A black Escalade was parked out front. Eddie had followed it from the shooting range, keeping the vehicle just on the edge of the horizon, until they were back on the north side of Chicago.

He'd watched his man tail Mason all the way up Lincoln Park West until the Jaguar pulled into the open garage door beneath the town house and the Escalade pulled over on the street.

Eddie watched for four hours, wondering how the hell this man could stand doing this. *Must be getting paid well.* Finally, as the sun went down, he saw a gray sedan pull up on the street. The driver of the Escalade got out, giving Eddie his first good look at him: middle-aged, Latino, in a T-shirt despite the cold weather. Faded tattoos on his arms. He walked over to the sedan and stood by the driver's-side window until it rolled down. A few words were exchanged, then the man came back and got behind the wheel again. He pulled out and made the turn around the town house, leaving the sedan to take the parking spot. Eddie followed the Escalade.

He stayed behind the vehicle as it crossed the river and went south, down to the Lower West Side, with more and more Spanish on the store signs as they crossed into South Lawndale and then here. This modest little house with a little kid's seesaw in the front yard.

Eddie wrote down the address. The first piece of information he would gather for Nick Mason to help him find a way out.

10

WHILE MASON WAITED FOR EVERYTHING ELSE TO FALL
into place, there was one thing he needed *now*. A place of
his own. Beyond the reach of Sandoval, Quintero, even
Diana. A place where no one could touch him. Not even
Darius Cole.

"I've got five apartments for you to look at," the
woman said, reaching for an envelope on the cushion next
to her. Her name was Alexa, and she was sitting across
from Mason at a two-top booth at the back of the restaurant. With the bleached hair, the bleached teeth, she was
obviously trying too hard to look twenty years younger.
"They all meet your specifications and they all fall into
your—"

"Great," Mason said, rolling the bottle of Goose Island Ale in his hands. "You pick."

"But Mr.—"

"I'll be okay with whichever one you choose. The cash
will be delivered to your office this afternoon."

"Works for me," Alexa said, raising her dirty martini in a toast. "You just need to fill out the paperwork and—"

"I'd appreciate it if you could take care of that, too. And remember, everything in your name."

For the first time since she sat down, her plastered-on smile vanished.

Mason revived it. "There'll be a cash bonus in it for you."

As Alexa waved to the waitress for another martini, Mason saw Diana standing in the shadows, eyeing him. Not for the first time, he was struck by how beautiful she was in the most effortless way he'd ever seen. From that first moment in the town house, a day after he walked out of that prison . . . She had been the one person who could understand the life he had found waiting for him. Because she was living through her own version of it herself.

There was something else he had noticed about her: she never smiled. Not really. Even now, as she stood watching Mason's table, she was still just as much a mystery as the shadows she was bathed in.

As the meal progressed, Alexa got drunker and flirtier as she totaled up the windfall she would make on the deal—"Are you sure you don't want to see the units? We could test each one out. See how sturdy the bedroom floors are"—Mason caught glimpses of Diana. At times, he swore Diana's expression was that of a jealous woman. *Odd*, he thought. *I never saw that look when Lauren was around. Not once.*

"A little old for you," Diana said, coming to the table only after Alexa had gone.

"It was business."

"What kind of business?"

"My business."

Diana looked wounded—the first time he'd ever seen it. This was a rare day.

"If I didn't know better, I'd swear you were jealous."

"Maybe I am, but not of that woman," Diana said. "Of your freedom. You can move around. Do whatever the hell you want."

"Mobility and freedom are two different things."

"And I don't have either. I'm on a tether that allows me to travel between the town house and this restaurant. That's it."

"Listen," Mason said, putting his hand on hers. He wasn't sure how much he could tell her yet. The secret apartment, the ongoing project with Eddie . . . It wasn't a fully realized plan yet, with one clear step laid out after another. It was more like a crudely drawn map with a starting point in one corner and a big X marking a spot somewhere on the other side of the mountains. A spot that meant real freedom for Mason—and, by extension, for Diana. Because saving his own life meant saving hers, too.

But he didn't want to raise her hopes yet. She'd been living in this cage for twelve years, a lot longer than he had. She'd probably left more false hopes behind her than she could count.

Diana looked down at his hand on top of hers. It was a gesture more intimate than he had intended, but she hadn't moved her hand away. He could feel the warmth of her skin.

"Hang on," he said. "This won't last forever."

"I need to get back to work." She pulled her hand away, not roughly, just the simple movement of a woman shifting her focus back to business.

Mason watched her as she decanted a bottle of wine on the other side of the restaurant with the care and precision she brought to even the smallest tasks. The charming mask she wore for her customers, so unlike the woman Mason saw at home. Not for the first time he was moved to wonder:

How well do I really know her?

AS EDDIE SAT IN HIS JEEP waiting for the bank to open, he wondered how a man would carry himself if he was delivering ten thousand dollars in cash to a safe-deposit box.

Eddie watched the first customer of the day, a middle-aged man in a gray suit, walk through the front door of the First Chicago Bank on Western Avenue. Eddie was the second man inside. He paused for a moment in the lobby, clocked the man doing his business at one of the tellers' cages. Another teller caught Eddie's eye and asked if she could help him.

"I'm thinking about opening a safe-deposit box," Eddie said. The teller called one of the assistant managers, who took Eddie through the process, which included a look inside the room and the fact that he'd be left alone to access the box's contents in complete privacy. Eddie thanked the woman and told her he'd think about it.

Eddie sat in his Jeep for another two hours, watching through the glass of the bank's front door, waiting to see who else would walk across the lobby to the assistant manager's desk. During that time, he saw three men go into the safe-deposit box area. One was empty-handed on the way into the room and carried a small black case on the way out. Another was at least ninety years old, bent over and shuffling with a cane—not a likely candidate. A third looked promising—a man in a leather jacket, bald as a cue ball, with a ring in one ear. Eddie went inside and stood in the lobby, watching the man carefully, but his impression of him shifted when the man sat in the chair across from the assistant manager and chatted with her for a solid ten minutes. He had a canvas messenger bag at his side and he went into the safe-deposit room for just enough time to drop something into a box and then leave. But the chattiness didn't feel right.

Like Nick said, this guy will be a pro. In and out. All business.

Eddie didn't want to raise suspicion by spending too much time waiting in the bank lobby, so he went back out to his Jeep and kept watch.

Thirty minutes later, he knew he had the right man.

A gray sedan pulled up in front of the bank. The same gray sedan—Eddie was sure of it—that he had seen parked outside Mason's town house the night before. He remembered seeing a white man behind the wheel when the window had rolled down. It looked like the same face now as he got out of the car. The man was wearing a gray suit, tailored to accommodate his huge frame. He had a buzz cut, so short his head looked like a dirty tennis ball. Eddie picked up the digital SLR camera with the 300mm lens from the seat beside him and started taking photographs.

The man carried a leather bag into the bank. Then the passenger's-side door opened and another man got out. He was black, bald, wearing dark sunglasses, and his suit was a lighter color of gray. Eddie took more photographs as the man waited on the sidewalk, looking carefully up and down the street.

The first man came out of the bank eight minutes later. Both men got back in the car and took off. Eddie pulled out into the late-morning traffic behind them, working his way through town, north to south, until the car got off the Skyway and made its way west.

A few minutes later, he was parked just outside the Bedford Park rail yard, the biggest in the city and one of the biggest in the country. There were thousands of railroad cars from all over North America, cranes rising high above them, and a huge wicket-shaped tower in the center of it all. Eddie had tailed them to the north side of the yards, and he took more photographs as they walked into the International Exposition Services office, then came back out a few minutes later and drove to a loading dock attached to a warehouse. There was a large panel truck with a built-in loader waiting. The driver got out and worked the loader, putting several large crates into the truck, while the other man stood by and watched, his expensive suit looking out of place in the noise and dust of the yard.

When the truck was done loading, the driver stayed in the truck and the second man got behind the wheel of the sedan. They left the rail yard in a convoy and Eddie followed as they made their way south again until the car and the truck finally pulled in behind a store on 111th Street. Eddie stayed a block away, waited for a few minutes, then pulled up and stopped his Jeep on the street. He took more photos, focusing first on the sign next to the front door:

Imperial Import/Export, LLC.

He took more shots of every vehicle he could see in the parking lot. Besides the truck and the sedan, there was a silver Porsche Panamera. *Must have run someone at least eighty grand,* Eddie thought. *Not what you'd expect to find parked next to an anonymous concrete-block store on the back-ass end of town.*

Eddie stayed on the street and watched the place for another hour. He saw nobody else coming or going, decided to go in for a closer look. He laid the big camera and long lens on the floor of his Jeep. If he had to move quickly, he couldn't have a camera hanging around his neck. If he had to take more photos, he'd use his cell phone.

He got out of the Jeep, walked around the block, and approached through the side alley next to a muffler shop, so he was looking at the loading dock of the store. One of the bays was open, but he didn't see anyone moving inside. As he came closer, he looked for security cameras. He stopped at the dock, fished out his cell phone, and took some shots of the crates that had just been unloaded. He tried to focus on the shipping labels, but he wasn't quite close enough, so he climbed up over the edge of the dock.

Eddie moved around the crates, taking photographs, until he came to one that had already been opened. Lifting the top, he saw boxes of automotive air filters.

He wasn't thinking about how far inside the loading area he had come. *Bad idea,* he thought just in time to hear the voices.

Eddie ducked down beside the crate as the two men he'd been following came into the bay, laughing roughly about some private joke, as the white man jumped down off the dock and stepped outside. The black man pulled down the overhead door with a loud clatter. It banged shut, trapping Eddie inside the bay.

He heard the truck start up outside. That left him inside with just the one man—an even match, at least, if that's what it came to. Eddie waited and listened until he heard receding footsteps and was reasonably sure the man had walked back into the interior of the building.

What now?

Raising the door was not an option. The sound of the corrugated steel would be so loud that every person in the building—however many that was—would hear it. His next best option was to stay right where he was until everyone left. Which could be hours.

Screw that.

Eddie stood up and went to the hallway, put his back

to the wall when he heard a voice. He froze, waited another beat, then started moving again. He felt sweat sticking his shirt to his back as he came to a doorway. The voice grew louder. He peeked around the edge and saw a different man sitting in an office chair, surrounded by a computer screen and a bank of video monitors. This one was younger, white, dressed more casually in jeans and a sweatshirt. He was distracted, talking on the phone, staring at the ceiling, not the monitors.

Studying the angles, Eddie wanted to make sure there was no reflection that would give him away when he crossed the doorway and moved down the hallway away from the control room. He was set to move when he took one last look at the man on the phone. That's when Eddie's focus drifted to the monitors. His eyes locked on the screens because what they displayed was familiar to him: Nick Mason's town house. The back deck, the kitchen, his bedroom.

Eddie already knew there were cameras in the town house. They weren't hidden, and Nick had even asked him how easy it would be to disable them, if he ever needed to, or how they'd go about finding the people who were watching on the other end.

It's all here, Eddie said to himself. *This is the command center.*

I can tap into their Secure Sockets Layer just like a wiretap on a phone. See what they're doing here.

But first I have to get out of here.

Eddie put his head down, crossed the doorway, and turned down the hallway. He didn't let out his breath until he was twenty paces down the hall. He heard footsteps. He stood still, listening. The footsteps were getting louder. Eddie pushed through the first door on his left. It was a bathroom with old-fashioned black-and-white tile, two stalls, and one big porcelain urinal. He stayed close behind the door, listening. The footsteps grew louder still, a man's shoes clacking against the terrazzo floor. The footsteps stopped outside the bathroom door.

Damn it!

The door pushed in a few inches. Eddie moved as quietly as he could so that he would be covered by the door until whoever was coming in was in. He felt his body preparing itself, his adrenaline rising. His mouth was cotton, his heart was pounding in his chest. As the door swung open, Eddie readied himself to take the man down.

"Hey, man, Quintero's on the phone," a voice shouted from farther down the hall. "He wants to talk to you. Now." It was the white guy from the control room.

"I gotta piss."

"You want me to tell him that?"

"Fuck no."

The bathroom door swung shut.

Eddie listened as the footsteps went down the hall in the direction of the control room. He waited a few beats before opening the door a slit. He looked toward the control room. His path was clear, and he made his way to the front of the building and out the door without encountering anyone else.

Eddie hopped into his Jeep and got moving. When he was sure he wasn't being followed, he pulled over and dialed Mason's cell.

A THOUSAND MILES TO THE SOUTH, as Bruce Harper looked into the face of the man who'd once been second-in-command in one of the biggest criminal enterprises in the country, he saw one thing and one thing only:

Raw animal fear.

He was sitting at the man's tiny dining room table in a one-bedroom apartment in the small town called Liberty, just outside Houston, Texas. Rachel Greenwood was sitting next to him. Across the table sat Isaiah Wallace, who'd aged the same way an NFL lineman would: once tall and powerful, now reduced to walking with a cane after a hard life first protecting his corner, then as the one man most responsible for watching Darius Cole's back on his rise to power, finally as a man in hiding, always wondering if a knock on his door or a turn of his car key would be the last sound he would ever hear. He went by the name Harold Douglas now. Most WITSEC clients kept either their first name or their initials, but Isaiah Wallace wasn't like most clients.

"I always knew this day would come," Wallace said. He gripped the edge of the table, holding on like a man already slipping into the abyss, even as his residence was surrounded by six heavily armed deputy marshals—not to mention a USMS Assistant Director and an Assistant U.S. Attorney.

"I know I should be trying to hide it," Wallace said, sounding just as tired as he looked, "trying to act all cold about it, but I'm too old to lie about this shit anymore. I spent too many nights waiting."

"Mr. Wallace," Greenwood said. "You might be the safest man in America right now. Next to the President."

On the way over there, Harper and Greenwood had actually discussed the pros and cons of telling Wallace that Ken McLaren had been gunned down in Chicago—weighing the risk of spooking the man against what would happen if he found out they were trying to keep it from him.

"You don't think he's going to read about it in the newspaper?" she'd said.

"The last time I saw him, he didn't strike me as a newspaper kind of guy."

"Doesn't matter if he reads the papers or not. If he's

got access to the Internet, he already knows about Mc-Laren."

Harper knew she was right. The Internet was one of his biggest ongoing headaches and a danger his old friend Director Shur never could have imagined when he founded WITSEC. It made isolating witnesses a hundred times harder.

"And besides," she continued, "he's going to know something's going on when he sees six deputy marshals parked outside."

Which is exactly what had happened. Harper could see it on Wallace's face the moment he opened his door. The first break he'd seen in the man after twelve years into his new life.

Harper hadn't been part of that original trial—Wallace was just one more CW out of the hundreds that went into the Program every year—but Greenwood's story made him wish that he'd been in the Chicago office the day Wallace flipped. They'd already had McLaren and were holding that over Wallace's head. *You and Cole can both go down, Mr. Wallace. Or just Cole. It's up to you, and we honestly don't care.*

Standard U.S. Attorney line of attack, which worked on most men. But not Isaiah Wallace. Not the man who'd been Cole's most trusted confidant going all the way back to their days as fifteen-year-old boys on the corner in Englewood. Cole had the mind, the vision, to see something much bigger. Wallace had the muscle—back when he was a younger man, anyway—the willingness to do anything necessary to protect his corner. And the belief in his friend Darius Cole, to stick with him no matter where he went.

That belief was rewarded more than he ever could have imagined. He had as much power, as much money, as any Mafia *capo bastone* ever had in any of the Five Families.

After arresting him and reading him a list of enough charges to send him away for life—in a prison that, just as a little extra fuck-you, would be on the other side of the country from Cole's—they started playing a Greatest Hits compilation from all of the wiretaps they'd collected. These were all conversations that Cole and Wallace believed to be encrypted, conversations with specific details about drug shipments, about money transfers, about hits on key members of rival organizations.

Wallace remained unmoved until somebody accidentally played him ten seconds of a conversation that hadn't even been identified as evidence. It was just Darius Cole talking to some woman he called Shortcake about getting together with her on an upcoming Friday night and some unsubtle hints about what he had planned for her.

Those accidental ten seconds turned Isaiah Wallace. Because Shortcake was Cheryl Wallace. Isaiah's wife.

Wallace testified at the trial, staring down Cole from the witness stand. Cole drew double life at Terre Haute, and Wallace, after some initial hesitation, agreed to enter WITSEC. That's when Bruce Harper had first met him, as a high-priority client, and the first thing Harper did was ask Wallace for a top-five list of where he'd like to relocate. Harper listened to all five choices and then immediately crossed them off the list. Las Vegas, the Monterey Peninsula . . . If you want to live in any of these places so badly, chances are you've told that to someone along the way. Harper wanted to make sure Wallace went somewhere *nobody* would ever think to look for him.

That's how Wallace had come to spend the last twelve years here in this little shitbox of an apartment in the sweltering oil slick that was southern Texas. Long divorced from his Shortcake, with no kids, he was a man leading a solitary existence, working as a night-shift stocker at the local Walmart. Not much of a life, but it was a lot better than federal prison, and at least marginally better than being dead. And he'd just been promoted to supervisor, for an extra fifty cents an hour.

"Doesn't matter how many men you put outside this place," Wallace said to them. "Outside, inside. You can have two marshals sleeping in my bed at night. If he wants me dead—"

"If he wanted that," Harper said, "don't you think it would have happened already?"

Wallace let out a breath. "He didn't *need* me dead before. Now he does."

"You're going to be moved to the most secure location we have," Harper said. "You'll be untouchable."

"Where's that?"

"We're not going to say where," Harper said. "Or even when we'll be moving. We don't want any leaks."

"I still need to show up for the trial."

"I'll be filing a request to have you give your testimony remotely," Greenwood said. "You'll be on a live video feed. Miles away from Chicago."

"You realize you won't be coming back here," Harper added. "For your own security, we'll be relocating you after the retrial."

"And now if you don't mind," Greenwood said, taking a legal pad out of her briefcase, "I'd like to go over some things that might come up in the courtroom . . ."

Wallace gave them a wry, tired smile as he shook his head.

"Look," Harper said, "I know you've made a life here—"

"I stack boxes in the fucking Walmart at two o'clock

in the fucking morning," Wallace said, "then I come home to an empty bed. That's not a life."

"Maybe this is what you need," Greenwood said. "Wherever you go next, you can—"

"You people still don't get it," Wallace said, cutting her off. "There ain't gonna be no *after the trial*. And nothing's going to *come up in the courtroom* because I won't be there. Not even on a video screen."

"Mr. Wallace, I assure you—"

"I've known Darius Cole for forty years," Wallace said. He stopped and closed his eyes as if bringing it all back. Every one of those years. Greenwood put her pad down, and she and Harper both waited for the rest.

"You know what he told me once? He'd just got off the phone with this crazy little Irishman he had working for him back then and he said to me, 'I don't have to be the Angel of Death, Isaiah. I just have to have him on my payroll.'"

He opened his eyes.

"Which means God Himself won't be able to save me."

AS THE SHADOWS grew longer in La Villita, Marcos Quintero sat on the front porch of his house holding his daughter, Gabriela. She was dressed in a brightly colored flower dress, red and yellow and orange. She had just turned eighteen months old.

As Quintero watched his daughter falling asleep, he knew his wife wouldn't be happy. *She sleeps now, she won't sleep at bedtime.* But this was what Quintero lived for, every single day, this simple act of holding his daughter, feeling her tiny weight in his arms. All of his *hermanos* from La Raza, how many of them were gone now? How did he alone survive and find a way out of that life and end up sitting here on this porch and given this last chance to have a family as a forty-three-year-old father?

El milagro. The miracle.

He didn't look up at the car rolling down the street, but it registered on his radar. Just one of many reasons for that miraculous survival, animal instincts, always being aware of what was happening around him. He glanced up from his daughter's face to see a large panel truck rumbling by. He waited for it to pass, and when it did there was a figure standing on the other side of the street. Watching him.

Nick Mason.

Quintero stood up quickly, went inside, and handed Gabriela to his wife, Rosa. He grabbed his Nighthawk Custom 1911 from beside the door, a no-fucking-around semiautomatic he had taken off a member of the Latin Kings, how many goddamned years ago, but it was still the only gun he trusted. He tucked it into the small of his back.

"*¿Lo que está mal?*" she asked him, but he didn't answer. Instead, he pushed the door open, went down the front steps, and stood in the driveway. Mason was still on the other side of the street.

The two men faced each other for a full minute. Neither man moved. Another truck passed between them. Then Mason finally crossed the street.

Quintero met him at the end of the driveway. "What the fuck do you think you're doing here?"

"Holding a mirror of my life up for you to look at," Mason said.

"What's that supposed to mean?"

"It means I want you to know how I feel every time you go near my family."

"You're gone. Now. And if you ever come near this house again—"

"I'm coming back tomorrow. And the day after that."

"I'll kill you, I swear to God—"

"Not the first time you've said that. I'm still waiting."

Quintero stepped closer, so that his face was just inches away from Mason.

"Turn around and walk away now."

Mason stood his ground, his eyes locked on Quintero's.

"I do everything I'm asked to," Mason said. "Now I need something in return. The same thing you have. Time with my family. Alone. Without you or anyone else watching me."

"You don't get to change the rules," Quintero said, taking the Nighthawk from his belt. "Nobody does."

"Your wife and your daughter are watching us," Mason said, nodding toward the front window of the house. "But if you really want to kill me right now, go ahead."

"Yo mierda en la leche de tu puta madre," Quintero said under his breath.

"It's not an insult if I don't know what the fuck you're saying."

Quintero put the gun back in his belt.

"We got a new deal now," Mason said. "You understand that, right?"

Quintero shook his head, almost smiling. "You think I don't know what it's like, Mason? You think Cole doesn't know where to find us? What do you think happens to my family if I don't do what I'm told?"

"So maybe we both need to get out," Mason said. *A seriously bad idea to even say it out loud, but maybe it was worth a shot.*

"You think it's that easy?"

"I'm just talking here."

"It's a bad habit."

"You walked away from La Raza, didn't you?"

Quintero laughed. It was a laugh without joy. "Nobody walks away from La Raza. Cole bought me. He owns me like he owns you."

"He doesn't own me tomorrow afternoon," Mason said. "I'm seeing my daughter. And you won't be there. We got a deal?"

Quintero looked back at his house, made a gesture to his wife as if telling her to step away from the window, to stop worrying about this stranger in the driveway.

"You can have one day with your daughter," Quintero said as he turned back to Mason. "*One*. That's it."

Mason looked Quintero in the eye, saw that he was giving him his word. Mason nodded, turned, and walked back to his Jag.

When Mason drove away, Rosa came down the driveway, carrying Gabriela, who was still asleep with her head on her mother's shoulder.

"*¿Quién era ese?*" Rosa asked him. Who was that?

"*Nadie,*" he said. Nobody.

But in his mind, he was thinking something else. *El Ángel de la Muerte.*

The Angel of Death.

11

WHEN MASON WOKE UP THAT SATURDAY MORNING, HE
knew it would be a day like no other day he'd had since
walking out of that prison. It was the kind of day he'd
think about constantly while staring at the gray walls of
his cell every waking hour for five and a half years. The
kind of day he never thought he'd have again.

Mason didn't notice anyone following him as he pulled
up in front of the house in Elmhurst. Not only had Gina
kept her promise but so, too, had Quintero. He tried not
to let himself believe it, that the thing he had sold his soul
to the devil for was actually going to happen: a day alone
with his daughter.

He was a few minutes early, but he went up the driveway to the porch, rang the bell, and waited. Gina answered the door, and then she stood there and stared at
him for a long moment, looking like a woman who was
already trying to find a way to change her mind.

But Mason tried looking past her ambivalence and

back in time to see the long, lean girl he'd fallen deeply, stupidly in love with. The woman he had planned to be with forever.

Was "his" Gina still alive inside this pretty suburban housewife? Could she have survived what he put her through? Or had life in the land of big houses and minivans swallowed her up forever?

"Adriana will be safe with me," Mason said. "I'll have her back here by three o'clock."

"One o'clock."

He knew that voice, knew it would be useless to argue with his ex-wife. If he even tried, he'd be bringing her back at noon instead.

"Where's Brad?"

"He's back in Denver already. We'll fly out in a couple days."

"You're really moving there?"

"We are."

"She's still my daughter," he said, knowing this was a bad idea but saying it anyway. "Legally, I'm not even an ex-felon."

That's when the Canaryville girl he'd been looking for reappeared.

"You won't fight it," she said, her voice transformed.

"How do you know that?"

"Because this is the best thing for your daughter," she said. She reached out to him and brushed her hand through his hair. "And because I know you're still a good man."

It was an intimate gesture, making Mason forget about everything else in the world for that one moment. It was something beyond sexual, a brief reconnection between two people who knew each other better than anyone else in the world.

Another voice from behind her: "Is that him?"

Adriana appeared, dressed in blue jeans and an orange

T-shirt. Her hair was out of the ponytail Mason always saw on the soccer field and down on her shoulders. She looked impossibly grown up for a nine-year-old. For Mason's little girl.

"Hello," she said to Mason, the little pistol who had clocked the cop in her playground suddenly turning awkward and shy.

Gina bent down and gave her a big hug, told her to behave, told her that she'd see her at one o'clock.

"Can I please stay longer?"

"Next time," Gina said, "okay?"

"If there even *is* a next time!"

"Just go," Gina said. She stood up and faced Mason with one more painful look of doubt and regret.

"We'll be back soon," he said to Gina. "Thank you."

She nodded and watched them walk down to the driveway to Mason's car. Even as he drove away, he looked in the rearview mirror and saw her standing in the open doorway, watching until they had completely left her sight.

EVEN IN THE MIDST of realizing his dream—time alone with the daughter he thought he'd lost forever—the doubts crept in.

Will she really be safe with me?

Who am I fooling?

Nothing about me is safe.

It won't last. It can't.

"This is a nice car!" Adriana said, bringing him back into the moment. "When did you get it?"

"That day I saw you at the school, that was my first drive."

"Really? What happened to that other car you had? The old one?"

Mason wasn't even sure which car she had seen. But it didn't matter because the answer was the same: Quintero had his men obliterate it, like it never existed.

"I just liked this one better," he said as he revved the engine and pulled away from the stop sign.

His daughter laughed.

That's all I need out of life right there, he said to himself. *That sound.*

"Where do you want to go?" Mason asked her. "You want to get some ice cream?"

"I can't eat ice cream before lunch."

"Well, how about lunch and *then* ice cream?"

"I want to see where you live," she said. "Let's have lunch there."

Mason pictured her in the town house. She'd love the place, of course, especially the pool. But then he thought about the security cameras, imagined someone sitting in a room on the other side of the city, just as Eddie had described, only now that person would be watching Adriana on the screen.

Mason couldn't bear it.

"It's such a nice car," Mason said. "How about we just drive around for a while? I can take you to the beach."

"Mom says you live by the zoo."

Now I'm stuck, Mason said to himself. But then the answer came to him.

"I got an idea," Mason said. "But you have to promise me something . . ."

"What's that?"

"Where I'm about to take you . . . you can't tell *any-body* where it is."

She thought about it for a moment. "Not even Mom?"

"Not even Mom," Mason said. "Nobody else will know about it except you and me."

"Okay, let's go!" Adriana said, and she laughed again as Mason hit the gas.

THE APARTMENT BUILDING was south of the Loop, a block off Michigan Avenue. Mason circled the block three times, watching the traffic carefully to make sure he wasn't being followed. He parked the car and he and his daughter rode up the elevator to the twelfth floor.

It was the first time he'd seen his "safe house." Hadn't even mentioned it to Eddie yet. Alexa, the real estate agent, had messengered an envelope to the restaurant with the address of the apartment and a set of keys.

"There's no furniture!" Adriana said when he opened the door. She ran into the empty room, then down the hallway to the two bedrooms, both just as empty.

Mason went to the window and looked out toward the lake. Through a sliver between two other buildings, he could see a corner of Soldier Field.

"That's where the Bears play," Adriana said as she came up and pressed her nose to the window just below his face.

"That's right."

"Daddy says they stink this year."

Mason stopped breathing.

"I'm sorry," she said. "I'm just used to calling him Daddy."

"It's okay. I'm glad you have him to take care of you."

While they were still gazing out the window, Mason reached down and stroked Adriana's hair. She hugged him. And suddenly all of his doubts about this day disappeared.

She looked up at him. "If you really live by the zoo, can you hear the animals?"

"Sometimes. Mostly at night."

"I would *love* that. But why do you need this place, too?"

"Just to have another place to go. Haven't you ever wanted that? Like a secret room in your own house?"

She let go of him, stepped away from the window, and did a quick cartwheel on the empty expanse of carpeting.

"How long have you had this place?"

"It's my first time here."

Her eyes lit up. "Really?"

"Yeah. Remember what I said. This will be our secret, okay?"

"Deal."

Mason sat down on the floor, watched her do two more cartwheels. Then she sat down on the floor, facing him, looking shy again.

"How do you feel about moving away?" he asked her.

"I don't want to leave my friends," she said. "But Mom says we have to go."

I'm the reason for that, he thought. *I took this deal so I could see her again. And now I'm driving her away. But there she is, my girl, sitting right there, talking to me.*

"Denver's in the Rocky Mountains. Mom says it snows there, just like here. But the snow is different."

"That's what I've heard."

"I just thought of an idea," she said.

"What's that?"

"Instead of having a secret room here," she said, "you could have it in Denver."

An apartment in Denver—it seemed impossible. But, then, today was the one day Mason could actually imagine it happening.

That was the exact moment his cell phone rang.

You have got to be fucking kidding me, he said to himself as he looked at the screen. This sudden act of violence, shattering the entire day and bringing him back to

his life, was worse than any punch, worse than any gunshot.

PRIVATE NUMBER.

Quintero.

He swiped the screen and put the phone to his ear.
"What is it?"

"I'm at your town house," Quintero said. "Where
are you?"

Mason hesitated. "I'm out."

"Then get back here."

"We had a deal, Quintero. You gave me your word."

"And mine ain't the final word, Mason. You know that.
I'm taking you to the airport, so be here in thirty."

Mason did some quick math in his head and realized
two things:

*It would take him an hour to drive to Elmhurst and then
back to the town house.*

*And no matter how he played this, there was no way he
was going to let Adriana or Quintero see each other.*

That left one possibility. Diana's restaurant was on
Rush Street, just a few blocks from the apartment building and on the way to the town house.

"I'll be there," he said and hung up.

"Who was that?" Adriana asked.

"Somebody I work with," Mason said. "I'm sorry,
sweetie, but I have to go now."

"We just got here!"

"I know. I'm really sorry."

"Where do you work, anyway?"

Mason got up from the floor. "I'll tell you in the car."

They went down the elevator and got into the Jaguar. "I
work in a restaurant," he said as he pulled out onto Michigan Avenue. "I thought we could go there right now."

"You're a chef?"

"No, I just help out."

"Doing what?"

Doing nothing. I don't even show up. I get a paycheck, anyway, so the IRS won't wonder how I live in a Lincoln Park town house and drive around in restored vintage cars.

"Doing whatever they need me to do," Mason said. "It's pretty boring. But see, I have to go do something right now. A restaurant emergency. So I need to leave you there for a little while. Your mom will come and pick you up."

"But I don't have to be back until one o'clock. I heard Mom say that."

"I know," Mason said. "But we'll do this again as soon as I can—"

"We *can't* do it again," she said, crossing her arms and looking out the window. "I'm moving to Denver."

A tense silence hung in the air as Mason kept driving. Adriana had retreated back into her shyness with a new layer of disappointment. It killed Mason to look at her, knowing today would probably undo every inch of progress they'd made since his release. He picked up his cell phone and dialed Gina's number, trying to find the right words to explain to her what he was about to do.

There were no words to explain it to Adriana.

IT WAS THE MIDDLE of a busy lunch rush when Mason walked into Antonia's. A hundred diners, most of them men and women in power suits, were sitting at every available table, while a dozen waitstaff swarmed around them. Mason asked the maître d' for Diana, was told that she was way too busy to spare even a minute.

"Tell her it's Nick," he said. "It's an emergency."

Adriana stood beside him, watching the mayhem. "Is this really where you work?"

"I'm not here every day. But it's a nice place, isn't it? I'll bring you here sometime."

Another promise he might never get to keep.

He was waiting for another comeback about how she was moving to Denver. It never came.

"What is it, Nick?" Diana had appeared from the kitchen, was wiping her hands with a towel. She was in her usual workday uniform, a dark suit with a brightly colored blouse. Today it was coral pink.

"I'd like you to meet Adriana," Mason said. "My daughter."

Diana's face was unreadable. Mason saw a lot of things in it—confusion, envy, hurt, anger—and then it all faded away in an instant as she looked down and saw Adriana.

"I'm so pleased to meet you," she said, bending down just enough to shake her hand. "I've heard a lot about you."

"Are you my father's boss?"

She laughed. "Not really. We work together. And we live in the same town house."

Now it was Adriana's expression that was hard to read. "You live with my father?"

"Oh, not really," Diana said, blushing. "I mean, not *together*."

"That's too bad," Adriana said. "You're very pretty."

"Well, thank you," Diana said, blushing even more. She seemed at a loss for words, the woman who ran the entire business that even now was humming all around her, suddenly reduced to shyness by one nine-year-old girl.

Diana finally looked up at Mason. "So what's going on?"

"I need to ask you a favor," Mason said. "Her mother's on the way over, but I have to go now."

"Nick, are you kidding me? It's the middle of lunch."

"I've got no other choice."

"What's so important that you have to—"

She stopped dead when she saw his eyes.

"Okay," she said. "I'll take care of her."

"Thank you. I owe you one."

"You already do, remember?"

Mason got down on one knee and gave Adriana a hug. He held on to her tight, wanted to stop everything else in the world and stay right there on the floor of the restaurant. But he made himself let go.

"Come on," Diana said to Adriana. "I'll show you the kitchen, get the chef to make you your favorite meal. What do you like most in the world?"

"Chicken nuggets."

"We'll see what he can do," Diana replied as she took her hand and guided her away. Mason stood there, watching her. She didn't say good-bye. She just waved and turned away from him.

A FEW MINUTES LATER, he pulled the car into the garage and came out to the street, where Quintero was waiting for him.

"You're late, Mason," Quintero said as he got in the Escalade. "The clock is ticking on the next target. You may have already—"

"I don't give a fuck," Mason said. "You know I was with—"

He stopped himself dead, didn't even want to talk about her. Didn't want to say her name out loud in front of this man.

"Plane tickets," Quintero said, giving him an envelope as he pulled away from the curb. "A driver's license and credit card under another name. You're landing in Atlanta, going to this motel, registering under this same name."

"What's in Atlanta?"

"Everything you need will be in the hotel safe. The combination's in here."

Mason stayed silent as Quintero wove through traffic to get to the Kennedy Expressway, then opened it up all the way out to O'Hare.

Mason spoke up as Quintero stopped in front of the Delta terminal. "Does Cole really think he can take out every witness who might testify against him?"

"Not your job to worry about that, Mason."

"You know I'm not getting within a hundred feet of this guy, right? They'll have a dozen marshals all around him every fucking minute."

"If they do," Quintero said, "you deal with it. Now get out of the car. Your plane's leaving."

As Mason opened the door, he felt Quintero's hand on his forearm, stopping him short.

"Don't get yourself killed," he said, looking Mason in the eye. "That wouldn't be good for either of us."

"I didn't know you cared," Mason said.

"Vete a la mierda."

Quintero sped away as soon as Mason closed the door behind him. It occurred to him that something had changed, some fundamental aspect of this relationship between Mason and the man who gave him his assignments. The man who was sworn to kill his ex-wife and daughter if he ever failed.

But he didn't have time to think about it now. He had a plane to catch. And another target to kill.

12

NICK MASON STEPPED OFF THE PLANE IN ATLANTA CAR-
rying the name of James L. Wilson, rented a full-size
Ford Expedition SUV, and drove to a hotel three miles
from the sprawling airport complex to retrieve the sup-
plies he'd need for this assignment.

When he was in the hotel room, he opened the closet
door and then the safe that was built into the back wall.
The first item he pulled out looked like a thin black back-
pack. As he put it on the bed and unrolled it, he saw the
components of a Remington Defense bolt-action sniper
rifle, with a carbon fiber–wrapped barrel with suppressor.
He assembled the rifle, flipped open the scope, and
looked through it. The weapon felt impossibly light in his
hands, but he knew Eddie could put one of the 7.62mm
NATO rounds through a quarter from three hundred
yards out. Mason, maybe two hundred.

The next item from the safe was a smaller gun case,
containing an H&K USP Full Size Tactical semiauto-

matic loaded with nine-millimeter rounds. It was the same model he'd used in his last mission at the Aqua. The gun he'd used to kill Ken McLaren.

Mason took out the final two items—a pair of Leica 2,000-yard binoculars and a large envelope with several documents inside. He spread the documents out on the bed next to the sniper rifle.

The first was a mug shot of a large black man with a look on his face that was a combination of disgust and world-weariness. He held his own name in front of him, white letters on a black placard: ISAIAH JEREMIAH WALLACE.

Then a series of printed photographs, of rough quality and with haphazard angles, likely taken with a cell phone. As he looked through the images, he saw that it was a detailed itinerary, with a list of destinations and waypoints, each scheduled down to the minute.

Then a map showing a route almost exclusively on secondary roads, from a small town just outside Houston, Texas, to a location in the Appalachian Mountains about sixty miles north of Atlanta. Mason checked the itinerary again, peered at the map to see the final destination.

Then he threw the map back on the bed and looked out the window.

"Son of a bitch."

AS MASON DROVE NORTH, he picked up his cell phone and dialed.

Quintero answered on the first ring. "What is it?"

"Tell me this is a joke," Mason said. "An Army Ranger camp?"

"On the phone? What's wrong with you?"

"What's wrong with me is I don't know how to get into an Army Ranger camp."

"You don't," Quintero said. "You have their route, you make the hit before they get there."

"How did you get the route?" Mason paged through the itinerary with his free hand while he kept the phone to his ear with the other.

"That's need-to-know and you don't need to know," Quintero said. "Just do your job."

"If they get to that camp, I'm fucked. You know that."

"I do know that," Quintero said. "And you know if you don't want to get fucked, don't drop the soap."

The call ended before Mason could say another word. He threw the phone on the seat next to him and kept driving. When he looked at his watch, he added an extra hour for the time change. He had five hours, the seconds ticking away loudly in his head.

THREE HUNDRED MILES to the southwest, a small convoy of vehicles was making its way through the state of Alabama. Bruce Harper sat in the front passenger's seat of an unmarked Chevy Express passenger van, specially modified for the U.S. Marshals Service with a turbo-diesel V-8 engine and heavily tinted bulletproof side windows.

Four other deputy marshals rode in the van with him. Isaiah Wallace sat in the middle row, a deputy on either side. They'd been rotating drivers every four hours to stay fresh. It would be fifteen hours on the road today, with a lead vehicle ahead of the van—an SUV with two deputy marshals—and another SUV behind them with two more deputies.

In case Darius Cole's people were watching, Harper had taken the unprecedented precaution of flying a decoy prisoner—actually, a retired marshal who resembled Isaiah Wallace—to the West Coast. As far as the marshals working the detail knew, the man they were guarding *was*

Isaiah Wallace. *Would it work?* Harper wasn't sure, but anything he could do to lower the risk of the real Wallace becoming the second fatality in the WITSEC Program in less than a week, he was going to do.

It wasn't the first time in his career Harper had gotten creative. He couldn't even count the number of times he'd brought high-profile witnesses to and from courthouses using newspaper vans, catering trucks, anything that didn't look like an official federal vehicle.

But now the stakes felt higher than ever, and when Harper had contacted his staff back in Arlington, he'd asked them to find the best possible location to keep Isaiah Wallace until the retrial was over. One of his administrators called back an hour later with an idea.

The man had been an Army Ranger before joining the Service and he told Harper about this intensive sixty-one-day training program they'd had, running obstacle courses and doing night patrols at Fort Benning, then rappelling down mountains at Camp Merrill, in the Appalachians, then finally parachuting into Camp Rudder, in Florida, to swim through the swamps with the alligators and snakes.

"That mountain phase at Camp Merrill . . ." the administrator said. "I remember thinking, this is one of the most isolated places I've ever seen and there's nobody there but Rangers in training. Except for two small civilian guesthouses."

Harper had placed high-risk clients at military bases before, but never somewhere quite like this. As soon as he heard the idea, he knew where he was taking Isaiah Wallace.

Harper looked at his watch.

Five more hours and he could relax.

*   *   *

MASON TOOK THE COUNTY HIGHWAY out of a small town called Dahlonega, turned onto a winding road leading up into the mountains. He passed a farm stand selling boiled peanuts, then the trees closed in tight, making a natural tunnel overhead. He turned on his headlights and kept driving as the time leaked away. He still had no idea how he'd hit a three-vehicle convoy, which, according to the documents, would be carrying eight deputy marshals to protect Wallace, along with the Assistant Director of WITSEC himself, a man named Bruce Harper.

As he went farther up the road, the elevation continued to rise, until he saw a sign indicating that Camp Merrill was one mile away. As he got closer, he came to an intersection. Straight ahead was the entrance to the camp. A gate with a man standing on either side of a green transport truck, the back of the truck filled with Army Rangers, some of them turning to clock him as he took the hard right and headed up the mountain. A quarter mile later, the road doubled back again and Mason pulled over.

Mason took the binoculars with him as he made his way through the trees and underbrush to a vantage point overlooking the camp, which sat half hidden on level ground just beneath him, the mountain rising steeply on the other side. The transport truck was inside the camp now, the two sentries back inside the guard shack. He traced the fence around the perimeter, saw four long barracks laid out parallel inside it, another dozen buildings, a small clearing with a helicopter standing idle, and a lone water tower high above the camp. A long line of Rangers dressed in forest camos waited at the door to what must have been the mess hall.

It all just confirmed what he already knew. *If Wallace makes it to this camp, I don't have a chance.*

Mason went back to the SUV and took out the map

and the itinerary. He didn't have a lot of time and needed to find a place to ambush the convoy. He tried to put himself inside the minds of the marshals. Then it hit him.

Any ambush would have to come between them and the base.

They'll be looking for a frontal assault.

They wouldn't be thinking about an attack from the rear.

He looked at his map and found an S-shaped stretch of road that might work. He checked his watch and drove to the area he'd selected on the map. It wasn't perfect—the road was a little too wide, the turns not sharp enough, the drop-offs not steep enough—but it could work. What it had going for it was that it was tree-lined and uphill in the direction of the camp. They'd have to slow down, and their focus would be on the road ahead and the base just beyond—not on what was coming from behind them. Or so he hoped.

It was time to go find the convoy.

IT WAS LONG AFTER SUNSET when the convoy reached Dahlonega, the last outpost before the long climb up the winding road to Camp Merrill. After driving eight hundred miles from Houston, they were barely twenty miles away. Harper should have felt relieved to be so close.

He was anything but.

Ever since they'd left that morning, Harper had been running it through his mind: *That detective had been pretty goddamned sure it was Nick Mason who killed Mc-Laren in Chicago . . . But how did Mason know where to find him?*

Harper was still assuming it was a local security breach. A Chicago deputy marshal who said the wrong thing to the wrong person. Or maybe just plain dumb luck. Someone from his old life, in his old town, who just happened to see him walk into that building. Those were Harper's explanations to himself for the first, and only, such disaster in the Service's history.

But what if he was wrong? What if there was an internal breach, maybe even in his own office? It would have been an outlandish thought just a few days ago. That's why he'd gone through the elaborate charade with the decoy. But now . . .

He might be here in Georgia, Harper said to himself. *He might be waiting for us. And if he is . . .*

He looked at his map again.

This is where he'd hit us. Right here, on the road up the mountain.

"You're going to see a farm on your left," he said to the driver, looking at the map. "I want you to turn in there."

"Are you serious? We're almost at the camp."

He's here, Harper said to himself. *Mason is here.*

I can feel it.

"That's an order," he said, his voice all business now, as he picked up his radio to alert the lead vehicle. "I'm going to call the commander and ask him for a favor."

MASON PASSED THE CONVOY as he drove south down Highway 400. The three vehicles were lit up for one brief moment in his headlights: two SUVs and a large passenger van in the middle. Just as the documents had specified. He kept going for another half mile until they were out of sight. Then he slowed down and made a U-turn.

Mason accelerated to close the gap, staying a quarter mile behind. He went through the moves in his head: *Run the trail vehicle off the road before the van has time to react.* Even if the driver hit the gas, the lead vehicle wouldn't be able to react as quickly. On the tight road, the van would have nowhere to go, and Mason could take it out. The lead vehicle would probably stop, but Mason would already be out of his own vehicle. At that point, all he would need was panic and luck.

It was his only shot.

The convoy was on the last road approaching the camp now, moving quickly without being reckless. Mason pulled closer, waiting for the convoy to pass the open farm and plunge back into the thick forest just before slowing down for the curve. Mason's exact moment to make his move.

He pressed down on the gas pedal, closing the distance.

A quarter mile from the target zone.

A hundred yards.

Then Mason saw the brake lights glowing in the dark.

What are they doing?

He watched all three vehicles turn off the road and head down the farm's long driveway. There was a cluster of buildings at the end—a large barn, two metal sheds, a house with a warm light glowing somewhere inside. Mason had no choice but to keep going. He passed the farm and followed the road into the trees.

This wasn't supposed to be their route, Mason said to himself. *Did they make me?*

He gunned it for another half mile, came skidding to a stop, and managed a tight U-turn in the narrow opening between the trees. He doubled back, headlights off, rolling as silently as he could. When he was almost to the farm, he pulled over, putting two wheels on the soft shoulder. He grabbed the sniper rifle, got out and closed the door quietly behind him, worked his way through the thick trees and underbrush, now completely dark, scratching his face on tree branches and briars, until he had found the edge and could see the farm.

All three vehicles were stopped dead. Lights off, doors closed.

Three hundred yards away, he thought. *Maybe more.* It was hard to judge the distance in the dark.

Mason stayed kneeling at the edge of the woods, the air cooling down in the darkness, insects buzzing around his ears, moisture from the ground seeping into his pant leg, and he waited.

Then he heard the sound.

Faint at first, a distant rumble, then louder. A low thrumming that turned into the violent, deafening whir of rotors beating the air, churning up dirt, pebbles, fallen branches.

A helicopter.

Son of a bitch.

Two minutes later, it landed. And not just any helicopter. A large Black Hawk chopper, lighting up the sky and directing a spotlight to the ground as it descended. Mason rested the barrel of the sniper rifle on a nearby branch, keeping the weapon steady and level as he took a deep breath and sighted down the scope. He passed the crosshairs across the long body of the helicopter, four windows, God knows how many seats inside but plenty of room for every passenger from all three vehicles.

He saw the doors open on one of the SUVs, two men wearing black windbreakers running toward the chopper, their heads bent down against the whirlwind of dust kicked up by the rotors. Another long moment, Mason waiting, watching, until the passenger doors opened and this time five men emerged. He saw them moving toward the chopper, illuminated in its spotlight, and he scanned them one by one in his crosshairs. Windbreaker, another windbreaker.

Then him. It was Wallace. The biggest man, the man moving not with the trained confidence of a U.S. marshal but like a hunted animal scurrying to safety.

Mason put the crosshairs on the target, moving left to right. He started to squeeze the trigger.

Then the target was gone. *What the . . .* He looked up over the sight as Wallace moved behind the helicopter. He was boarding through the open door on the side facing away from Mason.

Two more marshals came running from the third vehicle. As soon as they boarded, the helicopter would lift off, and Wallace's next step on solid ground would be within the confines of the camp. Although Mason wouldn't see it because by the time he got back to his own vehicle and up the road, the marshals would have Wallace inside one of the camp buildings.

He watched helplessly as the helicopter slowly rocked back and forth on the ground. It was going up.

As Mason aimed at the rear of the helicopter—he couldn't see the tail rotor, could only make an educated guess at its location—he heard Eddie's voice in his head.

Center mass. Center mass.

Whenever you try to pull off one of those Hollywood shots, you put your own life at risk.

And this was more than a Hollywood shot. This was a Hail Mary. Mason's comfort zone was two hundred yards and that was in daylight shooting at stationary paper targets with Eddie's rifle. The tail rotor was swerving side to side more than three hundred yards away in the dark.

Following the line of the fuselage, aiming above that, even a little higher to account for the drop, he fired one round, the sound only partially dampened by the barrel. Were the roaring rotor blades enough to drown out the rest?

As Mason slid the bolt and fired another round, he thought he saw one brief spark. Contact with the rotor? He slid the bolt and fired another round. And another. The shell casings ejected from the rifle, landing somewhere in the underbrush. No need to pick up his brass—they were untraceable. The helicopter, its skids only a few feet off the ground, stopped ascending. It seemed suddenly unstable, its tail swinging sharply left, then right. Mason held his breath and watched until finally the helicopter thumped back onto the ground. The twin engines cut off, the rotors still spinning.

He kept waiting. He didn't see any movement. *The smart play,* Mason thought. *Wait inside the helicopter, call for backup. Every Ranger in that camp will be swarming down that road. They'll find my wheels. Then they'll find me.*

Mason aimed at the chopper again, high along the side, just above the windows. He fired one round after the other, sliding the bolt as quickly as he could. He wanted a riot of sound inside the chopper, one ringing impact after another. No doubt in the occupants' minds that they were under attack, maybe even from multiple shooters.

Anything to get them moving.

He fired three more rounds. Then the exterior lights on the helicopter went off. He had to struggle to see in the darkness now, a slim ray of moonlight coming down through a gap in the clouds. Two shadows moved from the helicopter to one of the SUVs. Mason saw the interior light flash on for one instant. He couldn't tell who was inside, but it didn't really matter. He didn't want that vehicle moving, at least not with any speed, so Mason took sight on the right front tire. One shot and he saw the explosion of air and rubber.

The vehicle pulled forward, rolling across the grass on three good wheels. Now Mason had a sight line on the back right tire of the second SUV. He put the tire in his crosshairs and fired, saw another explosion of air and rubber. That left only the van, but he didn't have a good shot at any of the tires. He waited to see what their next move would be. More shadows moving from the helicopter. Impossible to see who was a marshal, who a Ranger, who Isaiah Wallace was. The van started to move, and Mason aimed at the road side of the SUVs, figuring that's where it would go. But, instead, it rolled toward the helicopter. It took Mason a moment to realize that they were pulling the van close to load Wallace, they didn't want him exposed for even a second. *That was a mistake*, Mason thought, because now he had a shot at the tires. He aimed and squeezed off a round but didn't see it hit. He slid the bolt one more time, fired at the back tire as the van was just about to disappear behind the helicopter.

Missed again.

Mason was tired, hungry, and cold. Everything was working against his aiming at a moving target, especially the bad light. He shook himself, closed his eyes for a few moments. Then he slid the bolt one more time, felt and heard the clunk of an empty chamber.

He didn't have time to swear at himself because the van was already in motion. He could hear the tires spinning angrily in the dirt and grass, could see the van gaining purchase when it hit the paved driveway. Mason was on his feet when the van got to the road. It turned right. Away from the camp. The driver was heading back the way it came.

Mason fought his way through the dark forest, branches whipping at his face no matter how hard he tried to shield himself. Every second felt like an eternity as he tripped and pulled himself back up and clawed his way back to his SUV parked on the shoulder. He pictured the van already miles down the road as he opened the driver's-side door and climbed behind the wheel.

He hit the gas and started the chase.

*   *   *

HARPER WAS DRIVING. He didn't trust anyone else to do this. Not now, not when the safety of yet another witness hung in the balance.

It had been his call to make a run for it as the bullets rang out against the outer shell of the helicopter and he had no idea where they were coming from. As much as it sounded like a full-scale war going on outside, his gut told him it was just the one man again. Nick Mason. But he couldn't rule out an accomplice this time, one or two, or God knows how many, and for all Harper knew, the bullets were just cover to keep them pinned down while the rest of the crew moved closer.

He wasn't going to wait for more Rangers to make it all the way from the camp down here. He was going to put Wallace in that van and get the hell out.

Now he was gunning it down the long winding road, retracing his route and trying to remember how many miles it would take them to get back to the town. He pushed hard around a tight curve, felt the momentum pull against the van, and hit the brakes too hard in reaction. Looking into the rearview mirror, he saw the eyes-wide-open animal fear all over Isaiah Wallace's face.

"Nobody's going to touch you," Harper said to him without turning his head. Wallace stayed silent.

As he hit another straightaway, Harper pressed the gas pedal all the way to the floor. The van had a powerful motor, but it was top-heavy, and Harper was starting to regret bringing so many men—four of his marshals and one of the Ranger captains.

He checked the side mirror as he took another curve. There was no sign of anyone behind him.

Another straightaway.

That's when he saw the headlights.

*   *   *

MASON GUNNED THE SUV, cutting off every turn and brushing against the trees. He'd run from the police on the streets of Chicago, usually while driving a stolen car, but that was years ago when he was young and foolish enough to think he could live through anything. Today he knew better. One turn too sharp, or one patch of oil on the road, and he'd hit one of these trees head-on going seventy or eighty miles an hour.

But he also knew that once they reached the town, his chances would go from one in a million to zero. He had to catch them *now*.

He pushed it harder, feeling the car sliding sideways for one sick moment as he rounded another curve. He regained his traction, overcorrected, and swerved back and forth until he finally had it going straight again.

He took another turn, thought he saw a brief flash of red, gunned it down another straightaway, and then white-knuckled another tight curve.

Until he saw the taillights a quarter mile ahead.

Mason went even faster, throwing every last bit of caution to the wind. He figured he was maybe two miles away from that last break in the trees before the road came to a four-way stop at the edge of town.

The brake lights flashed as the van took another curve. Mason tapped his own brakes for barely a millisecond and came out of the curve having gained noticeable ground. He was two hundred yards behind the van now and used the opportunity of one more straightaway to take the semiautomatic from the seat next to him.

Another curve, more ground gained. One more curve and he'd be close enough. As he hit the buttons to lower both front windows, the night air rushed into the cab and swirled around Mason's head like a hurricane.

They were coming to a big right turn, meaning the van would swing left, meaning Mason could cut the turn tighter and get his nose to the right side of the vehicle. He leaned into the turn, and branches hit the window frame, spraying Mason with twigs and leaves. Then, as he came out of the turn, he grabbed the wheel hard to keep the SUV on the inside track and suddenly he was next to the van.

The van swung back to the center of the road and swiped Mason's left front fender. He had to fight hard to keep control of the wheel and stay straight until he was able to hold the gun with his left hand.

Fucking left-hand shot, he thought as he fired at the van's back tire and missed. But then the van swung right and made contact again, and he felt everything slipping away. He cut back and hit the van hard with a sickening crunch of metal, but the impact knocked his own vehicle back on track and gave him one more chance to fire at the van's tire. Time slowed down as the bullet ripped the tire apart and the van's driver lost half of his speed and control in one instant, cutting right across the front of Mason's vehicle. He felt another impact, but this time it was enough to take the wheel from his hands as he saw the underside of the van exposed to him and then it somehow was upside down and then right side up again and then upside down, turning and turning, as he jabbed at the brakes and followed the van into the trees.

The van hit first, then Mason, the air bag exploding and slamming against his face like a heavyweight's right cross.

Then everything stopped.

FOR A WHILE, there was nothing. Black silence. Then a ringing sound and two thin beams of light. The beams merged into one, and Mason focused on the single map light next to his sun visor. He shook his head clear, waited for the pain to arrive and overtake him in a sick wave. But as he looked down at himself, he saw all four limbs still attached. His heart was beating. He was breathing. When he tried to push open the door, it wouldn't move, so he twisted his body around, his head spinning with the effort, until he had the leverage to kick it open.

Mason got out of the vehicle and looked at the van lying upside down in front of him, one of the wheels still turning. He reached back into the SUV and picked up the semiautomatic. As he approached the van, he took the balaclava from his back pocket and pulled it on over his face.

He didn't know how long he'd been out or what he'd find as he got down to one knee and looked into the van's interior. Through the cracked window he saw the bodies of several men, crumpled and folded over themselves. He saw blood but no obvious gaping wounds. No idea if these men were dead or alive. And no time to check.

Six men, he counted. Five in marshals' windbreakers. One in army camo.

Nobody else.

Mason stood back up and circled the vehicle. The window was completely gone on this side. Large enough for a man to crawl through. He got down closer to the ground and saw a drop of blood reflecting back the moonlight.

Wallace got out.

He's gone.

WHEN HARPER OPENED HIS EYES, he tried to twist his body free, but he couldn't move. He was trapped upside down against the steering wheel. The Ranger was next to him, his eyes closed.

"Captain," he said, but there was no answer. Harper felt along the man's neck. A pulse. He was alive.

"Who else is here?" he said. "Who else can hear me?"

Nothing. He turned his head, counting bodies. Someone was missing.

Wallace. *Fuck.*

Harper worked against the steering wheel again, trying to get himself free. Then he heard the sound of footsteps. He stayed quiet as he heard a man circling the van. A few seconds later, he saw the man's shoes, his pants. Then the barrel of a gun as the man bent down to look through the window. Harper made himself stay still, caught one quick glimpse of the face. But it was covered by something black.

Mason, he thought. *I know it.*

Harper waited until the man walked away from the van. He made one more attempt to free himself, with little success. The next challenge was whether he could get to his phone. It felt an eternity, but he was finally able to pull it from his pocket, then it clattered to the floor. Another eternity to reach it again. When he had it in his hand, he dialed the marshals' emergency hotline. Better than 911 because he knew that not only would they be sending police and ambulances, they'd also call Camp Merrill. They'd already sent down one truck full of Rangers to rescue the helicopter. Now every other Ranger in the camp would be woken up and sent out to find Nick Mason.

A few hundred highly skilled Army Rangers, all of them interrupted from their precious few hours of sleep, all of them storming into the forest in a seriously bad mood. Not a training exercise this time but a real enemy.

No way Mason gets out of this one, Harper said to himself. *I just hope they find him before he finds Wallace.*

The next thought hit him as he started to work his way free:

The leak couldn't have come from Chicago after all. I have a bad marshal in my own office.

MASON TOOK OUT his pocket flashlight and followed the trail of blood. He had no idea how badly hurt Wallace was, or how fast he could move, but Mason could already hear the emergency sirens in the distance. He was running out of time.

He followed the blood a hundred yards into the forest as it grew darker and more foreboding. Mason stopped for a moment and listened. He heard something up ahead. He kept on moving, walking several yards, seeing signs that someone had fought through the same underbrush just moments before him. More blood on the ground.

He's close. I've got to be—

He felt the impact before he could finish the thought. Something heavy on the back of his neck, driving him forward into the ground. The gun came out of his hand as he rolled onto his back just in time to see something coming down at his chest. He rolled farther and felt it glance across his ribs, saw the huge figure looming over him, blocking out the moonlight.

Mason grabbed at the man's leg, felt fabric, the weight of muscle and bone. He pulled just as the man was swinging the branch again and the man fell backward, letting out a cry of pain as he hit the ground. Mason rolled up onto his knees and hit the man in the face. He hit him again, then one more time just to be sure. He found his flashlight on the ground next to the man and used that to search for his gun.

When he found it, he brushed it off and pointed it at the man, who was sitting up by now. It was Isaiah Wallace.

"Let me see your face," Wallace said.

Mason pulled up the balaclava.

"Why's the Angel of Death always gotta be a white boy?"

"You know who this is from," Mason said.

Wallace nodded. "Yeah, I do."

He said it with something that sounded almost like relief, then let out a loud breath. "You gonna do it, white boy, do it. You ain't, I can find somewhere else to—"

Mason shot him twice in the chest, twice in the head. Then he put the gun in his belt and started walking.

A hundred yards later, he started to hear the movement in the forest. Behind him. To the left. To the right. They were suddenly all around him.

He quickened his pace and tried to remember the way back to the road.

You get lost out here, he told himself, *you'll be wandering all night.*

Unless they find you first.

He tried to pick up the trail of blood again, but he didn't want to turn on his flashlight and risk giving himself away. The road ran roughly from the southwest to the northeast, he remembered, and through the gaps in the clouds he was able to find the North Star and orient himself. He kept working his way in what he thought was the right direction, listening for more footsteps around him, trying to stay quiet.

Mason came to a steep ravine and almost lost his footing in the soft dirt at its edge. That's when he heard someone dangerously close. Easing himself down the ravine and into a slight depression under the exposed roots of a tree, he sat there for a moment and listened, hearing the unmistakable sounds of a man walking just above him.

Mason waited until it was quiet again. Waited another minute to be sure, then eased himself the rest of the way to the bottom of the ravine. There was a small stream that he crossed slowly, careful not to splash. He climbed the opposite side of the ravine and kept working his way toward what he hoped would be the road.

He heard more footsteps around him. The men moving without talking, without using artificial lights. Like he was the prey being hunted by silent animals.

That's when the truth came to him, the basic knowledge he could feel all the way to his bones:

The first Ranger who saw him would kill him.

A police officer is trained to disarm a suspect, detain him, bring him back alive unless deadly force is absolutely necessary. But these weren't police officers swarming the forest around him. These were pissed-off soldiers in training, jarred from their beds to track down an unknown enemy. It didn't matter that this was Georgia, not Iraq or Afghanistan. Mason was dressed in black, not green. That's all it would take.

He kept working his way toward the road. Every three or four steps, he would stop and listen. He pulled himself up into a tree and made himself one with a thick branch, held his breath for a long minute while a Ranger passed right beneath him, so close he could have reached down in the darkness and touched him.

When he eased himself back to the ground, he had to duck into the thick underbrush to let two more men pass.

He thought about Adriana, remembered how it felt to hug her before getting on the plane to come to this place. Just hours ago, according to the clock, but it felt like another lifetime.

I have to get out of here, he said to himself. *I'm not going to go down this way.*

He kept moving, stopping and listening, moving again. Until finally he came to the road. He ducked behind a tree as a pair of headlights swept across him. When the transport truck had passed, Mason started working his way down the road, staying close to the edge, not even sure if he was north or south of the overturned van and his own SUV. His question was answered a few minutes later when he saw both vehicles ahead. There were two ambulances on the scene. One of them pulled away, followed soon after by the other. It was quiet for a long minute as Mason waited, not sure if he was truly alone now. He was about to step out of the woods when he heard the rumble of another vehicle. A Jeep came around the curve and ground to a halt. A single Ranger got out and stood there regarding the mayhem.

Mason moved quickly, staying as quiet as he could. The Ranger was just about to turn when Mason pressed the barrel of his gun to the back of the man's head.

"If you don't move," Mason said, "I won't have to kill you."

"Key's in the ignition," the Ranger said. "But you won't get far."

Mason swung the gun hard enough to take the man down for at least a minute or two. Then he got into the Jeep and sped off.

He roared by a group of men, heard them yelling behind him. Then another group, one of the men inches away from getting run over when he took too long getting out of the way. Mason knew he had to ditch the Jeep as soon as he could, so as he got close to town he turned off in the first driveway, pulled the Jeep all the way up behind a detached garage.

The house was dark except for one porch light left on. Mason tried the door. It was locked. One kick and it was open, and Mason's next potential obstacle was the homeowner coming down the stairs with a loaded shotgun. But as any experienced car thief can tell you, there's often a set of keys by one of the doors. As Mason moved through the silent house, he saw them hanging on a hook in the kitchen. He went out the back door and found the car in the garage. A silver Toyota Camry, perfectly nondescript and forgettable. He opened the door and drove off, leaving the Jeep behind.

He stayed alert as he rolled down the dark streets of Dahlonega. When he made it to the highway, he pointed himself north. But not toward the airport in Atlanta because he knew this car would soon be reported stolen and someone might be looking for it there. It was eleven hours to Chicago, the last drive he wanted to make right now but the only smart choice.

As the adrenaline started to wear off and his heartbeat came back down toward normal, he felt the stinging, bleeding scratches on his arms and face, the burning in his neck and shoulder where the bullet wound was still healing. On top of that, Mason's ears were ringing, his head still fuzzy from the impact of the collision.

He waited for something else to come to him, too. That familiar feeling after doing a job, after standing in front of another man with a gun in his hand—with everything turned off, every emotion, every circuit breaker in his own humanity, just long enough to pull the trigger. There was always the inevitable moment when it would all turn back on at once and it would hit him, the realization of what he had just done.

Mason drove through the night. He drove and he waited.

The feeling never came.

13

FOR THE SECOND TIME IN HER CAREER, RACHEL GREEN-
wood had to genuinely restrain herself from hitting a man
in the face.

The man in question was Jay Starr, a high-priced defense attorney based out of New York, a man who made
John Gotti's mouthpiece, Bruce Cutler, look like Clar-
ence Darrow.

"Your Honor," Starr said, "the people would have you
believe that Darius Cole was somehow responsible for the
murder of these two witnesses despite the fact that he's
been sitting in a federal penitentiary for the past twelve
years."

They were speaking *in camera*, meaning privately inside the judge's chambers on the twenty-first floor of the
Federal Building, just down the hall from the courtroom
itself. For Assistant U.S. Attorney Greenwood, going to
the federal court meant riding seventeen floors up the

elevator. Except today she took the elevator ride with a U.S. marshal standing on either side of her.

It wasn't the first time—protecting federal court officers was one of the primary duties of the Service. She'd even had a car with two marshals inside parked outside her house overnight. But this was different. Her husband had a marshal stationed outside his private law practice. Her stepson had a marshal literally following him as he made his rounds of his hospital residency. Her stepdaughter had a marshal sitting outside her classes at DePaul.

And for the first time in Greenwood's career, none of this felt like a formality. Or an overreaction. It actually felt like something she and her family needed.

"McLaren and Wallace were both scheduled to testify in Cole's retrial," Judge Oakley said. "If you have another explanation, I'd love to hear it."

Judge Oakley was a black woman who'd grown up in Chicago, a woman who'd had to steel herself against whispers of preferential treatment ever since she graduated at the top of her class from Northwestern Law School. But Greenwood had been more than happy to hear she'd drawn Judge Oakley for the retrial. Not so much that she doubted the eventual outcome—she still believed, even with two dead witnesses, that she could win using only the physical evidence collected for the original trial—but because she was already imagining the scene in the courtroom when the retrial was over and Oakley had her chance to speak directly to Darius Cole. As a Chicago native who had grown up surrounded by gangs, drugs, and street violence, she had a now-famous habit of eviscerating any gang leader or dealer who happened to come through her courtroom. If she peeled the paint off the walls while sentencing a mid-level Latin King to twenty years, what would she do to a man like

Darius Cole before sending him back to federal prison for the rest of his life?

"McLaren and Wallace are two career criminals," Starr said after taking a moment to compose his answer. "Their pasts finally caught up to them."

Starr was a long way from his office in Manhattan, which instead of an elevator ride meant a limo to the airport, a first-class plane ride, then another limo downtown.

And he didn't need any U.S. marshals watching his back.

"Both of them," Greenwood said. "In the same week. Just before Cole's retrial—"

"It is a hell of a coincidence," the judge said.

"If Mrs. Greenwood has information that can connect these crimes to my client, she would have already produced it," Starr said. "And knowing her somewhat aggressive tendencies as I do, she would have already filed new charges against my client. Given the fact that she's done neither, I suggest that she either put up or shut up. The next sound you hear will be her resounding silence."

"Enough," the judge said to him. "We're in my chambers, Counselor, not open court."

"I'm feeling a little ganged up on here," Starr said, straightening his tie. "You'll have to forgive me."

"I'm sure this isn't the first time," the judge said. "But let me remind you, Mr. Starr, that you are an officer of this court. And if you have any knowledge of witness tampering, witness intimidation, witness *murder*—"

"Of course I don't," he said, cutting her off. "And frankly, I find the implication prejudicial."

"You see those marshals outside my office," the judge said. "They're here for Counselor Greenwood. Mine is down the hall, getting me some coffee. It's a nice gesture, but I don't think it makes up for the fact that I suddenly feel like I'm living in Mexico, getting ready to preside over the trial of some cartel boss."

"I understand the concern," Starr said. "But I assure you my client has nothing to do with any of these occurrences."

"And Al Capone had nothing to do with the Saint Valentine's Day Massacre," Greenwood said.

"Your Honor!" Starr said.

Greenwood saw her suppress a smile. "I'll be filing for a delay," Greenwood said. "At least four weeks."

The judge's half smile disappeared and Greenwood knew why. For her, just as much as for Greenwood, a four-week delay meant another month living with U.S. marshals watching her every move, walking her to her car and starting it for her.

Another month living in fear.

"I have an even better idea," Starr said. "I'll be filing a motion to vacate the charges outright."

"Oh, you go right ahead," the judge said. "This court could use a good laugh today."

"Look," Starr said, taking another moment to straighten his tie, "I know there are some extraordinary circumstances surrounding this retrial—"

"Do we have any other business here?" the judge asked, already looking past him to the doorway through which he'd soon be leaving.

Starr cleared his throat and handed her a sheet of paper. Then he handed a copy to Greenwood.

"We're adding another name to the list of witnesses for the defense."

As Greenwood looked at the name, it took her a moment to process it. It had been thirteen years since she'd last seen this name.

Now, as she saw it again, the outcome of the retrial suddenly seemed a little less certain.

*   *   *

IN 2003, Rachel Greenwood had just joined the U.S. Attorney's office in the Northern District of Illinois after
eight years of putting in her time with the Cook County
State's Attorney. The move to federal was a big step up.

She was thirty-two years old. Not married yet. Ready
to work sixteen hours a day if that's what it took to make
it as an AUSA. Late one Saturday night, it was her turn
to cover what they called "duty day." The least favorite
part of the job for any AUSA, especially on a night when
everyone else in the office was home or out enjoying the
weekend. But it was an absolute necessity to have cover-
age at all times because federal charges can be filed twenty-
four hours a day, seven days a week—and in every arrest
that might involve federal charges, the law enforcement
officer must call the U.S. Attorney's office to have the
charges approved before moving forward. If it's after
hours, the AUSA on duty will consult the latest declination guidelines and either approve or decline the charges.
The bigger the office's current caseload, the tighter the
guidelines—a suspect might draw a federal felony charge
for possessing twenty ounces of marijuana one month,
then get kicked back to the street with a misdemeanor
ticket the next, all based on how much time the over-
worked AUSAs had to spare.

The federal agents in town—FBI, ATF, DEA—all
knew this routine, but even the local Chicago police officers would have to get on the phone if they wanted to file
federal charges. Which is why so few of them ever both-
ered.

But it was a local cop who called her that Saturday
night, a detective in what they called Area 5 back then,
before they'd consolidated the areas to North, Central,
and South. He'd picked up a recent immigrant from

Northern Ireland named Sean Burke after the man had allegedly assaulted three people in a South Side restaurant.

"Doesn't sound federal to me," Greenwood had told him.

"There's something going on with this guy," the detective had answered. "Something major. But I can't get any of the victims to cooperate. All three of them were taken to the hospital, but nobody's talking."

"Witnesses?"

"A whole restaurantful. But nobody will say a word."

"Look, Detective, I feel for you, but I still don't understand why you're—"

"I found an assault rifle in his vehicle. I want to charge him with that just so I have something to hold him overnight."

"You don't need me to do that."

"Yes I do. This asshole sergeant I'm working under right now, he wants to kick him. But if I can get a federal charge . . ."

This was a year before Congress would let the Federal Assault Weapons Ban expire, and possession of certain types of assault rifles was still a federal offense. But Greenwood was working off an especially tight set of declination guidelines that night and she knew what would happen to her if she let this detective file a federal felony charge for just one weapon in a backseat.

"Did he use this weapon in the commission of a crime?" she asked.

"Far as I can tell, it hasn't even been fired yet. But I've been doing this a long time, ma'am. I've learned to trust my gut and my gut is screaming about this guy."

"I hear Tagamet's good for that."

Greenwood heard the detective laugh on the other end of the phone. Something about that made him seem more real to her. Made him seem like what he was: a man trying to do his job.

"You know that sling your sergeant's going to have your ass in when he finds out you went behind his back?" Greenwood asked. "I hope there's room for mine, too. Go ahead and charge him."

The next day, Greenwood found out what her punishment would be for approving a simple weapons possession charge in the busiest month of the year. She was given the case, solo, on top of everything else she already had on her plate. There was no time to complain about it because she knew the clock was ticking, so she called the detective at Area 5 to follow up on the disposition of the arrest.

"Burke is being released," the detective told her in a voice that held none of the conviction of the man she'd talked to the night before. "I'm sorry for all of the trouble."

"Wait a minute," she said. "I thought you said—"

"Forget it ever happened, Counselor. It was a mistake."

Then he hung up. She sat there at her desk, thinking about the sudden reversal and what could have caused it, until she finally got up and left her office. She didn't have the time to spend half the day fighting traffic all the way down to the Area 5 station, but she had to see this detective face-to-face. And if possible, she wanted to see the subject, Sean Burke, before he got out.

She gave the detective's name to the desk sergeant, was told that he had left for the day. "Taking some personal time," the sergeant said. And that was the end of it.

Until she got back out on the sidewalk and saw a man standing there.

He was thin, with a rough, pockmarked face and disheveled red hair. Seemingly too small and too slight to put three people in hospital beds. He looked back at her, watching her watching him, with a slight smile on his face. She knew this must be Sean Burke.

A black Escalade pulled up and Burke opened the passenger's-side door. Before he got in, he turned back to Greenwood and gave her a little nod of the head. Then he was gone.

That night, she had drinks with an FBI agent named Tim Flaherty. She'd been seeing him off and on, nothing serious, just drinks after work, until the night he stayed over, leaving early the next morning without leaving a note. So they were officially off at the moment, which was actually fine for her because she didn't have the time to be on. But she wanted to ask him about Sean Burke.

He promised he'd look him up and get back to her.

The next day, Flaherty called her and told her he'd spent the whole morning tracking down everything he could find on Burke. "I've run into this other name a couple times now," he said. "It's like I'm touching a live wire, or something, every time I hit it."

"What's the name?"

"Darius Cole. You ever hear of him?"

"Can't say that I have."

"He's got a juvenile record from a long time ago, but then he just disappears. Right off the map. I'll keep digging and tell you what I find tonight. At dinner. Our usual place?"

When she got to the restaurant, she waited for a half hour at the bar. Flaherty never showed. Eventually, another man in a suit walked in and found her there. He was tall, with dark eyes and a thick mustache that should have been retired with Burt Reynolds.

"You're Greenwood?"

"Who are you?"

"Agent Flaherty sends his regrets. He won't be able to have dinner with you tonight."

"What are you talking about? What's going on?"

"He's been called away on an important case. He's already gone."

"Gone where?"

"I'm afraid I can't divulge that information."

"He wouldn't just leave without telling me," Greenwood said. Something about this man got to her. On the same level that Burke had.

"I'm going to give you my card," he said, reaching into his jacket pocket. "You have any more questions about Sean Burke or Darius Cole, I'd appreciate it if you could bring them directly to me, okay?"

Greenwood took the card. *Stanley Horton, Federal Bureau of Investigation.* Below that was the address and phone number of the field office on Roosevelt.

"You have a nice night," he said, pursing that mustache into some semblance of a smile before leaving.

As she sat at the bar and finished her drink, Rachel Greenwood kept looking at the card. And wondering.

She never did see Tim Flaherty again. The agent never came back to Chicago. And when she called the field office a week later, she was told he had left the Bureau.

That was the same day she took Agent Horton's card, still sitting on her desk, and taped it to the whiteboard in her office. She wrote down the name Sean Burke. And, above that, she wrote Darius Cole.

Over the next sixteen months, other names would be added. Burke's would be moved to the side, but Cole's would remain at the center, the single sun around which an entire solar system revolved.

Greenwood spent every waking hour thinking about Darius Cole, and running prosecutorial interference for the small team of DEA agents working on the case. Wiretaps, audio and video surveillance, garbage pulls—Cole was a careful man with an uncanny ability to keep his own name off every record. Greenwood was just as careful, keeping the investigation securely under wraps, with strict orders to everyone involved to be especially careful about any possible interaction with the FBI. Even then, as the evidence was slowly gathered, it became clear that this would have to be, ultimately, a pure "cooperator" case, built almost entirely on the direct testimony of at least two, and ideally three, witnesses who could be persuaded to testify against him.

The first to turn was Ken McLaren. The second was Isaiah Wallace. One man knew Cole's money better than anyone else, the other knew Cole himself, going all the way back to their childhoods. Sean Burke was briefly considered as the third cooperating witness, but Greenwood's boss at the time, the U.S. Attorney who personally tried the case against Cole, was confident that the testimony of McLaren and Wallace would be more than enough. And he was right.

In the fall of 2005, Darius Cole was found guilty under the Continuing Criminal Enterprise Statute, otherwise known as the Kingpin Statute, for trafficking drugs on a major international scale, along with conspiracy to launder money, evade taxation, and commit murder. The original judge handed down two consecutive life sentences and the Federal Bureau of Prisons placed Cole at USP Terre Haute, where he'd remained ever since.

NOW, TWELVE YEARS LATER, as Rachel Greenwood stood in Judge Oakley's office looking at the list of defense witnesses who would be testifying at Darius Cole's retrial, she zeroed in on the name that had just been added:

Stan Horton, retired FBI agent.

The surprise lasted for three seconds, quickly replaced by anger. *Killing witnesses was no surprise,* she said to herself. *But what the hell is this?*

And then her anger was replaced by raw determination. *They add a witness, we add a witness.* She went right back downstairs to her office and got on the phone. Within ten minutes, she had located Sean Burke at Rikers Island. Within twelve, she'd learned that Burke had not only killed his cellmate at Dannemora but had recently killed five more inmates while awaiting resentencing at Rikers, with a transfer to Southport in his immediate future.

This keeps getting better, she said to herself as she looked up the number for the U.S. Attorney for the Southern District of New York. *But at least we have some leverage. He's not going to walk away from six homicides, but we can offer him someplace a hell of a lot nicer than Southport.*

We need to protect this guy, Greenwood thought as she waited for the phone to ring. *Keep him out of General Population, move him to a Protective Custody Unit.*

She was already thinking about Jay Starr's smug face and how his expression would change when he saw her own addition to the list of witnesses.

That's right, Counselor. Sean Burke.

Yes, he's a killer. One killer testifying against another. And helping me make sure that Darius Cole stays locked up forever.

14

AFTER ELEVEN STRAIGHT HOURS ON THE ROAD, DRIVING all night long through Appalachia and then the long straight flats of Indiana, Nick Mason crossed the Skyway Bridge and saw his hometown again, lit up in the Sunday morning light. He couldn't help but remember when he walked out of prison after five and a half years and crossed this same bridge. On that day, he'd had no idea what his new life would look like. Now, just a few months later, he knew all too well.

Would I do it all over again?

He didn't have an answer. Not that it mattered, anyway. There was no going back.

He was close to the Chicago State University campus, found a crowded parking lot and abandoned the silver Camry. He got on the Red Line and rode uptown, got off at the Clark/Division stop, and walked the rest of the way up Lincoln Park West to the town house. He needed a shower, a bed, and a cold Goose Island, and he didn't care what order they came in. But when he walked through the front door and up the polished wooden stairs, Diana was waiting for him. She was dressed for work because Diana was *always* dressed for work. But there was something different about her, obvious to him even in his exhaustion. Something in her eyes that made him stop dead.

"We need to talk," she said.

In eight years of marriage to Gina Sullivan Mason, that was his least favorite four-word combination.

"How about later?"

"How about now."

"Look," he said, "I'm sorry about—"

"You left your nine-year-old daughter in my restaurant," she said. "In the middle of my lunch rush."

"I had no choice."

"The last time you did this to me, I had to come rescue Lauren, send her away to God-knows-where. Do you have any idea what you did to that woman? She can never come back here, Nick. Ever."

"It was a mistake being with her. I know that."

"If you knew it, you wouldn't have done it!"

"Look," Mason said, taking a beat to calm himself down, "I just drove for eleven hours straight. And if you had any idea what I had to go through down there—"

"I don't want to know where you were," she said, "or what you were doing."

"You know exactly what I was doing."

"Just shut up," she said, turning away from him. "I said I don't want to know."

"It's my job, Diana. You know what I do. We both work for the same man."

"We don't *work* for him, Nick."

He waited for her to go on but she had run out of steam, at least for the moment. As she turned away from him, Mason could hear her breathing, could practically hear her heart beating, from six feet away.

Mason took a step closer to her, placed his hand on her shoulder. He felt her flinch on contact, but she didn't move away.

"What's wrong?" he asked her.

"He's here."

"What are you talking about?"

"Darius is here. In Chicago. They moved him up here for the retrial."

"How do you know that?"

"Somebody from the Federal Bureau of Prisons called me. Darius asked them to, I guess. But it doesn't matter. I think I already knew. As soon as I woke up this morning."

"Diana . . ." He put his other hand on her other shoulder, tried to look her in the eye, but she kept her gaze fixed on the floor.

"I can feel him here," she said. "In this city."

"Where are they keeping him?"

"Downtown."

Meaning MCC, the Metropolitan Correctional Center, on Van Buren Street. Hell, he'd just passed right by it when he was on the Red Line, that strange, triangular monolith with the narrow slits in the otherwise unbroken gray walls, looking nothing like the other tall buildings that surrounded it. In 2012, two bank robbers actually made a long rope out of sheets, like in some old movie, and rappelled seventeen floors down to the street. A security camera caught them getting into a taxicab. One of the men was recaptured a week later, the other remained at large for two more weeks after that. Nobody had ever escaped from that building before they did and nobody had done it since.

But of course Darius Cole would never rappel down the side of a building. That wasn't his style. Darius Cole was going to find a way to bend the retrial in his own favor and then walk out the front door a free man.

"You're helping him," Diana said as if reading his mind. "I know that's what your assignments have been. That man who was killed downtown a few days ago . . . He used to work for Darius."

"I thought you didn't want to hear about it."

"How many of those marshals did you kill, Nick?"

"None. Didn't you watch the news?"

Mason felt his own anger spiking. He'd taken a bullet in his shoulder, inches away from killing him, to avoid taking any more lives than he had to.

"Darius is going to walk through that door," she said, looking down the stairs. "I always knew he would, no matter what anyone said. And you're the one who's going to make this happen."

"It's not just me doing this . . ."

"Twelve years I've been alone, Nick. That restaurant was nothing more than a place to launder Darius's money and now it's one of the best in the city. I did all of that myself, built my whole life around it. And now it's all going away."

"Diana, he's not out yet. We have time to think about this."

"I've already thought about it. I'm leaving."

"No you're not. Not yet." He tightened his grip on her shoulders.

"Your daughter told me your ex-wife is taking her to Denver. Is that true?"

"Yes."

"So they'll be gone. You already sent Lauren away. You even sent that dog away. How come I'm the one who has to stay?"

"Because you're the one who chose this," he said. "You made your own deal with the devil just like I did."

"No, Nick. It's not the same. Your deal doesn't include sleeping in the man's bed."

Mason let that one go.

"There's no way out of this," Diana said. "Not if we stay."

"We can't run," he said. "You know anywhere he can't reach out and touch us?"

"Who said anything about *we*?"

"You can't do this alone," he said, spinning her around, hands on her hips. He had never stood this close to her. Never held her. Even through her panic and his exhaustion, there was a buzz. "Diana, I'm working on this. Every day. Trying to find a way out."

"I've already packed a suitcase."

"Go unpack it. Right now."

"Why? What do you think—"

"You have to trust me," he said. "We'll find a way out."

"Why should I trust you, Nick? You're nothing but a . . ."

She hesitated.

"A hired killer."

"Don't say that."

"I'm not going to wait here," she said. "I've been alone for twelve years. A prisoner in solitary. He did that to me, Nick. Darius did that to me. And now . . ."

She stopped, looking for the right words.

"I can't be what he'll want me to be. Not anymore. Not ever. By the time he gets out, I'll be a thousand miles away."

She bolted out of his grasp toward the door. Mason took a step sideways to block her path.

"It won't work," he said. "You know that."

"Get out of the way, Nick."

Mason held his ground. As he looked her in the eye, he remembered the first time he saw her, in his bathroom. He was in the shower and she appeared out of nowhere, holding a towel. He didn't know then that she would become so much a part of his daily life without ever really letting him in. An intimate stranger.

On some nights, he couldn't help wondering, as she slept alone in her own bed on the other side of the town house—

The phone rang, breaking the spell.

He stepped away to answer it, but she made no further attempt to leave.

"What is it now?" he said.

"This isn't over yet," Quintero said. "I'll be there in five minutes to take you back to the airport. You're going to New York."

EIGHT HUNDRED MILES EAST, Sean Burke was in motion. But that was all he knew. He didn't know what kind of vehicle he was in or how many men were in the vehicle with him. He sure as hell didn't know where he was going or how long it would take to get there—because there was a blindfold wrapped around his head like he was some kind of goddamned Guantánamo Bay terrorist.

Maybe forty-five minutes later, the vehicle stopped. A wide radius from Rikers Island, even with traffic. Burke heard a door slide open, then he felt two pairs of hands take him by the arms and guide him roughly out the door.

His hands were cuffed behind his back, but he wasn't wearing leg-irons. As he stepped down, he didn't know how high he was and he nearly lost his balance when the ground surprised him.

"Take it easy there," he heard a man say with a sharp

edge in his voice. "Wouldn't want our little friend to get hurt."

Burke felt cold air on his face, heard the distant hum of traffic. He was led across a concrete surface, felt himself kicking leaves as he walked. A breeze picked up, stirring the leaves and sending a chill down his back.

I'm someplace away from the main roads, he said to himself. *Someplace still in the city, or close to it. I wonder if they've brought me here to kill me . . .*

Burke believed these guards to be capable of anything. Put a bullet in his head right here, tell their supervisors that he tried to escape. He didn't panic because panic wasn't useful. He needed to play this out, see where it led. Keep his senses wide open.

He was led across more concrete, took one step onto grass, then back onto concrete. He was on a path. Maybe a park? Not Central Park—there'd be sounds of other people around.

Another hundred yards maybe, until a hand touched his chest and stopped him. He heard a key going into a lock. A door opening. He was pushed forward again and felt the air change as he was taken inside. It had a stale antiseptic smell that took him back to someplace from long ago. A school? A museum?

He heard an elevator door slide open, listened to the footsteps, and counted two other men joining him.

"You try anything," the man to his left said, "you'll be tased."

Burke smiled, imagined himself taking the Taser from the man and putting it right up his ass. *Does this qualify as trying something?*

He sensed the elevator moving down. He was going underground. When the elevator opened, he was taken forward, stopped for a moment while another door opened, and Burke felt the vacuum of the air being pulled into an enclosed space. He heard voices. Maybe half a dozen men.

"This is him?" he heard one man say. "You gotta be shitting me."

He was walked forward onto a hard tile floor until he was finally stopped again, and this time the blindfold was taken off his face.

"Do not move," someone said to him. "Do not turn around."

Burke blinked in the harsh artificial light. He was facing a metal cell door, with the standard slot for meals and handcuffs. The door was opened and he was pushed inside. There was a bed with a thin pad, a steel sink-and-toilet unit. A small ventilation grate high on the concrete wall. No windows.

He'd seen worse. A lot worse.

The door was slammed shut and he heard the bolt being slid across it. When the slot in the door was opened, they didn't have to tell him to back up to it and extend his hands behind him so they could uncuff him.

"Welcome to the bunker," the man said. Then the little access door slid closed and Burke was alone.

AS MASON WAITED OUTSIDE the United terminal at LaGuardia Airport, he saw the rusted-out Subaru idling in the pick-up line. Mason didn't move, so the vehicle pulled up and stopped in front of him. The man behind the wheel was maybe fifty years old, with thinning hair in a bad comb-over. His face was red from weather, age, alcohol, God knows what else. He was wearing a tan raincoat and staring straight ahead until he reached over and pushed the front passenger's-side door open.

"You waiting for an invitation?"

Mason looked in the backseat and saw the suitcase there. He closed the front door, pulled open the back door instead, and got in.

"I'm a goddamed chauffeur now?" But as soon as Mason closed the door, the driver put the car in gear and pulled away without another word.

The car smelled of cigarette smoke. Mason studied the man from behind as he kept driving without turning his head.

He's a deputy marshal, Quintero had told him. *Thirty-two years on the job. Just got transferred out of WITSEC, wants to retire, but certain habits have made that impossible. He's motivated to help us.*

Mason didn't want to know what the habits were. Or how he was motivated. While the man drove, Mason turned his attention to the suitcase. There were two combination locks, one on each side. After he'd keyed in the right numbers, he hit the buttons and the two locks flipped open. He lifted the top of the suitcase.

"Holy shit," he said out loud as he looked down at a fully automatic M4A1 carbine with three high-capacity magazines and a black tactical vest with six attached grenades—three round fragmentation grenades on one side, three cylinder-shaped concussion grenades on the other.

For the last assignment, he'd been given a sniper rifle with a scope. A weapon of skill and accuracy.

This time, he was being given the tools to become a one-man army.

"Where are you taking me?" Mason said as he closed the suitcase.

"You're going underground," the man said, turning his head to sneak a look at the contents of the suitcase. He shook his head. "One way or the other."

* * *

BURKE LISTENED CAREFULLY to the sounds outside the door. He'd separated the voices, counted five or six of them in total. He added that information to the map he'd already constructed in his head—he'd taken approximately ten steps from the elevator to the inner door, another thirty steps to the cell door with a left turn roughly in the middle.

About three hours after his arrival, the slot in the door opened and a tray of food was pushed through. A Subway turkey sub, a bag of chips, and a Coke. Not prison food at all, which told Burke there weren't many other prisoners here. In fact, he might even be the only one. Which just added to the mystery of why he'd been brought to this place.

He picked the onions off his sub and couldn't help thinking that as long as they were going out to buy him food, they could have brought him a Guinness instead of a watered-down Coke. But by far the most interesting part of the meal was the tray it came on. He had never seen a tray like this in a regular prison. It was metal, first of all, and as he put pressure on one edge, he felt it starting to bend.

This will do quite nicely.

When the access door was opened a few minutes later, Burke slid the tray back through and then got down on one knee to look through the opening. He saw the belt of the man taking the tray and, behind him, a wall of lockers and a wooden bench.

Burke still had no idea where he was. But an hour later, the access door slid open again and he was told to back up for his handcuffs. He complied, but instead of taking him out of the cell, they told him to stand against the far wall with his back to the door. The door opened and he heard someone step inside.

"You can turn around now." It was a voice he hadn't heard before.

When Burke turned, he saw a middle-aged man wearing a dark windbreaker with the U.S. Marshals' seal on the chest. He'd brought in a folding chair with him, had to hold it with his left hand because his right arm was in a sling. There was a white bandage taped to his forehead above his left eye.

"I'm going to take your cuffs off," the man said, showing him the key in his left hand, "so we can talk like two men."

Burke turned around and let him unlock the cuffs. It took an extra moment with one arm in a sling, but he'd obviously done it before.

"Please sit down," the man said, putting the cuffs and the key in his pocket.

Burke sat on his bed and watched the man unfold the chair and sit down facing him, about three feet away.

"I'm Marshal Bruce Harper," he said. "I'm in charge of the WITSEC Program. Do you know what that is?"

"Witness protection."

Harper nodded. "Technically, I only handle clients out of the prison system. A case like yours, that falls under the Federal Bureau of Prisons."

"Where am I?"

He watched Harper consider his response. "You're in a Protective Custody Unit," he said. "In fact, the most secure PCU ever built. You're the very first man to come here."

"Should I be honored?"

"I understand you killed five men at Rikers."

"It was them or me."

"I also understand you once worked for Darius Cole."

Burke just looked at him. The name burned in his mind, had been burning ever since the inmates had tried to kill him in the elevator.

"Cole's retrial is scheduled for two days from now," Harper said.

The information hit Burke harder than any guard's Taser. "He's getting a retrial?"

"Why else would you be here?"

"I'll wager you're about to tell me."

"I don't know if you're aware of this," Harper continued, "but the U.S. Attorney's office was actually thinking about asking you to be a witness at the original trial."

An even bigger surprise. "Nobody ever said anything to me about that. If they'da asked me, I would have said no."

"They can be persuasive about these things."

"I'm not a rat."

"Well, apparently Cole isn't so sure."

"You know the two worst things you can call an Irishman?" Burke asked. "The first is an Englishman. The second is an informer."

"How did you end your relationship with Cole? I'm guessing there was no retirement party? No gold watch?"

He sent a half dozen men to find me, Burke thought. *I killed them all.*

But I still wouldn't have testified. My father would have crawled out of the grave and slit my throat if I had.

"I want to ask you something," Harper said. "Because the two men who did testify against him . . . They're both dead now."

The picture was getting clearer. Burke leaned forward, listening to the man across from him. Absorbing every word.

"The second hit was last night," Harper said. "I was there."

Burke smiled as he nodded at the sling holding Harper's right arm.

"Do you know a man named Nick Mason?"

Burke's smile faded as he ran the name through his head. He had a feeling this name would be important to this man and he didn't like the fact that he was a stranger. "No," he said, "I don't know that name."

"But you know the kind of man Cole would hire to do this."

"He doesn't 'hire' people," Burke said. "He acquires them. Owns them. Forever. Or at least, that's how he sees it."

"Is it fair to say this man effectively took your place as Cole's personal assassin?"

"I'm not sure anyone could take my place," Burke said. "But it sounds like this Nick Mason is doing his best."

Harper looked at him with a level of discomfort he hadn't shown since entering the cell.

He may be having second thoughts about taking the cuffs off me, Burke thought.

"Don't mind my boasting," Burke said. "Those days are behind me."

"They weren't behind you at Rikers," Harper said, "but what I want to know about is this new man, Nick Mason, and what you think he'll do next."

"That's easy. If I'm the next name on his list—"

"He can't touch you here."

"You probably thought the same thing about the other two."

"I don't think you understand where you are right now," Harper said. "Nobody can find this place. Nobody. And even if they did find it, they can't get down here. And even if they did get down here, there are six armed men outside this door."

Six armed men, Burke thought. *Thanks for the information*.

"When Napoleon was exiled to Saint Helena," Harper said, "he spent the rest of his life on this little island in the middle of the Atlantic Ocean, a five-day sail from Africa, with five hundred British troops watching him. Which made him probably the most well-guarded prisoner in the history of the world."

Harper leaned back in his chair.

"Until now."

Burke waited for the rest of it. He knew there was something else coming.

"So now I want to ask you," Harper said, "now that you know you're safe . . . What are you going to do about Cole?"

Burke didn't answer.

"You testify at the retrial, we *keep* you safe. Forever."

"What," Burke said, nodding to the concrete walls around him, "you're going to keep me here?"

"Once we've put Cole away for good, you'll be moved into another Protective Custody Unit. Someplace a lot nicer than this. And a hell of a lot nicer than Gen Pop at Southport."

"But I'm still in prison for the rest of my life."

"That's better than being dead."

"You've never been in prison," Burke said. "I need some time to think about it."

"Not too long," Harper said as he stood up. "Remember, the retrial's in two days. And they'll need some time to prepare you."

As Burke stood up, he waited to see Harper's reaction. Any Corrections officer would keep Burke seated until the door was closed. But Harper wasn't a Corrections officer.

"I'll be here for the rest of the day," Harper said. "Let

the guards know when you're ready to finish this conversation."

Burke watched Harper go to the door and knock three times. Watched the door open and this time he caught a better glimpse of the room outside the cell. More of the lockers. And what looked to be the edge of a case mounted on the wall.

A gun case.

I don't know where I am, Burke said to himself, *but when they built this place, they were obviously thinking about one thing: how to keep someone out.*

Not how to keep someone in.

TWO HOURS LATER, Burke had it all worked out in his head, based on two rock-solid facts.

Fact number one: Whoever this Nick Mason was, he was coming after him. It didn't matter if he was on a submarine at the bottom of the ocean, Mason was coming.

Fact number two: Burke was not going to sit around and wait for it to happen.

When the dinner tray came, Burke quickly ate the food. He had no hunger at that point, but once things were in motion, he had no idea when he'd be able to eat again, so better to take in the calories while he could for stamina and mental clarity. When he was done, he stood on one edge of the tray, pressing it flat. Then he worked the edge of the tray against the concrete wall, careful to use the outside wall to minimize any sound that might carry to the rest of the bunker.

Then he knocked on the door. He couldn't wait for them to ask for the tray back. He needed this to happen *now*.

"Get me Marshal Harper," he said when the slot was opened. "I want to make a deal."

He was happy not to hear the guard tell him to turn

around for cuffing. Harper must have laid down a new law out there, which probably pissed off the guards. But for Burke it was just one less obstacle.

Burke heard the footsteps, heard the door opening.

It was time.

15

AS MASON STUDIED THE BLUEPRINTS OF THE UNDER-
ground bunker, he went through a hundred different details, trying to force them into something other than an outright suicide mission.

The car was parked at the old fairgrounds in Flushing Meadows, in an empty lot facing the giant Unisphere. It rose over a hundred feet in the air, hollow and gray and surrounded by the drained bed of its fountain. Beyond that was the abandoned pavilion, looking like New York's answer to the ruins of Rome's Colosseum, and next to that the two towers—which stood together as if holding each other up, the highest rising two hundred and fifty feet in the air. On the top of each was a round viewing platform that looked like a giant flying saucer, stalled out and fallen into disrepair.

Mason went over the blueprints one more time, then focused on the mug shot of Sean Burke. The man was pale and lean—it was hard to imagine him as a killing machine. But then Mason, of all people, knew that the talent for killing could be found in the most surprising places.

This was the man who once did my job, Mason thought. *Somehow, he got away alive. Too bad I won't get the chance to ask him how he did it.*

Mason put Burke's file together and returned it to the suitcase. He looked at the blueprints one more time, tracing the route of the air vent—it rose from the opposite side of the bunker, fifty feet from the entrance, but there was no denotation for the size of the opening. That was something he'd have to figure out on the fly.

He put on his black gloves and the balaclava, rolled up into a skullcap. Then he took the tactical vest from the suitcase and slipped it on. A new and discomforting sensation to have grenades hanging from his body—like he was a suicide bomber approaching an enemy's checkpoint.

Though maybe that's exactly what he was.

He slid a magazine into the M4, put two extra magazines in the vest's pockets, one on each side. The marshal sat in the driver's seat, silently smoking a cigarette and looking out at the leaves blowing across the empty parking lot.

"How many men?" Mason asked him.

"Hell if I know."

"What *do* you know?"

"The location of this place, you prick."

Mason tried to stare down the marshal, but the man wouldn't look him in the eye.

"Used to be a bomb shelter," he relented. "Now it's a top secret Protective Custody Unit. Only a few people in the Federal Bureau of Prisons know about it. And even fewer marshals."

He took a bitter drag off his cigarette.

"Just the marshals they really trust," he said, looking out the window. "Like me."

Mason waited for more. He had to fight off the urge to reach forward and slap the cigarette from the man's mouth.

"This is the last time I do this," the marshal said. "You can tell your boss that."

He lowered the window and the cold rushed in as he threw the cigarette out against the wind and ended up spraying himself with sparks. He swore and brushed the embers from his coat.

"That's not the way this works," Mason said. "But you want to try telling him that yourself, go ahead."

The marshal turned to him. "You think you're any better than me? I'm not the one about to kill some good men in that bunker."

"Shut the fuck up and show me where it is."

"It's out there." He pointed through the windshield at the crumbling path leading into the fairgrounds. "Just follow the Yellow Brick Road."

"The ventilation outlet is fifty feet away from the entrance. Where is that?"

"You know what? I'm done with this. I told you, I got enough blood on my hands already."

Mason weighed his options. Even if he dragged this man out of the car, he'd be nothing more than a liability. But if he left him here . . .

"Give me your car keys," Mason said.

"Why?"

"So you'll still be here when I'm done."

"I'm not giving you my keys."

Mason exhaled as he shook his head and stuck the barrel of the M4 in the marshal's ribs. The man fumbled in his pockets for a moment, then handed them over.

"Now," Mason said, "the entrance . . ."

"It's one of those two towers over there."

"I can see that from the blueprints. Which one?"

"I don't know. Take a shot. You got a fifty-fifty chance."

Mason swore under his breath as he got out of the car. "Take off your coat," he said, opening the driver's-side door. When the marshal hesitated, Mason grabbed him by the back of the neck and pulled him out.

"This is my good coat," the marshal said as he took off his full-length gray mackintosh. "Try not to get bullet holes in it."

"You're going to sit in this car until I get back," Mason said as he slipped the coat on over his vest. "If you run, I'll find you."

The marshal shivered in the cold, got back in his car, and shut the door. *He's betting I won't make it back,* Mason thought as he made his way across the parking lot. *He's coming up with his story right now about how I forced him to bring me here.*

Mason put the marshal out of his mind, tucked the M4 under the coat, and focused on his surroundings. He couldn't see anyone else around—this part of the park was essentially abandoned, and you wouldn't come out here on a gray, windy day, anyway. But Mason still felt exposed as he walked across the open ground, the wind swirling a small hurricane of dead leaves all around him.

No matter what happens, he said to himself, *this is going to be some version of a nightmare.*

On every other mission, he had done everything he could not to kill anyone besides the intended target. Even now, he was walking with a reminder, the still-healing gunshot wound in his shoulder, of how much he put his own life in danger to avoid taking an innocent life.

As he approached the looming towers, weighted down with more weaponry than a Special Ops soldier, he knew that this personal code of his was about to be obliterated forever. If he left this place alive, he would leave as another kind of man.

There's no other way I live through this. I take out everyone. Or they take out me.

Mason paused by the great Unisphere, its globe rising high above him as he stood in the dry concrete bed of the fountain. The towers were two hundred yards away, rising even higher, a single light blinking at the top of the taller one—a warning to any aircraft passing by. Otherwise, the towers looked completely deserted.

Mason knew there was no way to approach the towers without being seen by the surveillance cameras. And there *had* to be cameras. He wondered if he could have used a better disguise right about then—something to make himself look like a homeless person wandering by. With a shopping cart to hide the weapons.

He looked back to the car behind him, decided to go ahead with the hand he'd been dealt. Moving quickly, keeping his eyes wide open for any movement, any sounds, anything at all that would indicate a reaction from the men in the bunker, he walked toward the towers.

Fifty feet from the entrance. I don't even know what this ventilation outlet will look like, or how big the opening will be.

He scanned the ground as he walked, circling the towers, and finally found it on the far side. It was a pipe, about four feet high, maybe eight inches in diameter, topped with a fitting to keep out rain and debris and anchored in a metal plate that was only slightly larger around.

I can't fit through this. And if I try to blow the opening any bigger, I might as well be ringing the doorbell.

That left Plan B. When Mason went back to the larger of the two towers, he found a double set of glass doors, and, looking inside, he saw an elevator door and the bottom steps of a long spiral stairway that presumably went all the way up the tower. He didn't see a surveillance camera, but when he pulled on the handle, the door didn't move.

He went to the other, slightly shorter tower, pausing at the wastebasket next to the door. When he looked inside, he saw a dozen fast-food bags and coffee cups. He reached in, picked up the cup closest to the top. Even through his gloves, he could feel that it was still warm.

This was the tower.

Mason stayed out of view for as long as possible, keeping his back to the wall. He waited, listened, heard nothing but the wind and the leaves. He pulled the balaclava down over his face and then he moved.

There was another double set of glass doors, as in the first tower. A similar elevator door and stairwell. But this time, he could see the surveillance camera mounted over the elevator. The red light was on. If there was someone actively watching a video screen in the bunker, he was looking right at him.

It doesn't matter, Mason said to himself. *There's one way into this place. One way out. No matter what else happens, I'm going to have to fight every inch.*

Mason tried the door. It didn't move. He didn't want to stand there for the two or three minutes it would take him to pick the lock, so instead he rammed the glass with the barrel of the M4. With the glass shattered, he reached in and turned the latch, then pulled the door open. He took off the marshal's coat as he moved under the camera's range. No need to hide anything now, and it would only get in his way. He paused there for another moment, listening for some response to his entry.

Nothing.

He brought the blueprints back into his head. The elevator, taken ninety-nine and nine-tenths percent of the time straight up to the viewing platform, also had a secret capacity to go down to the bunker, a capacity accessed only by a special key. The compromised marshal hadn't been able to get Mason a copy, but even if he had, there was no way Mason was going to ride down the elevator and let the doors open to whoever would be waiting for him. The blueprints showed an alternate set of stairs, from its time as a bomb shelter. Mason saw the door set into the wall, painted the same mid-century shade of institutional green. He pulled on the handle, felt it catch against a lock. He took one step backward and kicked it open, stepped inside.

As his eyes adjusted to the dark, he saw fuse boxes, circuit breakers, a panel of controls for the elevator.

No stairs.

He'd seen no other door in the lobby. This electrical closet was the only possibility. Unless . . .

He took a few slow steps across the floor. On his third step, he felt it give with a slightly different degree of resistance. Mason went down to one knee and examined the floor, flipped up the recessed ring and lifted the trapdoor. He had found the bunker's secret emergency exit.

Mason went down the dark concrete stairs, leading with the M4. He saw a dim light that grew brighter as he neared the bottom. Then as he turned the last corner, he saw a small alcove with the elevator door inset next to the opening in the wall that provided access to the stairs, and, on the far wall, a metal door that must have led into the rest of the bunker and a security window with thick glass.

Above the door was yet another surveillance camera. Another light blinking red, another chance for whoever was inside to see him.

If they've clocked me, Mason said to himself, *why have they let me get this far?*

The answer came to him immediately.

Because this alcove is the killing room. As soon as I take

*one step forward, that door will swing open and they'll gun
me down.*

It was fight-or-flight time: either make a bold move
forward or get the hell out of there and deal with the
consequences of failing his first mission.

Mason turned off his mind, put every ounce of his
humanity into a hard black box, and closed it.

Then he took one of the fragmentation grenades from
his vest, pulled the pin, and rolled it to the door, ducking
back into the concrete stairwell and covering his ears.

The explosion was more powerful than anything he'd
ever experienced, far more intense even than what he'd
been through at the Aqua. The noise and heat were stag-
gering, lighting up the confined space with a sudden
blinding flash and pressing needles into his eardrums.
Fragments of metal flew in every direction, some of them
chipping right through the corner where he was hiding
and drilling holes into the concrete just inches behind
him. Mason came out into the alcove with the M4 drawn
and ready to fire.

The smoke hung heavy in the air. Mason moved
through it to where the metal door had once been. It was
blown backward into the interior of the next room, and,
as he stepped over it, he saw the first body. He trained the
barrel of the M4 on the man's chest, but it wasn't necessary. His entire body was torn apart, from his abdomen
to his neck, his head bent back at an impossible angle, the
blood already pooling around him. The humanity Mason
had locked away was straining against the box's lid. Mason kept it shut tight.

He stayed low, waiting for any sense of movement, not
even sure if his ears were working again yet. As he took a
few more steps down the hallway, the smoke began to
clear and he saw the second body, twice the distance from

the blast but just as torn up as the first. With just as much blood on the floor.

Something was wrong. This wasn't adding up.

Two more steps and he came to a doorway on his left. He peered around the corner and saw the bunker's control room, with the two video screens corresponding to the two surveillance cameras he'd seen on the way in, and the window looking into the alcove. Another man lay dead in another pool of blood. A pistol lay a few inches away from his right hand.

The explosion didn't touch this room . . .

He kept moving until the hallway opened up into the largest room of the bunker. Four folding chairs were toppled around a table in its center, with three more dead bodies on the floor.

Mason scanned the rest of the room and saw several lockers against one wall, a gun case against the other with its glass doors ajar. There was room in the case for eight weapons, Mason saw seven—a full array of shotguns and assault rifles. One slot was empty.

He noticed one other odd detail: a metal tray lying on the floor, one edge slick with blood.

Hearing a noise somewhere to his left, Mason spun with the M4 raised and saw the metal door half open, a pair of legs visible on the floor inside the next room. He went to the door and carefully pushed it open with his foot, ready to fire at anything that moved.

It was a makeshift cell, with one bed and a stainless steel sink-and-toilet unit. The man on the floor was lying on his back, his eyes closed. Mason moved closer, watching the man's hands. He was wearing a black windbreaker with the U.S. Marshals seal on its chest. One arm was in a sling, and it looked like his head had also been bandaged—although now the bandage was hanging by a single piece of tape. And there was a fresh scrape running all the way across his forehead.

Mason bent down and put his gloved hand against the man's neck. He was alive.

As he stood back up, Mason pieced together the whole sequence of events, running everything backward. The marshal was in here alone with Burke. When the door was opened, Burke surprised the marshal and incapacitated him by ramming his head against the wall. Or else possibly he took out the marshal first and then knocked on the door. Either way, he surprised the man on the other side of the door—the man who, along with five other guards at his side, had been so concerned about the threat *outside* this bunker they'd become complacent about the threat *inside*.

Burke had slashed the guard's throat with the tray, moved quickly toward the gun case, probably slashing one or two of the other guards on the way. As soon as he had one of the weapons in his hand, the war was all but over. He killed every one of them on his way out. Only this marshal, lying on the floor at Mason's feet, was left alive.

When he looked back down, he saw that the marshal's eyes were open. Mason stepped back and aimed the M4 at his chest.

"Where is he?" the man said, his voice ragged.

Mason shook his head.

"The others . . ." The man tried to sit up, but then he brought his free hand up to his head and lay back down on the concrete floor again.

"Please," he said. "Help them."

Mason didn't bother telling him that the other men were beyond help. He'd find out himself soon enough.

"Don't move," Mason said. "I'll call someone after I leave."

As he stepped away, Mason felt the marshal reach out and grab him by the ankle with his left hand. Mason stopped and looked back down at him.

"You're Mason," he said.

Mason didn't respond. When the marshal let go, he left the cell, stepped over all of the dead bodies, and went up the stairs.

When he was back on ground level and out of the tower, Mason sucked in a big gulp of air, hoping it would clear his head.

Those men weren't dead for long, he said to himself, *and that marshal was just regaining consciousness.*

Meaning I just missed Burke. By, what, five minutes? Ten?

A chill swept over Mason as he wondered what would have happened if he'd gotten there in time to meet him.

As he walked back to the car, Mason took the keys from his pocket. When he was a hundred yards away, he saw the driver's-side door open. When he was ten yards away, he saw the marshal slumped behind the wheel, a bullet hole in his head.

Burke wanted this car, Mason thought. He scanned the horizon in all directions, looking for some sign of him. But there was nothing to see but an abandoned park. Mason pulled the marshal from behind the wheel, left him on the concrete staring up at the sky with unblinking eyes as the wind blew dead leaves across his face.

When Mason closed the door, he saw the file on the passenger's seat beside him. Burke's mug shot on top. Burke now knew with absolute certainty that someone had been sent to kill him.

I don't know what he knows about me, Mason told himself as he started the car and put it in gear. *But he knows who sent me and he knows where I came from. Which can mean only one thing.*

He's heading to Chicago.

16

EDDIE WAS BACK ON THE JOB, SURVEILLING COLE'S OP-
erations at the storefront on 111th Street, gathering more
counter-intel for Nick Mason's exit strategy.

The gray sedan pulled out of the lot, and Eddie tailed
it across town to the Irish neighborhood of Beverly in the
southwest corner of the city. He clocked the two men
parking the car and entering one of those neighborhood
places that don't even need a sign—just a single neon
shamrock glowing in one window—because all the regu-
lars know where to find it, and nobody else has any reason to be there, anyway.

He waited a beat, then followed the men inside. It was
a place out of another time, dimly lit, an unused jukebox
in one corner and an unused pool table in the middle.
There were a dozen hard drinkers arranged at the other
tables, and the two men he'd followed were at the rail,
their expensive suits making them look like aliens from

another planet, while the bartender stood on the other side, his tattooed forearms on the top of the bar.

Eddie went right up to the bartender, a man in his sixties with disheveled white hair and red eyes. He seemed distracted and out of sorts as he drew Eddie a pint glass from the tap like a man trying to remember how to perform a routine task he'd done ten thousand times before. He put the glass down on the bar, and Eddie slid him a twenty, told him to keep the change. The bartender didn't even blink.

The two men watched Eddie with a look that was cool and patient. Eddie gave them a nod and sat down at one of the tables. He couldn't hear much of their conversation, and after another few minutes, one of the men led the bartender through the door to the kitchen. The other man remained at the rail and announced that the bar had just been closed.

Eddie left with everyone else, hung back by his Jeep and watched the place. A full half hour passed. When the two men finally came out, got in the sedan, and drove away, he gave it another minute, then went inside. The front door was still open.

He went through the empty bar, pushed open the kitchen door with his shoulder, saw the splash of blood on the floor first, then the red lake surrounding the man himself, the lifeless eyes looking up at him. There were burn marks on his face. His fingers were gone. Eddie had seen dead bodies before in the army, had seen a few more through his scope when he backed up Nick in that quarry, but this . . .

He eased the door closed, grabbed a bar towel, went back to the table and wiped down his glass. He picked up the phone behind the bar, still holding the towel, called 911 and gave the operator the bar's address, told her there'd been a murder. When she asked him for his name, he hung up.

He went out quickly to his Jeep and drove away, hoping to put as much distance between himself and the dead bartender as quickly as he could.

He'd barely gotten on the Skyway when he saw the police lights behind him.

A FEW HOURS after leaving the marshal's car in the long-term parking lot at LaGuardia, Mason walked through O'Hare, the first time he'd ever come home from an assignment without blood on his hands. It should have felt like a relief to him. But, instead, it felt like failure.

And something else. Like he was a different man walking off that plane. A man who would have done the unthinkable if he had been given the chance.

The fact that he hadn't gotten that chance didn't play well with Quintero when he called him from New York, but Mason he'd made it clear: you can't kill a man who's not there to kill.

Now as he made his way down the long terminal hallway, in the midst of the other travelers with regular lives, Mason tried calling Eddie, but the calls kept going through to voicemail.

You always answer your phone, Mason thought. *Where the fuck are you?*

Mason hung up, kept walking until he came to the security checkpoint. A half dozen valet drivers stood in a line, holding names on placards. At the end of the line stood Detective Frank Sandoval. He wasn't holding a name, but Mason knew exactly who he was waiting for.

MASON AND SANDOVAL sat across a small table from each other at the airport bar. Neither man was drinking.

"If you're trying to call your friend Eddie," Sandoval

said, "I arrested him about two hours ago on suspicion of first-degree murder."

It hit Mason like a bucket of ice water. "What the fuck are you talking about?"

"Victim owned a neighborhood bar down in Beverly. Eddie was the last man to leave, and when I went inside, I found the man dead in his kitchen."

Mason sat there looking at him with no idea what to say next.

"Name was Eamon Burke. His cousin is Sean Burke, who just escaped from his Protective Custody Unit in New York about five hours ago. But you knew that already."

"Eddie's got nothing to do with this."

"That's what his wife said. Gonna be tough on her and their kids. The charges, the trial . . . But I can tie Eddie to you and you to Cole."

Mason glared at him. "Why are you doing this, you son of a bitch?"

"Help me and I'll make sure your friend goes home tonight."

"How?"

"Come in with me, give me sworn statements on everything you've done for Cole."

"Why don't you do your fucking job and go get Cole yourself? Whoever killed your vic, it wasn't Eddie."

Sandoval leaned forward in his chair, shaking his head.

"I don't care," he said. "Cole's going to walk because you killed two of the key witnesses, and the third witness just escaped and slaughtered six guards. Why do you think he chose today to break out, anyway? He knows about the other two witnesses, knows he's next on the list, and that you're coming after him. Rather than wait, he's coming after *you*. My guess is that Cole's pretty nervous, too, which explains the hit on Burke's cousin."

"Why are you telling me this?"

"Because this is coming to your door and I'm the only way out," Sandoval said. "You don't even have Eddie anymore."

Mason shook his head, still working hard to keep a grip on himself.

"This guy will destroy everything in your life," Sandoval said. "He'll move when you move, go where you go. Maybe your ex-wife's house. Or your daughter's next soccer game."

Mason clenched his fists at the thought, and in his mind saw Adriana standing on the other side of that fence in the playground, remembered how he thought that anyone could get to her there.

Anyone.

"Even that woman you live with now," Sandoval went on. "Everyone's in play. And you're the one who brought him here."

Mason let that one go.

"If we take Burke alive," Sandoval said, "we might be able to turn him. That's why he was in that place to begin with."

"He's just killed six guards. You're going to make a deal with him?"

"Sammy the Bull killed nineteen people and the Feds granted him full immunity. That's how much they wanted John Gotti. And that's how much I want Cole. Personally, I think you'd make a better witness. But I can't help you if you won't let me."

Mason took a long breath, picturing the dead guards he'd seen in the bunker, the long line of them on the floor, the bodies torn up by an assault rifle, throats slashed with the sharpened edge of a metal tray.

That's the man who was on his way to Chicago.

"Full immunity in exchange for your testimony in court," Sandoval said. "Full protection for your family—"

"WITSEC?"

"We've got our own program in Illinois. Not federal. I'll check up on your family every day, make sure they're safe. I don't have anything else in my life except this job, Mason. If part of that job is protecting your ex-wife and your daughter . . ."

Sandoval left it hanging in the air. Another thing for Mason to think about, a real chance for Gina and Adriana to be safe.

I can't protect them, he thought, *if I'm dead.*

Sandoval took out a business card from his breast pocket and put it on the table.

"You're running out of time," Sandoval said as he got up to leave. "If Burke's on the road, he'll be here in seven hours."

17

RACHEL GREENWOOD WAS DRIVEN ACROSS TOWN, WITH
a U.S. marshal sitting on either side of her, to do something that could technically get her disbarred. But today,
she had no choice. She had one last chance to stop the
man who was about to torpedo *United States vs. Darius
Cole*.

She found the office on the second story of the
anonymous-looking office building on Roosevelt, just
down the street from the FBI building. The lettering on
the door read *Stanley Horton, Private Security*. The re-
ceptionist asked her to sit down and wait for him, said it
wouldn't be more than a moment. Thirty minutes passed.

When he finally came out to the waiting room, Greenwood saw little of the man who had approached her in
that restaurant thirteen years ago. His hair was gone, including the Burt Reynolds mustache, and his jacket was
filled out with at least seventy more pounds. The only

thing he had left was his height and that same condescending half smile she still wanted to slap off his face.

"AUSA Greenwood," the retired agent said. "This *is* a surprise."

"So is this," Greenwood said, holding up his deposition.

She'd received it an hour ago, the supporting deposition that was hand-delivered to the court by Jay Starr, along with an official motion to vacate all federal charges against Darius Cole.

At last, Cole's whole legal plan had become clear:

Retroactive jury tampering to win the retrial.

Then the murder of every key witness.

And now this.

"What kind of bullshit is this?" she asked, waving the deposition. "McLaren and Wallace were both informants?"

In the deposition, Horton had made the stunning claim that back in 2004 the FBI had already been conducting its own investigation of Darius Cole, long before Greenwood and the DEA became involved. And then an even more incredible statement: Ken McLaren and Isaiah Wallace had both been working not just as FBI informants but as TE informants—*TE* for *Top Echelon*—meaning that their identities were protected under the strictest of FBI protocols. Only the FBI agent directly in charge of the investigation, Stan Horton, and his immediate supervisor, Jonathan Lancer, were ever aware of McLaren's and Wallace's involvement in the case.

"You waited all this time," Greenwood said, "to bring this up now?"

"Lancer was afraid the original case would fall apart. He sat on it, even though he knew it was wrong. Now that he's dead, I had to come forward. It's my last chance to tell the truth."

She looked at him with raw amazement. "Do you even remember that oath you took? The part about 'bearing true faith'?"

Horton straightened his tie. "I think you should leave, Counselor."

"You know what this does to the retrial," she said. "This is the Scarpa Defense all over again."

Named after Greg Scarpa, the "Grim Reaper" of the old Colombo family, an FBI informant who had a thirty-year relationship with a single agent—a relationship that destroyed fifteen otherwise airtight cases against other members of the family. Hundreds of years of prison time down the toilet all because of the simple principle that in the eyes of the law an informant working for the government effectively becomes an agent of the government himself and anything he does must follow the same rules of evidence.

In other words, if your informant keeps committing criminal acts—like transferring money overseas to avoid taxation or coordinating the delivery of illegal narcotics—even *after* he signs the cooperating witness agreement, every piece of information that informant collects for you is worthless.

A mountain of evidence suddenly turns into a pile of shit.

It had all happened before Greenwood even went to law school, but the "Scarpa Defense" had been sending chills down the spines of U.S. Attorneys ever since, and now this one retired agent was about to use it to blow up the retrial.

"You tried to run me off Cole thirteen years ago," she said. "So just tell me one thing: how long have you been on Cole's payroll?"

Finally, that condescending little half smile left his face.

"Good luck in court," he said.

"I can help you," she said. "What does he have on you?"

He shook his head and didn't say another word. Then he turned and walked away from her.

"Horton," she said, going to the door just as he opened it. "I'm throwing you a lifeline. Grab it before you sink so deep you can never come back up."

"You're too late," Horton said. He pulled the door closed and was gone. Greenwood stayed there for a full minute, composing herself. On her way out the door, she turned the ringer back on her phone, saw that she had gotten a call from Marshal Harper.

She called him as she walked back to the two marshals waiting for her by her car. "We need Burke," she said to him. "He's our last chance."

She listened carefully to what Harper told her. When the call was over and she was sitting behind the wheel, the sickening truth washed over her.

Darius Cole is going to walk.

IT WAS AFTER DARK when Mason got back to the town house after a long cab ride across the city, him staring out at the streets and thinking about everything Sandoval had said to him.

When he was inside, he went to his room and slid out the gun case from beneath his bed. He took out the Browning Black Label 1911 Eddie had given him, loaded it with .45 ACP shells, and stuck it in his belt.

Mason went back out to the refrigerator and pulled out a cold Goose Island, slid open the door to the terrace, and went outside. The pool was lit up a bright aquamarine, vapor hanging in the cool night air above the warm water. Mason went to the railing and looked out at the lights of the city to the south and at the dark horizon of Lake Michigan to the east. Above him, the red lights of the two surveillance cameras blinked.

He looked down at the street, feeling the weight of the weapon tucked into his belt. *It's twelve hours from New York to Chicago, once he finds a vehicle.*

Sandoval was right. He'll be here soon.

Mason ducked out of the wind and sat down on one of the chairs. A few minutes later, the door slid open and Diana came outside. She was in her dark suit, finishing her own version of a long day at work. She went to the rail and looked out at the lake as Mason had done, shivering in the cold.

Mason broke the silence. "I need to ask you something."

"What is it?"

"Do you know a man named Sean Burke?"

As she turned to him, even in the dim glow of the pool's light he could see the sudden panic, first in her eyes, then in her whole body. "Where did you hear that name?" Her voice was brittle.

He didn't answer her.

"He used to work for Darius," she said, "then he disappeared. Why?"

"He's coming back."

She went completely still. The panic he'd seen in her turned into something else, something more like a sudden, galvanized resolve, as she turned and headed back inside.

Mason followed her. She was already at her bedroom door by the time he caught up with her.

"Diana, wait!"

"No," she said, reaching for the handle. "I'm leaving."

"We have to stay together," he said as he took her by the wrist. "It's the only way you'll be safe."

"I was *safe* before you got here, Nick. I'm not safe anymore."

Their faces were close enough that he could feel the warmth of her breath against his cheek. He felt her heart pounding.

"I'm working on a way out," Mason said. "For us."

"*Us?* I don't need your help, Nick. Or your protection. I don't need *anything* from you."

She yanked her wrist free and swung open the door. She took a step into her bedroom. Mason grabbed her by both arms and spun her around to face him again.

"You're hurting me," she said.

He let go of her, but he didn't leave. It was the first time he'd ever seen her bedroom. A four-poster bed, a vanity, a chair with a reading lamp. Everything elegant and functional. Beautiful in its own unassuming way.

Just like her.

"I'm scared, Nick."

"I know . . ." Mason hesitated before saying what he said next because it was something he didn't want to admit even to himself. "So am I."

"I have to leave this place. I can't take it. Not another minute."

He looked at her one more time and said, "Let's go."

MASON OPENED THE DOOR to the apartment. It was only the second time he'd been here. Diana stepped past him into the emptiness, looked around at the bare walls and then out the window at the lights and the nighttime traffic streaming by twelve stories below.

"What is this place?" she said.

"A place to get away. From everything."

When she turned to face him, Mason could see that she was shaking.

"What's wrong?"

"You're going to kill me," she said, "that's why you brought me here. You have a gun in your belt. You've never carried a gun before."

"I've never had Sean Burke coming to kill me before."

He took a step closer to her, looked her in the eye.

"I would never hurt you," he said. "I would kill anyone who tried."

He whispered in her ear: "We both know what I do. But I still know what I *wouldn't* do. If he ever told me to kill you . . . I would kill everyone else I had to instead. Including myself. I swear to you."

She stopped trembling and leaned into him. He could feel the tension leaving her body. For just one moment until she tried to push away from him. He kept holding her, looking in her eyes. There was just enough light coming from the city outside to see the tears coming down her cheeks.

"I don't want him to touch me," she said, her voice barely loud enough to hear.

"I won't let that happen."

"What are you going to do, Nick? You can't stop him."

It was an idea that had first come to Mason when he was running down that hallway after killing McLaren, had taken form when he was working his way through those woods with a whole platoon of Army Rangers hunting him down. Had been brought to undeniable life when he walked through that bunker and saw a half dozen dead men and realized that the blood on the floor should by all rights have been his own.

The idea was direct, and simple, and as clear in his mind as the bell at St. Gabriel's:

As soon as Darius Cole walks out of prison.

Within twenty-four hours.

Even if it means going back to prison myself . . .

"I'm going to kill him," Mason said.

From the look on Diana's face, she seemed to be running through a dozen different emotions in quick succession: shock, then horror, then a desperate single moment of hope that died and turned right back to horror. She shook her head, tried to step away from him.

But they had come too far together, were already too close, to be pulled apart. There was no turning back now, and as Mason drew her body against his, she didn't resist. His mouth was close enough for him to breathe in her breath, his chest against hers and their hearts beating in counterpoint. She put one hand flat against his chest, not to push him away but to push him down to the floor. He put his hands on her shoulders and brought her down with him.

They finally kissed each other, cautiously at first, then with more and more passion, until they were tearing off each other's clothes. Diana dug her fingernails into his back as they came together. All of the fear and the tension melted away as they willed each other to feel something else, something real and immediate and good, at least for these few moments in the dying light.

Afterward, Diana felt along the lines of the bandages on Mason's shoulder and neck. Mason looked up at the ceiling and didn't break the silence, didn't disturb this moment of stillness he never thought he'd experience that day.

"There has to be another way," Diana said. "What if you . . ." She pulled herself up onto her side so she could look at his face. "What if you can't do it? What will happen to you? And to me?"

"I won't fail."

"Let me help you," she said.

"No. I have to do this."

She lay back down with her head on his shoulder while the city of Chicago, beautiful and terrible all at once, waited for them outside the twelfth-story window. He knew they could only stay hidden away for a few more hours.

Nobody can help me.

The words kept ringing in his mind. Over and over again, the words collided and then finally connected to something else. Until suddenly, for the first time since he walked out of that prison, Nick Mason could see the one way to set himself free.

Nobody can help me.

Except one man.

Sean Burke.

18

THERE AREN'T MANY MEN WHO CAN CHANGE THE LIFE OF a whole city.

The President. The Pope. They come to the city, everything stops, everybody knows about it. Everything *feels* different just for those few hours. Then the man leaves and everything goes back to the way it was.

When Sean Burke came back to Chicago, there were only a handful of residents who even knew his name. Even fewer who had any idea what chaos he was about to bring with him.

But for those people, he would change the city forever.

Sean Burke didn't give a shite about Chicago, his old hometown, or how much it might change that day. He only wanted one thing:

The man named Nick Mason.

*　　*　　*

IN LA VILLITA, Marcos Quintero closed the suitcase packed with his daughter Gabriela's clothes. His wife, Rosa, had an old friend from the church on Twenty-eighth Street, lived across the border in Hammond, Indiana, now, and that's where he'd be taking them until he was absolutely certain they'd be safe.

As he helped carry the suitcases to the car, Quintero looked up and down the street. Ever since Mason had shown up there, he'd known just how vulnerable his family was, how easy it would be for anyone to find them.

Especially the man to whom he once relayed orders from Darius Cole. The man who came before Nick Mason. The man who would set the standard for every assassin Darius Cole ever hired.

Sean Burke was the original *Ángel de la Muerte.*

IN LINCOLN PARK, Detective Frank Sandoval pulled out behind Nick Mason and followed him down the street. Sean Burke had now been out of the Protective Custody Unit for sixteen hours, and Chicago was twelve hours from New York City. This was the math that made Sandoval realize it was a great day to take some personal time. The sergeant who ran his six-man crew wasn't happy about it. The sergeant hadn't been happy about a lot of things lately.

Neither had Sandoval. He honestly didn't know how long he could keep doing this job.

But today, that all took a backseat to the one thing that was most important: never letting Nick Mason out of his sight.

MARSHAL BRUCE HARPER checked himself out of Forest Hills Hospital with the official designation of AMA, meaning "against medical advice." He had a freshly taped-up head and a Grade 3 concussion, which gave him intermittent nausea and blurred vision. But he was doing a hell of a lot better than the six Corrections officers who were lying on metal slabs in the basement.

Travis Claiborne. That was the name of the marshal they'd found shot in the head, lying on the ground in the parking lot outside the bunker.

Travis Fucking Claiborne, a man Harper had transferred out of WITSEC months ago, burying him in Prisoner Operations. His instincts about the man's basic integrity had been proved correct, but not about the man's ability to somehow break into his old office wing.

Harper swore to himself for the hundredth time as he got himself dressed. He had to hold on to the railing of the bed for a full minute until he could start walking. When he did, he went downstairs, got into a taxi, and headed toward the airport to catch the 11:43 a.m. flight to Chicago.

ASSISTANT U.S. ATTORNEY Rachel Greenwood looked at the boxes stacked in her office's biggest conference room. The hearing was scheduled for the next morning, when the motion to vacate the charges against Darius Cole would be considered by Judge Oakley. That gave Greenwood one full day to go through all of the evidence from the original trial.

If Starr's Scarpa Defense really works and most of this gets excluded, Greenwood asked herself, *what will I have left?*

She started going through the first box. Arrest records. Police reports. She pulled out a mug shot. A thin, pockmarked face. The face of a starving animal.

Sean Burke. Her last chance to turn a witness against Cole.

I have nothing, she said to herself. *This is going to be a bloodbath.*

DARIUS COLE WOKE UP seventeen stories above street level, a thin ray of sunlight coming through the thin slot in the wall. Twelve years after the long trip to Terre Haute, he was back in Chicago. Back in the city he still owned.

He should have felt good that morning. He could look back and see every successful step in his plan, one after another, from the day the plan had been born as he sat reading legal journals in the prison library and had found the one legal exposure in trials heard by anonymous jurors. Then realizing that somewhere in Chicago one of his own twelve jurors must have boasted about the case to the wrong person in the wrong place at the wrong time.

That was the one simple idea that had put everything in motion and now he had one of the best lawyers in the country walking into that hearing the next morning fully armed for battle . . .

COLE DID SOME QUICK MATH in his head—if everything went the way he'd orchestrated it, plus processing time—it added up to a genuine possibility he'd be free in approximately thirty hours. Not a sure thing, not yet, but there were other moves to make if this one didn't produce a checkmate.

Because if you're Darius Cole, there are always other moves. Other pieces on the board.

The one piece on the board that troubled him that morning was Sean Burke. It had been a mistake not to go after him harder when he had first left Chicago. He should have sent an army to hunt him down. Whatever it took.

Cole looked out the slit in the wall, could see only the building across the street and a fleeting glimpse of the pavement if he stood up tall enough. Sean Burke was out of his bunker, the rogue piece moving across the board. And there was no doubt in Cole's mind where Burke would end up.

SEAN BURKE SAW the devil's horns of the Sears Tower in the distance as he crossed the Skyway Bridge. The last time he'd been on this bridge he was heading in the opposite direction out of Chicago. That was the day he had driven east to start a new life in New York City, putting the only home he'd ever known since coming to America behind him.

He didn't think he'd ever have a reason to come back. When he got sent to Dannemora, it became an impossibility, anyway. No way he'd ever see Chicago again. Yet here he was, driving over the Calumet River in a Ram 1500 pickup truck, previously owned by the man behind the counter at the service station in Flushing Meadows, wearing clothes also previously owned by that same man.

As soon as Burke crossed the city line, he headed west to his old Irish neighborhood of Beverly. He recognized most of the old buildings, but that didn't surprise him. It was a part of the city that didn't exactly embrace change.

He stopped the pickup truck half a block down from the bar on the corner, got out, and walked the old sidewalk, came up to the front of the building and saw the darkened windows and the crime scene tape still stretched across the door. This was his cousin Eamon's place, the man who'd taken him in when he had to run away from Crossmaglen, who let him sleep in the spare room upstairs and introduced him to certain people in the neighborhood. On this morning, Eamon should have been cooking up eggs for the housepainters and plumbers and serving up the first drinks of the day to the other men who couldn't, or wouldn't, work at all. But, instead, the place was locked up tight. Burke was about to walk across the street, but then a Chicago PD squad car drove up and parked in the lot.

He didn't need to see anything else to know that Eamon was dead.

Burke got back in the pickup truck and drove across town with clenched teeth and white knuckles on the steering wheel. He had the assault rifle he had brought with him from the bunker on the passenger's seat beside him, and as he glanced down at it he tried to estimate how many rounds he had left.

I don't want to use a gun, anyway, he thought. *I don't want it to be quick.*

Burke remembered the office's location on Canal Street, not far from the Chicago River. It was in an industrial park, set between low-traffic manufacturing sites. He remembered crates being unloaded on the dock, unpacked, repacked, some thrown away, others sent to different locations Burke knew nothing about. It was not his area of responsibility, and he got the idea that he wasn't supposed to even know about this place at all. But it didn't matter now because as Burke drove through the entrance he saw a new refrigeration business in the old building. He didn't bother getting out of the truck to ask if anyone knew where the old import/export enterprise had moved to. He was sure it was well hidden in another forgotten corner of the city.

Cole is too smart to keep his office in one place for too long, Burke thought to himself. *But I wonder how many*

*of the same people are still alive and still working for him.
And who can lead me to Nick Mason?*

Burke drove west through the city to La Villita. He
turned onto Trumbull, passed the old house in the middle
of the block, parked, and waited to see some sign of Quintero. Burke had spent many a night in his cell thinking
about settling the score with that fooker, the man who'd
call him up in the middle of the night and order him about
like some kind of white slave. Burke didn't know how
much it would take for Quintero to give up Mason, but he
found himself hoping the man would be stubborn about
it. That he would make Burke torture him, and maybe his
whole family, until he got the information he wanted.

He kept waiting, but there were no signs of life, and
he wasn't about to go ask the neighbors if Marcos Quintero still lived there. A neighborhood like this, they
wouldn't say shite to a red-haired stranger.

As he drove toward the restaurant on Rush Street, it
seemed every block he passed brought back memories of
different jobs he'd done, first working for the old man
who ran the bookmaking operation, then for Cole, who
paid him a lot better but had a certain problem when
Cole withdrew the hit on that rival dealer and Burke
killed him anyway. Burke had let himself believe the war
was over until, after all these years, Cole sent those men
to kill him in the elevator.

You actually believed, Burke said to the Darius Cole in
his mind, *that I'd turn into a rat?*

As he drove on, he tried to remember the name of that
restaurant where Cole laundered so much of his money.
Started with an *A* . . .

Antonia's. That's it.

The place looked better than he remembered. There
were red awnings on the windows now, a red canopy over

the door. Burke parked the truck in the lot and went in through the front door. He wondered if Cole still used the place to launder money and to give no-show jobs to his special employees. Only one way to find out.

"Good day, sir," the maître d' said in a tone that implied anything but. "Do you have a lunch reservation?"

Burke looked down and realized he was still wearing the work shirt and jeans of the service station attendant. Typical American snob who thought an expensive suit somehow turned him into a superior man.

"I don't, sad to say."

"Unfortunately, we're completely booked this afternoon."

Burke was looking past the man into the open kitchen. He caught sight of the woman. *Diana. Cole's woman.* She looked just as good as he remembered. Better than anything he'd seen in a long time.

"You mind if I use the jax?" Burke said.

"Excuse me?"

"The john. The facilities."

The maître d' didn't look pleased but pointed the way. Burke thanked him and made his way down the hallway toward the bathrooms, being careful to stay out of Diana's line of sight. When he saw the door to the office, he took a quick look around him and then pushed it open.

He was prepared to break into the filing cabinet if he had to but it was unlocked—his first bit of good fortune since that metal tray had found its way to his cell in the bunker. Riffling to the *M*'s, he looked at the address listed for Nicholas Mason.

And couldn't believe it.

WHAT BURKE HOPED WOULD BE his last stop wasn't far away. He was already north of the Loop, making his way along the shoreline. North Avenue Beach was mostly empty, a wind coming off the lake and making whitecaps in the water. Burke rolled up Lincoln Park West, slowing down as he approached the town house. He circled the block and pulled over near the entrance to the zoo on his second lap, just close enough to maintain a sight line.

Seeing the town house brought back a memory, the one time he was allowed inside, to go up those wooden stairs to where the great Darius Cole lived. The grand kitchen with the green granite countertops and the center island larger than the bedroom he'd shared with his brother back home. The plush leather furniture and the giant television, the pool area out on the terrace. *Who the fuck builds a pool two stories off the ground, anyway?* It was the kind of place Burke wouldn't have minded spending more time in.

Burke was a little surprised at the jealous rage he felt welling up inside him now. When he'd worked for Cole, he was handsomely paid, no arguing that. But he sure as hell wasn't invited into the king's palace to live with the queen as Mason obviously had been. Burke had lived in that little shite apartment above the bar in Beverly with no grand kitchen, no pool two stories off the ground, no views of the lake. And instead of coming home every night to a woman like Diana, he came home to his drunken cousin Eamon.

The thought of his cousin brought him back into the moment, blew a fresh wind onto the fire that was already burning inside him. He stayed in the truck, watching the town house, until he finally saw a face appear over the railing.

That must be him, Burke said to himself.

That's Nick Mason.

*   *   *

MASON GOT TIRED OF WAITING. It was after dark and time to move. He went down to the garage, got behind the wheel of the Jaguar, and hit the button to raise the door. He cleared it by inches as he backed out onto the street, hit the button again, and spun the tires on the pavement. The streetlights were all burning against the cold night.

He drove down to Rush Street, clocking the dark sedan behind him: Sandoval. If there was someone else following both of them, he couldn't see him. Mason parked the car on the street in the valet area directly in front of the restaurant, went inside, and found Diana closing up the kitchen. She looked scared.

"Everything's going to be okay," Mason said as he handed her the keys to his secret apartment. "Make sure you're not being followed."

She didn't look like she believed the first part, but she understood the second and gave him a quick kiss on the lips as she took the keys from him. The restaurant was otherwise empty. Nobody was here to see them, and Mason had a sudden urge to pick her up and put her on the prep table.

"We'll celebrate later," she said, seeing the thought in his eyes. "Take care of yourself."

He nodded, and then he took the gun from his belt as he led her to the back door. He went out first and let the door close behind him, waiting for a footstep, a shot, anything. The alley was quiet. He opened the door again and she came out, hurried to her black BMW, and took off.

Mason went back inside. When he looked out the front window, he was happy not to see Sandoval's dark sedan parked on the street. He didn't see Quintero's Escalade either or the gray car that sometimes took its turn following him.

But still no sign of Burke.

"Where the fuck are you?" Mason said. "I'm right here. The front door is open."

Mason had spent all day thinking like Burke, trying to get in his head. *What would I do if the situation was reversed?* That's why Mason wanted to stay visible without being too obvious about it. If Burke had worked for Cole, he'd know about the town house. And he'd probably know about the restaurant.

Again, thinking like Burke, the town house was a bad place to make a move. This may have been the man who just escaped from an underground bunker staffed with six armed guards, but those tactical disadvantages were unavoidable. There was no reason to attempt infiltrating a town house two stories above street level knowing that there were surveillance cameras and God knows what other security measures—not if you knew that the occupant would eventually have to leave the premises and make things a lot easier.

That left the restaurant. Mason's car was parked right outside. Everything short of a billboard announcing that Burke could find Mason there. But once he made his move, the next problem was how to isolate him. How to keep him away from everyone else, including Sandoval, and at the same time switch everything around so that Burke would be the one at a tactical disadvantage.

This would have been a great time to have Eddie watching my back, Mason thought.

He looked back out on the street. This time, he saw the dark sedan pull up half a block down, nose facing the restaurant. He didn't have to see through the windshield to know who was inside.

Sandoval.

As he took out his cell phone and dialed Sandoval's number, he played out in his head what was about to happen. Sandoval was just as exposed as he was. Even more so, sitting out there in his unmarked yet obvious car. Burke wouldn't even blink before putting a bullet in the back of Sandoval's head. It was the last thing Mason needed to think about right now—the image of some cop with his hat in his hands, ringing the doorbell at the house where Sandoval's ex-wife and kids lived.

"Listen to me," Mason said as soon as Sandoval picked up. "You have to get out of here."

"I'm not going anywhere."

"Sandoval, you have no fucking idea what you're doing. I don't have time to explain. *Just move.*"

Mason ended the call as he looked out the window again. It was time to hit the reset button and get the hell out of there. He opened the front door and stepped outside. It was colder now as the hour approached midnight. Mason barely felt it. He was about to open the driver's-side door to the Jaguar when he saw the wire leading down from the handle. He stopped his hand a half inch away from it, stepped back, and got down on one knee to look under the vehicle. The wire trailed all the way down and hooked under the chassis. No way in hell he was going to reach under and find out what it was connected to.

The phone in Mason's pocket rang again. He knew it was Sandoval, didn't even bother checking. He looked up and down the street, then started walking. With every step he imagined Sean Burke somewhere behind him already focusing crosshairs on his back. But, no, something in his gut told him Burke wasn't a long-distance kind of killer. Or at least he wouldn't be with Mason.

This is personal for him. He'll want to see my face. He'll want me to see his.

Mason heard a car coming up behind him as he walked south on Rush Street. He took a turn on Illinois and started walking the wrong way down the one-way street.

It was hard enough to tail a man on foot when you're in a car. In Chicago, it was almost impossible.

He was already counting the blocks to the apartment building, not that far once he crossed the river. Then he stopped. Mason was standing next to Nordstrom's, the building closed up but the windows lit up with an autumn display of pumpkins and leaves and a well-dressed female mannequin staring through the glass at him. He watched a single figure walk toward him, a lone shadow growing bigger with every step. It wasn't Sandoval. He'd do the cop thing, stay in his car and maybe get on his radio. Burke, on the other hand, he'd ditch a stolen vehicle in one second flat and keep coming on foot. Mason knew that because that's exactly what he'd do if the situation were reversed.

Mason reached inside his jacket, put his right hand on the grip of the Browning. The figure came closer, hesitating for a moment as he looked up and saw Mason standing there with his hand reaching for his belt. Unmistakable body language, in a city where someone was killed by a gun every day. The man crossed the street and kept walking, watching Mason carefully with every step.

That's when he noticed another figure, another lone shadow, standing at the intersection. Not moving at all.

Mason thought about the training he'd done with Eddie, wondered how close he'd have to be to have a realistic shot with the Browning. He studied the figure carefully, and as the wind picked up he saw the tail on the man's long coat moving. He remembered the empty slot in the bunker's gun rack, the wreckage of the bodies on the floor.

He's got an assault rifle under that coat. If we go Wild West in the streets, I'm a dead man.

Mason turned and kept walking, made a turn at Wabash and headed toward the river. The twin Marina City Towers loomed on one side of him, the garish Trump Tower on the other, as he turned again, saw the shadow a block behind him. He crossed the Wabash Avenue Bridge, the water glittering below him as it reflected the lights of late-night Chicago.

I need a play. I need an advantage.

He continued across the bridge, sped up as he made another turn on Wacker, moving down to the promenade next to the water. But he realized how exposed he was there, that the man following him could stop on the bridge and use the rail to steady his weapon, send a spray of shells at Mason and cut him down. The only question would be where his body would fall, if it would be on land or into the river. Mason picked up his pace and cut south onto State Street. He walked down another block and came to the intersection with Lake Street, saw a handful of barhoppers, still out on this cold night, converging on this one corner where the El train ran east–west and the subway north–south.

Mason went up the stairs to the El, stopped by the window facing north, and saw the man coming down State Street. In the dim light he saw the red hair and the way the long coat hung from his thin shoulders. He watched him come to the same staircase, so Mason went to the opposite end of the platform and went down the other steps. When he was back on street level, he crossed State, looking behind him as he took the stairs down to the southbound subway.

There was a train waiting as he hit the platform. He went through the doors and watched carefully behind him. An automated voice told everyone to stand clear of the closing doors, and at that moment a large group of college-age kids rushed down the stairs and boarded the train. When the doors were closed, Mason moved to the back of

the car and looked through the window into the car behind him. All of the kids were standing, at least a dozen of
them. Then they parted, and Mason saw Sean Burke, lit up
in the glare of the artificial light.

Their eyes met. Burke smiled at him. He opened his
coat just enough for Mason to see the assault rifle hanging from its shoulder strap. Then Burke's eyes scanned all
of the other people in the car around him—besides the
college kids, there were two older men in overalls and a
woman with a baby wrapped up in a shawl and held close
to her chest. Burke regarded every one of them with that
same smile on his face before his eyes met Mason's again,
and the message was clear: Burke would kill every single
person in the car, if he had to, without giving it a second
thought.

The two men stayed frozen to their spots as the train
rushed down the tracks. Burke finally broke the spell and
came toward the door. Mason backed up, moving away
from him. He went to the opposite end and went through
the door to the next car. Then again to the opposite end
of that car and through to the next car. When he turned
to look behind him, he saw Burke advancing, slow and
steady. Both men knew there were only so many cars Mason could go through before he hit the end.

But only one man had ridden the Red Line enough
times to know that the next station was only four blocks
away.

As Mason watched Burke reach to open the door of
the last car, he took stock of the other riders: one man
sitting by the door, another man apparently asleep, a
third man standing and holding the rail. The standing
man would be shot first, had no idea he had maybe five
seconds left in his life. Mason took the Browning out of
his belt and was about to yell for everyone to get down
when suddenly the lights flickered for an instant and the

train's brakes were hit a notch too hard. The man holding the rail swayed, and Mason saw Burke lunge forward, off balance, and hit his head on the glass. The train had come to a stop before Burke could get the door open. Mason moved quickly through the other, open door and out onto the platform.

Mason kept the gun tucked behind his back, still in his right hand, safety off, finger on the trigger. Burke had essentially been trapped between the two cars for several seconds, but as Mason eyed the exit he saw Burke coming out the open door. The barrel of the assault rifle was extended from his coat and he had an angle on Mason now—there was a flight of stairs leading up to the street, but Mason had no way to get there without getting cut down.

Mason looked behind him, saw a grimy metal utility door in the station wall. He tried the handle but it didn't move. There was no engine at this end—it was a "push" route instead of a "pull"—so the conductor was sitting at the far end of the train and wouldn't interfere with what Mason was forced to do next.

He took one more quick look behind him as everyone else on the platform filed up the stairs. Burke smiled at him. There was nowhere for Mason to go. Unless . . .

Mason knew it was his only choice as he squeezed himself onto the thin edge of the platform that ran beyond that final wall into the darkness. He listened for the sound of Burke following him, every step farther along the tracks, as Mason kept his back against the wall and moved as quickly and as silently as he could. When the platform ended, there were metal stairs leading down to the tracks. He looked back one more time, saw a shadow obstructing the light: Burke was coming after him. Mason climbed down the stairs onto the tracks.

There was another safety light somewhere ahead of

him but not close enough for Mason to see where he was stepping. He knew there was a third rail here somewhere, knew there were rats and filth and other things he didn't have time to bother with. He kept moving forward until the light ahead of him grew closer.

You're going to walk right under a fucking spotlight, Mason said to himself. *Might as well paint a target on your back.*

He went forward another ten yards before he saw the cutout on his right. He ducked in and put his back against the wall. He listened for footsteps, but all he could hear was the distant sound of a train on the rails. It was growing louder.

Mason's heart was pounding. He tried to slow it down. *Breathe. Focus.*

The roar on the tracks got louder. A light started to grow in the distance, getting brighter every second, along with the sound of the train. But it came from Mason's right, the track on the other side. As the light became visible, it was filtered through the support beams that separated the tracks. It flickered and became intensely bright as the northbound train came around a bend in the tracks and slowed down for the Monroe Street station. Mason moved closer toward the edge of the cutout, then receded when he sensed the shadow nearby. He waited with his gun held in both hands.

The train passed by on the other track and stopped. Mason watched and waited, ready to react in an instant.

He saw the barrel of the assault rifle first, swung both hands with the Browning and knocked the barrel upward. He stepped out, tried to grab the barrel with one hand while he swung his gun with the other. But Burke stepped away too quickly, and Mason felt the butt of the rifle before he saw or heard it as it hit him across the side of the head and knocked him against the wall. Burke kicked him in the gut and drove all of the wind from his body, then used the rifle again to hit him on the back of the head.

Mason was down on his hands and knees, in the squalor of the subway tracks, waiting for the shot, wondering if he'd even feel it.

"Stand up," he heard a voice say. A lilting accent to the voice, something almost musical, from somewhere far away. "Get on your feet."

Mason reached for the wall and pushed himself up. When he was standing upright, he took another blow to the face. The rifle again, the man's fist, he couldn't tell, and it didn't even matter. He fell back down into the filth and he saw his daughter's face, the way she looked up at him the last time he saw her when he left her at the restaurant.

If he'd only known it would be the last time he ever saw her.

He felt a hand grabbing his jacket, pulling him back up. From somewhere he heard another sound building. A thunderstorm in the distance, something far away, that wouldn't matter to him anymore. In the dim light he saw Burke's face, calm and composed. Studying him, lining him up for another shot. There had been a gun in Mason's hand. Where was it now? He didn't have it anymore.

"Are you telling me," Burke said, that same brogue, "that you're the man Cole hired to replace me? Are you fooking kidding me?"

Mason heard the swing, not that it helped. He took the blow right on the chin and would have gone down again if the wall hadn't held him up. The distant sound grew louder, and now a light appeared from beyond the north end of the platform. As Burke turned to look in that direction, Mason went down to one knee and drove his right fist into the man's groin. He'd learned it on the streets of Canaryville. You fight dirty when you have to. And even when you don't.

With Burke bent over, Mason put his shoulder into him and drove him into one of the support beams. Burke let out a cry of pain as Mason grabbed at the assault rifle, not so much to shoot him with it but to use its strap against him, pulling it and turning it at the same time to tighten it against his body.

The train came to a screeching stop in the station, bathing both men in a harsh white light. Mason kept twisting the rifle against Burke, tying him tighter with the strap. Burke kicked out with his right foot, catching Mason in the leg, then he came off the support beam and used the momentum to spin Mason around and drive him backward toward the far wall. Both men tripped over the rails but somehow didn't electrocute themselves as they went to the ground, Burke on top now and pressing the length of the rifle against Mason's neck. As the train left the station, Mason could see the interior of each car as it flashed by, the backs of heads, people on their way home to regular lives. The roar was deafening for those few moments when Mason struggled against the rifle, pressed against his throat and cutting off his air supply.

Adriana's face came to him one more time as the tracks rumbled beneath his back and the train left them behind. Adriana as a baby, coming home to that little house in Canaryville. Adriana as a four-year-old, sitting at the table and waiting for her pancakes on a Saturday morning. Adriana as the nine-year-old girl, sitting next to him in his car. And then even another vision of Adriana as a teenager, riding uptown on this subway and not even realizing that her father died right here on this very spot.

Another sound. Another light. Mason's eyes went to his right and he saw another train approaching, only this time on the tracks he was lying on. Burke looked up and then back down at Mason with a cruel smile. He said something but Mason couldn't even hear it, the roar of the train already too loud and the ground shaking beneath him as Burke changed his position, moving his own body off the rails and continuing to hold down Mason with the rifle. Mason knew he would pull the rifle away at the last moment, just enough time to fall backward and watch the train run over Mason's body.

Mason struggled against the rifle, trying to push it away. But then he saw that the strap was still looped around Burke's neck and he reversed his energy, pulling Burke's surprised face close to his.

"We'll both go together," Mason said, holding the strap tight and feeling Burke frantically trying to pull away. Burke didn't have enough leverage to work against Mason's strength, his eyes going wide as he looked up and saw the light growing brighter. Mason held on, held himself and his enemy on the tracks, the roar growing louder and louder, Burke fighting harder and harder to pull away, the train so close now that Mason could almost taste the metal in his mouth.

Burke screamed, and Mason curled himself upward, twisting the rifle as he did and turning everything around, Burke still trapped in the strap and losing his advantage now until he was on the bottom with Mason holding the rifle against him, his neck positioned perfectly across the outer rail. The simplest move in the world now for Mason to pull away, completely free, and let the train decapitate Burke right in front of him.

Burke looked sideways, still screaming, the train a hundred yards away from his head.

Fifty yards.

Twenty.

Mason grabbed him by the collar and pulled him away from the track. He kept his grip on the strap as the train rumbled by, kicking up a wind that washed over both of them, with its dirt and grime and rat shit, until the last car finally passed by and Mason could let out his breath.

Mason looked Burke in the eye. Neither man spoke.

Mason next cocked his right hand and hit Burke in the face again and again until he was unconscious.

Mason got up, brushed himself off, went to other side of the tracks and found his Browning. He came back and unraveled the strap from Burke's neck. Burke was starting to regain consciousness again. Mason took the Browning and stuck it in his temple.

"I just saved your life," Mason said, "but I'll blow your head off right now if you do anything stupid."

"What do you want?" Blood was trickling from Burke's mouth and his words were slurred.

"We're walking back to the restaurant," Mason said, pulling Burke to his feet. "And we're going to have a little talk."

19

MASON MAY HAVE TOLD BURKE THAT HE'D SHOOT HIM IN
the head if he tried anything stupid, but he still expected
it to happen, and Burke did not disappoint him.

Mason had pushed him up the ladder and along the
subway platform, drawing stares from the few after-
midnight riders who were there waiting for the next train.
Both men were filthy and bleeding, but Mason had kept
the gun out of sight, and nobody tried to stop them.

Burke had stayed silent when they were back up on the
street. The cold stung the fresh scrapes on Mason's face
as he'd directed Burke up State Street, all the way past the
original Lake Street station and over the Wabash Avenue
Bridge. Mason had intentionally stayed off Rush Street,
paralleling it on Wabash and cutting over to the rear of
the building. He didn't need Detective Sandoval involved. Not until he settled things with Burke.

When he'd opened up the back door, that's when
Burke tensed up and tried to backhand the gun away

from Mason. It might have worked if Mason hadn't already been thinking about how good it would feel to hit him again. He caught him right in the face with the butt of the gun. The fingers of his right hand hurt like hell, on top of everything else he'd been through that night, but it did a lot more damage to Burke, and now Mason had to physically drag the man through the back of the restaurant and into the kitchen. He propped him up on a chair, took off the man's belt and looped it crossways around his wrists. Then Mason took off his own belt and secured Burke to the chair. It didn't have to be a professional calf-roping job, just enough to keep him still for a while.

Mason put some ice in a plastic bag, then he filled a saucepan with cold water and threw it in Burke's face. He pulled up another chair and sat down in front of Burke.

"Wake up," Mason said. He winced as he pressed the ice bag against his own cheek.

"Why am I still breathing?" Burke said when he'd opened his eyes and shaken his head clear.

"I told you, we're talking."

Burke looked down and strained against the belts.

"I will take the heaviest thing I can find in this kitchen," Mason said, "and I will beat the living shit out of you with it if I have to. Now just sit there and listen to me."

Burke sat back, looking as defiant as a one-hundred-and-sixty-five-pound man can look when he's tied to a chair.

"First of all," Mason said, "what kind of bomb is in my car?"

Burke smiled. "There's no bomb."

"Bullshit, there's a wire going from the door handle down to the—"

"That's all it is," Burke said. "A wire. It's an old trick from Crossmaglen. When we were kids, we'd use it on the RUC."

Mason gave him a look and shook his head.

"The Royal Ulster Constabulary," Burke said. "You tie a wire to their door handle, make them think it's connected to a bomb. It's not, but you've just disabled their car for two or three hours while they wait for the patrol to clear it."

"How do I know you're not just feeding me a line right now and there's a real bomb under my car?"

"Take a mirror, hold it under your car. You'll see."

Mason didn't want to leave Burke alone for a second, but unless he wanted to risk untying the bastard and bringing him into the office, he had no choice.

"Don't move," Mason said, sticking the gun under Burke's chin to make the point. He went to the office, opened up the bottom drawer of the filing cabinet, and took out his backup copy of the information Eddie had given him.

He was gone for maybe thirty seconds total, and when he was back in the kitchen, he sat down in front of Burke again. He was about to open the envelope when he happened to glance at the floor. Something didn't look right to him. The positioning of the chair legs was slightly different now.

The chair had been moved.

Mason stood up, grabbed Burke by the shoulder, and looked at his hands. They were still bound by the belt, but as he looked closer he saw the long blade of a knife hidden against the inside of Burke's right forearm. He took the knife and held it in front of Burke's face.

"I oughta cut your fucking ears off," Mason said before he threw the knife in the sink. "You got any more tricks you want to play? 'Cause I'm getting tired of them."

"I got one more, boyo," Burke said, looking him in the eye. "I'm going to take your gun from you and empty every fucking bullet into your body. And you'll be alive until the last one."

Just one more minute, Mason thought. *One more minute hitting him in the face is exactly what I need right now.*

"I was never going to testify against Cole," Burke said. "He didn't have to send you to kill me. Or my cousin . . ."

Mason took a photograph from the envelope—two men on a sidewalk, one black, one white. He was almost certain that the white man was the one who drove the gray sedan and took turns tailing him. But, more important, it was these two men who Eddie had followed into the bar in Beverly.

"*These* are the men who killed your cousin," Mason said, holding the photograph in front of Burke's face. "Do you recognize them?"

"The black one is Patrick," Burke said. "Been with Cole a long time. The big dumb white one is Gordie. He was new when I was around."

Burke kept peering at the two faces in the photograph. "Gordie's the one killed Eamon. I know it. Not Patrick."

When Mason put the photograph back in the folder, Burke looked him in the eye. "He would have told *you* to do it. But you were in New York."

Mason didn't bother arguing.

"Would have been interesting if you had made it down the bunker while I was still there."

"But I didn't," Mason said. "And now you're here. Which means we both have a choice."

Burke narrowed his eyes. "About what?"

"About what to do next."

"There used to be an office," Burke said. "Over on Canal Street. It's been moved."

"It's down on 111th Street now."

"And Quintero. He still works for Cole?"

Mason nodded.

"And Cole's woman," Burke said, "still runs the restaurant. I saw her at lunchtime today."

"Diana has nothing to do with this," Mason said. "You're not going to touch her. Do you understand me?"

Burke smiled. "Tapping the boss's molly, are we? He's not going to like that."

Mason held the barrel of the Browning close to Burke's left eye.

"Easy, boyo," Burke said. "Put that thing away and we'll keep talking."

"I need to make this clear to you," Mason said. "Diana has no part in any of this. Whatever happens, she walks away."

"Understood."

Mason pulled the gun away.

"You're alive right now for one reason," Mason said. "It's because we both want the same thing."

"That would be?"

"We both want Darius Cole dead," Mason said. "We both want freedom. We can do that if we work together."

"You expect me to help you now?" Burke was smiling again.

"Cole has a hearing tomorrow morning," Mason said. "There's a good chance he'll be on the street by the end of the day."

Burke nodded, deep in thought.

"So, tell me the truth," Mason said, sitting back down on the chair and facing him. "Who do you want more right now? Me or Cole?"

Mason watched him carefully. Watched for that key moment when Burke's hatred for Mason redirected to his old boss. Just like a freight train switching tracks. Just as quick. And just as deadly.

"If we agree to work together," Burke finally said, "how are you going to trust me?"

"I won't," Mason said. "But I don't have any choice. Neither of us do."

Burke seemed to accept that. When Mason stood up and undid the belts, he stayed seated on the chair, rubbing his wrists.

Mason took out the burner phone he'd bought that day, gave it to Burke, along with a few hundred-dollar bills. "My phone number is already in here. Buy yourself some clothes. Find a place to stay."

Burke folded everything and put it in his pocket. "I'm taking orders from you now, am I?"

"This is my town," Mason said. "Now get the fuck out of here and be ready when I call."

When Burke left, Mason put together all of the materials Eddie had collected for him. All of the photographs, computer records, everything a man would need to bring down Cole's operation.

Mason knew that Burke was his best bet for Plan A.

But he was smart enough to know you always need a Plan B.

It was time to set up that insurance policy. Time to protect his family, and Diana, in case he didn't live to see the end of the next day.

He took out his cell phone and dialed Detective Sandoval's number.

"Where did you go?" Sandoval said after answering on the first ring. He didn't sound happy. "I was right behind you, and when you left the restaurant, then . . . What did you do, jump down a manhole or something?"

"Forget that," Mason said. "I'm back at the restaurant now. And I'm ready to make that deal."

20

AT NINE O'CLOCK IN THE MORNING ON THE WORST DAY OF
Rachel Greenwood's professional life, she stood in the
courtroom on the twenty-first floor of the Federal Building, thirty feet away from a man directly responsible for
the deaths of two people that week and indirectly for a
dozen more.

God only knows how many others over the years, she
thought. *Twenty, thirty, a hundred? And what about the
rest of it? The drug trafficking, extortion, money launder-
ing, corruption, the ruined lives?*

Thirty feet away from her stood Darius Cole, about to
walk out of this courtroom a free man.

But not before Judge Oakley delivered one of her fa-
mous tongue-lashings, even if to Greenwood it felt like
nothing more than empty words. She had failed. Harper
had failed. The system had failed.

"Mr. Cole," the judge said, looking down at him over
a pair of reading glasses, the perfect cinematic touch.

"You were found guilty by a jury of your peers twelve years ago in a case that exposed a vast criminal enterprise based on illegal narcotics, based on murder, based on intimidation, bribery, and corruption. To this court, you represent everything that is destroying our city. The drugs, the guns, the very culture of lawlessness. All of those things personified in one man."

Darius Cole stood motionless next to Jay Starr. He was wearing a perfect olive-green suit, with a pale lilac shirt and a red floral tie that matched the handkerchief folded in the jacket pocket. He was facing the judge without really meeting her eyes, looking as calm and undisturbed as a man waiting for a traffic light to turn.

"You are a cancer on this city," the judge went on. "A cancer that was once isolated and removed from our body, now tragically returned and metastasized."

"Your Honor . . ." Starr said.

The judge shifted her gaze to him and he stopped talking.

"Any reasonable person," she said, "would find reason to believe that you, Darius Cole, are directly responsible for the brutal murders of the two men who testified against you at the original trial. And that same person would have no doubt that *this* . . ."

She picked up the deposition from the retired Agent Horton, the same deposition that Greenwood had taken with her when she confronted the man yesterday. Even now, he was sitting somewhere in the courtroom, showing his true colors by hiding in the back row.

"That *this*," the judge said, seeking out the agent, "is nothing more than an opportunistic fantasy, about which I hope to have much more to say at a different time in a different venue."

Greenwood saw Cole giving his attorney a quick smile.

"But, at this moment, I am beholden to the law," the

judge said. "And the law requires this court to follow the Rules of Evidence at all times, no matter the circumstances."

Last chance for a giant meteor, Greenwood thought to herself. Something her first boss used to say whenever a case was about to take a turn like this one.

"In the case before this court," the judge said, "the U.S. Attorney has advised me that the vast majority of the evidence relies either directly or indirectly on the testimony of Mr. Cole's former accountant, Ken McLaren, and his former adviser, Isaiah Wallace. If those witnesses were, as attested . . ."

The judge paused for a moment. One brief second of total silence in the courtroom before the unthinkable actually happened.

"If those witnesses were functioning as paid informants at the time the evidence was developed, and if those witnesses will not be able to testify in a retrial, then this court has no choice but to disallow that evidence under the Exclusionary Rule as clarified in *Nardone versus United States.* The so-called Fruit of the Poisonous Tree."

Judge Oakley picked up her gavel, looked at it like she was in just as much disbelief as anyone else in the courtroom.

"Darius Cole," she said, "this court hereby vacates all federal charges against you and orders the Department of Corrections to release you immediately."

She brought the gavel down once and was already on her feet by the time the sound was done reverberating through the chamber. The door behind the bench opened and the judge disappeared. Greenwood wished she had her own special door to do the same.

The dozen journalists in the courtroom didn't rush out like they would have done a couple decades ago.

There were no calls to editors to stop the presses. Instead, they worked furiously on their smartphones and tablets.

The whole scene was much too quiet, much too restrained. It was as if the city of Chicago didn't yet realize what had just happened to it.

DETECTIVE FRANK SANDOVAL sat on the aisle, four rows back. Next to him sat the bruised and battered Marshal Harper.

Sandoval watched Darius Cole walk down the aisle. If you were making a Mount Rushmore of Chicago criminals, you'd start with Al Capone and John Dillinger, then consider figures like Tony Accardo and Sam Giancana. If Darius Cole didn't make the final cut, he'd at least be part of the conversation, and yet here he was, walking out of this courtroom a free man, passing maybe twenty inches away from Sandoval's right elbow.

"Enjoy it while you can," Sandoval said to him.

Cole barely slowed down, gave the cop a quick nod and a smile. Then he kept walking.

Harper pushed his way out into the aisle, past Sandoval, and stopped AUSA Greenwood before she left the courtroom.

"Marshal!" she said, not hiding her surprise.

"I know," he said, "I look like hell. Never mind that. I want you to meet Detective Frank Sandoval."

"Rachel Greenwood," she said as she shook Sandoval's hand. "But if you'll excuse me—"

"I know you're busy," Harper said, "but I thought you might be able to spare a few minutes—"

"I'm sorry," Greenwood said, already moving away from them. "I have to go talk to my boss, see if I still have a job."

"Are you sure? Detective Sandoval would like to talk

to you about putting Darius Cole back in prison. Forever."

That stopped her. "Then let's buy the detective some
coffee," she said, gesturing toward the door.

TEN MINUTES LATER, they were sitting in the back of a
coffee shop a block down Dearborn Street. A steady
stream of federal workers came in to get their cups to go,
most of them apparently blissfully unaware of what had
just happened in the district courtroom.

"Nick Mason killed Ken McLaren," Sandoval said.
"He killed Isaiah Wallace. He would have killed Sean
Burke if he had gotten the chance."

"Marshal Harper mentioned Mason before," Greenwood said. "He works for Cole?"

"Yes." Sandoval snuck one more quick look at Harper,
then he delivered the punch line facing Greenwood: "I
want to arrest Cole. And use Mason against him."

She stopped drinking her coffee.

"He's going to give us everything we need to make it
stick this time," Sandoval said. "And he's going to testify."

"In exchange for what, full immunity?"

"He's more worried about protection for his ex-wife
and his daughter."

"How long do you think it'll take to put this case together?"

"I don't want to wait," Sandoval said. "I want to arrest
him tonight."

She looked at him. "That's a joke, right?"

"Look," Sandoval said, "if we wait for a new federal
case to get put together, it'll take months. A hundred
people working on it. Your office, FBI, DEA. During that
time, what happens? He gets to somebody. Just like he

got to my partner. Just like he got to the marshals. Just like he got to that FBI agent. That's what he does."

"This is insane," she said. "You can't arrest him on your own."

"Watch me," he replied. "I've got an open murder investigation right here in Chicago. That's where I was going to start, but if you back me up, we can throw in federal charges now, put *everybody* on the spot. We bring in Mason, tell him the deal expires in twenty-four hours. Now everybody's got to make a choice: either get behind the charges *right now* or take an official position that Darius Cole should walk free again."

She looked at him for a long beat. "You really want to get fired," she said.

"I'm already on my way out, Counselor. What about you? How's your career path looking right now?"

Greenwood put her cup down and turned to Harper. "What do *you* think?"

"Sounds crazy to me," Harper said, "but Sandoval's right. All you need is one cop. And one Assistant U.S. Attorney."

"One way or another," Sandoval said, "Cole's going to have quite a night. Either he has a big party and goes home to sleep in his own bed . . ."

He leaned forward and looked at Greenwood with his intense dark eyes.

". . . or he goes right back in the cage. It's up to you."

SEAN BURKE SAT behind the wheel of the stolen pickup truck with New York plates, watching the storefront on 111th Street, when he saw a gray sedan pull up driven by the man he knew as Gordie. Patrick was in the passenger's seat. They got out and went inside, and Burke waited patiently, watching the building until Gordie came back out alone and got into the panel truck that was parked in the back lot. When he pulled out onto the street, Burke pulled out behind him.

He followed the truck to a major transport center near the southern border of the city just off the Skyway. When Gordie left, Burke noted that the truck was lower. It had a full load. But Burke didn't care about what was in the back of the truck. He only cared about the man driving it.

Burke stayed behind the truck as it made its way back toward the storefront, but instead of going straight back to work, Gordie made a stop at a Japanese restaurant. Burke pulled in and parked his truck next to Gordie's.

He watched through the window as Gordie went into the restaurant's bathroom, then he took out the toolbox that had been rattling around in the back of his pickup truck all the way from New York and went inside.

There were half a dozen people sitting at the tables having an early lunch. Two men were busy preparing sushi behind the counter, barely looking up at the newest arrival. Burke walked past the counter and into the bathroom.

Gordie was standing at the sink, washing his hands. Just as big a man as Burke remembered, just as ugly, with that same stupid look on his face. He had dark sunglasses on today, probably thought they made him look like a real badass.

Burke locked the door behind him.

It took Gordie a full second to recognize the man who'd just entered the bathroom. Gordie was ninety pounds heavier, six inches taller, and was carrying a Ruger in his shoulder holster—but within the span of that one second his surprise turned into the desperate fear of a cornered animal.

Before Gordie could reach for his Ruger, Burke swung the toolbox, shattering both the radius and the ulna bones in the big man's forearm, then quickly closed in on him in the confined space, broke two of his fingers and took the gun away. He hit him in the face with it until his nose cartilage was pulverized and several of his teeth were lying on the bathroom floor.

Burke stepped back, wiping the blood from his hands as he looked down at the man sitting slumped against the wall.

"It's nice to see you again, Gordie."

He picked up Gordie's sunglasses, which had been thrown to the floor, got down on one knee beside the man, lifted the jacket from his chest, and carefully slipped them into his inner pocket.

"Wouldn't want these to be damaged," Burke said.

Then he slid the toolbox over, undid the latch, and opened it.

"Now," he said as he rummaged through the tools, "what can we play with?"

He picked up a long screwdriver, then a hammer, then a pair of vise-grip pliers.

"These will do," he said. "For a start."

NICK MASON SAT at the kitchen counter, cleaning the subway dirt from his Browning. The town house was otherwise empty. Diana was at the restaurant preparing for the lunch rush.

And Mason knew that somewhere, in a little house in Bridgeport, Eddie Callahan was safe at home after being released from the Cook County Jail—no formal charges ever filed against him—but still with a hell of a lot of explaining to do to his wife.

The front doorbell rang. Mason went down the stairs and opened the door and was shocked to see Gina standing there, holding Adriana's hand.

"I thought you were in Denver," Mason said, looking over her shoulder at the vehicles on Lincoln Park West. It was the only thing that had given him any peace of mind the night before, believing they were a thousand miles away when he faced off against Burke.

"Good to see you, too," Gina said. Adriana didn't bother saying anything at all. She ran past her father and up the stairs into the town house.

"Come in," Mason said.

When he led Gina up the stairs, he saw their daughter was already outside on the terrace, dipping her fingers in the pool. It was something he'd imagined a thousand times, finally having her here. But now that it was happening, on this day of all days . . .

"This is some place," Gina said. "I had no idea."

"It's not mine." He went to the kitchen counter and covered the gun with a towel.

"Somebody else lives here?"

"Diana. The woman at the restaurant," Mason said. "But you have to understand—"

"I don't have to understand anything," Gina said, putting up a hand to stop him. "It's none of my business."

"I'm sorry about the other day," Mason said. "It was unavoidable."

"You really are a bastard, Nick. Do you know what it took to convince Brad to let you take Adriana for the day?"

"I know. I'm sorry."

"You've already let me down enough, so I'm used to it. But Adriana . . ."

Gina stopped herself for a moment, rubbing her forehead and wiping away a tear.

"She was heartbroken," Gina said. "It must have felt like you had abandoned her. Again."

"I'll make it up to her. I promise."

They both watched Adriana get up from the pool and

go over to the railing to look down at the zoo across the street. Mason had to fight off the urge to go get her, to bring her back inside where she'd be safe.

Or at least safer.

"Look," Mason said, "if you came here to make me feel even worse . . ."

"Brad says Denver is amazing," Gina said. "The houses cost a lot, but there's so much to do there. The mountains and skiing and hiking, and the schools are really good . . ."

Mason knew what she was doing now. There was something else on her mind, so she was spinning her wheels, talking about nothing, because she didn't want to say it.

"What is it, Gina? Talk to me."

She moved toward the door and looked out at the terrace.

"This is the only city I've ever lived in," she said, "except for that one year in college. And you know how much I hated that."

"Is there something else going on here? Between you and Brad? I thought you were the perfect couple."

She turned to look at him with those burning green eyes. "There's no such thing, Nick. You know that."

"I'm sorry. I shouldn't have said it."

"Brad is a good man. A good stepfather. He loves Adriana like his own."

"But . . ."

"But he's consumed with his work. And sometimes he makes me feel like I'm his charity project. You know, save the poor lost girl from Canaryville and raise her daughter to be something better."

"The girl I knew never needed saving."

She smiled and looked at him for a long time before speaking again.

"You know, we'd still be together," she said softly. "You and I. If you hadn't . . ."

She didn't finish the thought. She didn't have to.

"I know," he said. "I've been trying to do the right thing ever since I got out. That's all I can do now. But if Brad really wants to take you away from here . . ."

He couldn't even believe what he was about to say. But he knew it was right.

". . . go."

Gina hadn't come here to ask his permission. Mason knew that. But after everything they'd been through together, this was the one word she needed to hear. He could see it on her face.

Mason looked out at his daughter again, still looking over the railing. He couldn't help imagining a strange pair of eyes watching her on those video monitors Eddie had described to him. And though he'd made his deal with Burke, he couldn't help imagining the crosshairs from a high-powered rifle lining up his daughter's head even now from somewhere down on the street.

You made a deal with a madman, Mason told himself. *You're gambling with everything you have, everything that ever mattered to you.*

Mason went out to the terrace and grabbed his daughter, held her tight, and brought her back inside.

She whispered into his ear: "I want to go to the zoo."

"We will," he said. "I promise."

Gina stood and watched them. There were tears on her face.

"I will always be your father," Mason said. "Forever. You know that, right?"

He felt her nodding her head against his shoulder.

"No matter if we're together or far apart, you're a part of me and I'm a part of you."

"But we're not always going to be apart, right?"

"No," he said. *Probably a lie.*

"Not for long." *An even bigger lie.*

"Promise me," she said.

He pushed her away gently so he could look into her eyes. "I promise," he said. "You're going to have a great time in Denver. And I'll see you soon."

She smiled, wrapped her arms around his neck, and squeezed. "I love you, Daddy."

"I love you more than you could know," he said, hugging her as if this were the last time he would ever see her. "I love you."

When they separated, Gina leaned over to Nick.

"Thank you," she said so quietly he could barely hear her.

Mason grabbed onto Adriana again. He didn't want to let go. But he put her back down on the floor and he watched them go down the stairs, watched them get into their car and leave. He stayed out on the street, watched the car stop at the corner and turn. Watched his whole life drive away.

He stayed outside for a long time, ignoring the cold air. Finally, he went back upstairs to finish cleaning his gun.

21

WHEN DARIUS COLE TOOK HIS FIRST STEPS OF FREEDOM
after twelve years in federal prison, he knew he'd done
more than just beat the odds. He'd beaten the best prosecutor the federal government could throw at him, with
all of the resources of the U.S. Justice Department behind
her. He'd eliminated two key witnesses, turned a federal
agent into the wrecking ball of the government's evidence against him, turned a U.S. marshal into his own
eyes and ears inside the WITSEC Program.

He'd beaten them all. But on a day when he should
have been celebrating, he went right back to business.

Cole had two men waiting for him in the back row of
the court galley. They were just as large as the beefs he
had looking after him in Terre Haute, but instead of
prison denims, they wore gray suits. They joined Cole on
his way back down to the street level through the lobby,
one on either side of him, pushing away a half dozen

journalists who wanted to ask Cole questions, then ramming right through a camera crew that had been set up to block them.

Cole didn't need these men to keep him off the six o'clock news. He needed them to help keep him alive.

Burke was out there somewhere. Watching him, waiting for the perfect opportunity. Cole wouldn't see it coming. Wouldn't hear it. That's what Burke did, better than anyone Cole had ever known. Which meant that as long as Burke was still alive, Cole had to watch his back, conceal his movements, avoid exposed positions.

Cole had to be just as smart as Burke. Just as careful.

The attorney had already arranged for him to use the side exit from the Dirksen Building. As much as he wanted to go down those wide front steps onto Dearborn Street, he knew that Burke would have a perfect shot at him there. Four lanes of midday traffic, a throng of pedestrians on their way back from lunch. Tall buildings on all sides, a thousand different windows in which to set up a sniper rifle. Cole's newfound freedom might not last halfway down the steps.

Cole hated the idea of sneaking out the side door like a servant instead of walking out the front door like a king retaking his kingdom. But as he'd once told Nick Mason, pride will kill a man faster than any bullet.

When his men took him out the side door, he saw the black Town Car waiting on the street. Steel plates in the side panels and roof, polycarbonate tinted windows. One of his men opened the rear passenger's-side door and Cole slipped inside.

"Welcome home, boss," the driver said, and when the other two men were inside the vehicle, he accelerated away from the curb.

The man with Cole in the backseat handed him his

new cell phone—every important number already keyed in. Cole hit the number for Quintero and had him on the line after one ring.

"Mason and Sandoval cut a deal," Quintero said. As always, right to business.

Cole took a beat to let this sink in.

"How do you know this?"

"Horton," Quintero said. "He knows somebody in the U.S. Attorney's office, says that woman who led the retrial—"

"Greenwood. The AUSA."

"She's putting a new case together. Conspiracy to commit murder, another set of CCE charges for everything that happened in the last twelve years . . ."

The Kingpin Statute, Cole thought. *Postdated from the day they sent me away. Which means they won't need McLaren and they won't need Wallace.*

"Mason will be the cooperating witness," Cole said.

My samurai.

"Yes," Quintero said. "How do you want to handle this?"

"What's the cop's role?"

"He gets the arrest. Wants to do it at the restaurant tonight, make a Mongolian opera out of it."

Cole thought about what Sun Tzu said over twenty-five hundred years ago in *The Art of War*: "Make your enemies reveal themselves."

Burke is too smart to hit me at the restaurant. Too hard to get a clean shot, too many bystanders on the way out. But Sandoval's just another cop who thinks he can do anything because he's wearing a badge.

"Stay on Sandoval," Cole said. "Wherever he goes."

"And Mason?"

Cole sat back in his seat and looked out the darkened windows as Chicago raced by.

I gave him his life back, Cole thought. *And the man betrays me.*

"I'll deal with Mason."

FIVE HOURS LATER, Antonia's Restaurant had become the center of the city. A long line of limousines and Town Cars jockeyed for position on Rush Street, each vehicle stopping at the great red awning leading to the front door. Drivers opened doors, men stepped out and held out arms for women dressed like it was the event of the year.

Businessmen of every race, a dozen retired athletes, a handful of the more daring low-level politicians—they were all taking a calculated gamble that night, publicly celebrating the Second Coming of Darius Cole.

Inside the restaurant, Nick Mason sat on a stool at the bar, nursing a Goose Island. Just one, to take the edge off. No more than that. He needed to stay sharp.

He was wearing his Armani jacket, white shirt with no tie. He watched the front door of the restaurant as the guests all seated themselves and waited for Cole's arrival. He had been due here at eight o'clock. It was now after nine and still no sign of Cole.

Mason was getting nervous. Without knowing why, he had a sense that his plan was already starting to unravel. It was just another one of those gut feelings. But those feelings had helped keep him alive ever since he'd walked out of that prison.

His plan was to let Cole make his big entrance and work his way through the room. Mason would ask him into the office for a moment, while Diana improvised any necessary diversion—she even had a pan prepared for a small grease fire—to make sure Mason and Cole had that one moment alone.

Mason would take Cole out the back—he had the Browning tucked into his belt—put him in the Jaguar, and take him to where Burke was waiting. Mason would be back here in a matter of minutes, and then there'd be two hundred well-dressed witnesses, along with one homicide detective, to establish that Mason was right here in this room when they wrote down the time on Cole's toe tag.

Sandoval would know that Mason had lied to him, that he never had any intention of testifying.

Mason could live with that.

The backup plan if Mason failed was Sandoval still gets all the information on Cole's organization and Mason trusts him to protect Adriana.

And Gina.

And Diana.

Mason didn't want to use the backup plan because it meant trusting a cop and trusting the system.

The backup plan also meant that Mason was dead.

Mason looked at the door again. Then his cell phone rang. As he answered the call, he walked to the end of the bar to minimize the surrounding noise.

It was Cole. "Change of plans. I'm in Englewood. Bring Diana with you."

Mason's gut feeling was right. The delay had already thrown off the timing. Now the whole plan could be lost. Sandoval, who was waiting to arrest Darius Cole that night, would lose patience and go off script.

And God knows what Burke would do if Mason failed to deliver.

"Everybody's waiting for you here," Mason said.

Cole ignored that, gave him a street and a number.

"Twenty minutes," Cole said. Then the call ended.

Mason put his phone away, looked up and saw Diana standing near one of the tables filled with eight men, all of them already half drunk. As soon as he caught her eye, he gave her a nod and she came over to him. Her face was red from running around, trying to keep two hundred impatient guests happy, and from the same nerves Mason had been trying to deal with all day. From both of those things and more. She was a woman waiting for her captor to walk through the door. A captor she never thought would come back.

"That was Cole," Mason told her. "We have to leave."

Her face went white. "Nick, that's not—"

"I know," he said. He wanted to pull her close, but he knew couldn't. Not right there in the restaurant with two hundred guests watching. "We have to stay cool. Play this out."

"Nick, I don't know—"

"Do you trust me?"

"It's not a matter of—"

"Diana," Nick said, looking into her eyes, "do you trust me?"

"Yes," she said, trying to compose herself within that moment. It would have fooled anyone but Mason, who could still see the apprehension in the way she held her body. "Let's go."

SANDOVAL SAT in his unmarked blue sedan parked a half block down from the restaurant on Rush Street. He listened to the radio traffic, the second shift already busy at work as the sun went down on another day in Chicago.

Sandoval hated waiting. Always had. Surveillance was torture for him. And for everyone else around him—just ask any of his former partners.

But tonight he was alone. One man, one pair of handcuffs.

But still no sign of Darius Cole.

He looked up in surprise as Mason's black Jaguar came out of the parking lot, moving fast. Sandoval pulled in behind him, watched him make two left turns and then head south.

Sandoval picked up his cell phone as he drove, hit the speed dial for Mason's number. "What the hell's going on?" he said as soon as Mason answered. "Where's Cole?"

"I'll get him," Mason said. "Bring him back. Just stay by the restaurant and be ready."

The call ended. Sandoval threw the phone on the seat next to him. No fucking way he was going back to wait on Rush Street. He picked up Mason on the Wabash Avenue Bridge and stayed behind him.

QUINTERO DIDN'T MIND WAITING. He knew the value of patience. He'd seen enough men die on the streets because they didn't have enough of it.

Tonight he'd need every ounce of *la paciencia* because every other part of him wanted only to go inside that restaurant, grab Mason, drag him outside into the back alley, and beat him to death.

Quintero saw Mason's black Jaguar pull out of the parking lot, Sandoval's sedan pull out soon after. Quintero started his Escalade and joined them, tailing both cars across the Wabash Avenue Bridge all the way to Englewood.

ON THE FAR END OF TOWN, in the Irish neighborhood of Beverly, Bruce Harper rang the bell next to door number twenty. Or maybe twenty-one—Harper had lost count. His arm was out of the sling today but still sore as hell, and he still had the bandage going all the way across his forehead, hiding the raw scrape Burke had given him when he had hit his head against the concrete wall of the bunker.

A man who was at least seventy years old pulled open the door. He'd probably lived on this street his whole life, half a block away from the old corner bar owned by Burke's cousin.

Harper showed him his U.S. Marshals' badge, then Burke's mug shot, and asked him if he'd seen Burke around the neighborhood.

"I know his family," the man said, "but haven't seen Sean in years. Isn't he doing a murder beef out in New York?"

"He was," Harper said, "but I need your help." It was a good way to get a man on your side: by making him feel like he's part of the process. Like you're pinning a deputy's badge right on his chest.

"If you see him," Harper said, "or hear somebody talking about him, you give me a call, okay? There's a half-million-dollar reward."

If deputizing a man was a good way to buy his help, half a million dollars worked a hell of a lot better.

"Never liked that kid, anyway," the man said with a wry smile, putting the card in his pocket.

Harper thanked him and left. He was still walking around with the effects of a concussion, but he had more doors to knock on here in Burke's old neighborhood. Like every good U.S. marshal, Bruce Harper knew one dead-solid truth about how to find a fugitive:

Sooner or later, they always go home.

THE ADDRESS WAS a three-story apartment building on May Street at the corner of Sixty-eighth—the heart of Englewood. As Mason and Diana walked around to the front, they saw a large mural of Derrick Rose, a former

Englewood resident himself and the most popular Chicago Bull since Michael Jordan until he got traded away to the New York Knicks. The rest of the building's exterior looked worn out by the hard Chicago weather, but the mural had been freshly repainted with Rose still in his old red and black.

They rode up the elevator. Mason reached over and squeezed Diana's hand. He could practically hear her heart beating in counterpoint to his own.

No way Cole could have found out, Mason said to himself, *about the deal with Sandoval.*

About me and Diana.

No way. Not even him.

The elevator opened and they walked down the long hallway toward the light coming from beneath the very last door. The music grew louder with each step. A thrumming bass line Mason could feel right through the floor itself shattered by the sudden wail of a saxophone. Mason knew it well, one of Cole's favorites: Coltrane, *A Love Supreme*.

Mason looked at Diana, nodded, felt for the gun in his belt just to reassure himself.

He knocked on the door, pushed it open. Inside the apartment were a half dozen men, all black, all dressed in perfectly tailored suits that probably came from someplace like Balani's up on Monroe Street. Brightly colored ties and pocket squares. Newly shined leather dress shoes. Mason recognized one of the men Eddie had photographed—the man Burke had called Patrick.

As every man turned to look at Mason and Diana, an electric current seemed to crackle through the smoky air.

The music suddenly stopped, and he stepped forward.

Darius Cole.

He was the same man Mason remembered, a few inches shorter than every other man in the room but with a commanding air that more than made up for it. He was dressed in an impeccable olive-green suit, tailored so perfectly it was hard to imagine that he'd been wearing jailhouse orange just hours ago.

And that same look on his face. Calm and untroubled. How foolish it would be for any man to mistake that look for serenity, outright suicidal ignorance to mistake it for weakness. Mason could still remember Darius Cole looking as peaceful as a Buddha while ordering a fellow inmate beaten to death.

It had been months since that last morning at the prison when Cole came to Mason's cell one more time to give him his best wishes, telling him that even though they'd still be in touch, still be *connected*, he'd miss their afternoon walks around the yard when Cole would tell Mason about whatever recent book he'd read.

And Diana . . . The last time Cole had seen her was twelve years ago.

Cole gathered her into a full-body embrace. Then he stepped back and looked at her.

"You look good," he said, his voice low.

Diana gave him a cautious smile. From three feet away, Mason could see her shaking.

Hold it together, he thought, willing the words into her mind.

"Let's make a toast," Cole said, moving between them and putting one hand on each person's back. Mason looked around at the apartment as Cole led him to the table that had been turned into a makeshift bar. There was a large HD television on one wall, expensive furniture, photographs of young men on the mantel over a gas fireplace.

"This was my mother's place," Cole said, answering Mason's question before he could ask it. "Lived here her whole life, raised me and my brothers, God rest them."

He stopped and looked around the room like he was bringing back his whole life in that moment.

"Sixty-eighth and May," he said. "Never let me move her. Even with the shootings down here every night. Fifty, sixty murders every year right in this neighborhood. She said this was her home, always gonna be. So I bought the building. Made some rules, made sure everybody knew them. No drugs, no guns."

"Everyone's waiting for you at the restaurant," Diana said. Mason was glad to hear her speak, glad to hear her voice sounding normal.

"They can keep waiting," Cole said. "Those people are there for their own reasons. Got nothing to do with me."

He picked up a bottle of Krug champagne.

"These are the people who really matter to me," Cole said as he nodded toward the others in the room, the six men who probably went all the way back to his days on the corner, every single one of them—and now they were here to welcome back the Emperor of Englewood. "These are the people who stayed loyal from the beginning."

He poured two glasses and gave them to Mason and Diana. Then he poured his own.

"To freedom," Cole said, raising his glass. "The most priceless commodity in the world."

Says the man who just bought his, Mason thought as he clinked his glass against Cole's. He kept watching Diana.

When Cole put down his glass, he trailed two fingers of his right hand along Diana's hip. A simple, intimate gesture that said one thing: *It's been twelve years since I've touched a woman.*

Mason caught her eye. *Keep it together.*

"Isaiah's mother lived downstairs," Cole said, "until the day she died. Even after what her son did to me, I still let her stay here."

Cole pressed his whole hand against Diana's hip, then slid it down the outside of her thigh, moving so slowly it was almost imperceptible.

"Did you see that mural of Derrick Rose outside?" he continued. "He grew up right down the street, too. Used to ride his bike over to that arena, tell himself he'd be playing inside it one day. That kid was *born* for that team, just like any other kid around here, born into his colors. If you got enough talent, you can play a different game. But you still gotta play something."

Every man was listening. The only sound, as Cole stopped speaking, was the ticking of a clock on the mantel.

Breathe in, Mason told himself, in time with the clock. *Breathe out.*

"Derrick owned this town until he got hurt. Then they trade him away because he's damaged goods. He comes back home, now he's wearing a different uniform. Different colors. But everybody still loves him because they know he didn't want to leave. He would have stayed loyal to Chicago, but the owner of the team wasn't loyal to him. So now the Englewood boy plays for New York."

Cole put his other hand on Diana's hip.

Mason watched Cole's hands but stayed focused on his breathing.

"I don't own the Bulls," Cole said. "If I did, that kid would still be playing for me. Because there's something important I know, Nick, and that's that loyalty works both ways. A man like McLaren, a man I trusted with my money for years . . . Or a man like Isaiah Wallace. As close to me as one of my brothers . . ."

Cole's grip on Diana tightened. She closed her eyes.

Mason stopped breathing. *Keep your head on,* he told himself. *Don't make a move.*

"Nick," Cole finally said, "what did I say about no guns?"

"I didn't know the rule," Mason said as he took the Browning from his belt and handed it over, playing the part of the loyal soldier.

Cole examined the gun. "Quintero didn't give you this."

There's nothing I can do now. No matter what happens next, I have no play.

"I picked it up on my own."

Cole nodded and slipped the gun into his own belt. "I'm going to borrow it, if you don't mind. Diana and I are going up to the restaurant, make our appearance."

That can't happen. I have to stay with her.

"I'll drive you," Mason said.

"I have a driver," Cole said. "You're not a driver, you're a killer. Isn't that right?"

Mason didn't answer.

"I asked you a question, Nick."

"Yeah, that's right."

"So why would you volunteer for a demotion?" Cole asked. "Is it you want to drive me or you want to drive Diana? Have you been driving Diana around, Nick? Is that in your job description?"

"No."

"No," Cole said. "So I think you stay here . . . With the other killers. Diana rides with me now."

Diana put her champagne glass down too hard, rattling it against the table. Mason could see the raw panic in her eyes. He had to fight down the urge to pull her away from him. *You do that,* he told himself, *you're both dead.*

Cole nodded to the other men in the room. Two of them separated from the pack and led the way to the door, followed by Cole, one arm clinging around Diana's waist.

Mason caught her eye one more time.

Stay calm, he told her in his mind. *Stay strong.*

When the door closed behind them, Mason was left alone with the other four men. If they were football players, they'd be two huge offensive linemen, one solid, athletic linebacker, and one tall tight end.

"Have a cigar while you wait," the linebacker said, holding out a Cuban Cohiba.

"No thank you."

"Man won't smoke a celebratory cigar." He drew out the word *celebratory*. "Even on the day his boss gets out of prison."

There was a subtle undercurrent of laughter in the room like the sound of a distant storm.

"You know the real bitch of a thing here?"

Mason looked at him and at each other man in turn. Four pairs of eyes all watching him. Measuring him.

"What's that?" Mason said.

"We're not allowed to kill you. But you're gonna wish we were."

22

THE FOUR MEN CLOSED IN AROUND MASON, GIVING HIM no chance to get out of the room. No chance to go after Cole and Diana.

He tried to cover his head as he took the first shot, chose the man standing between himself and the door, lowered his shoulder and drove it into the man's chest, slamming him against the wall and rattling every picture frame in the apartment. He felt the man's breath leave his body, grabbed him by his jacket and tried to throw him back at the other three men as he broke for the door.

"Where you going?" a rough voice said as Mason felt two hands grabbing him by the shoulders. He turned to swing at him and took another shot right in the gut.

Desperately, he thought back to every other time he'd been outnumbered in a fight, every lesson he'd learned on the streets.

Keep moving, he told himself. *Don't give them an easy target.*

And whatever you do, stay on your feet.

But another punch to the side of the head drove him down to one knee. As soon as he got his feet under him, they pushed him back into the center of the room. Surrounded him. As he turned, one man hit him from behind. He turned again. Another blow.

He felt himself going down, braced himself as the next man came close and left himself open. Mason came up fast and drove his fist into the man's Adam's apple. The man clutched at his throat as Mason went for the door, but this time it was two men on him at once, one hitting him in the back of the head and the other aiming a kick at Mason's chest. He felt something give as the shoe made contact, tried to grab the man's belt and caught a knee in the cheekbone, making everything go white, and then another blow to the head sent him down. He tasted carpet in his mouth mixed with warm blood, and as another man lined him up for another kick, Mason rolled away from it, tried to get up, and felt a blast against his temple.

Protect yourself, he thought as he covered his head. *Stay awake.*

You have to get to Diana.

DETECTIVE SANDOVAL HAD THOUGHT he was one hour away from finally putting handcuffs on Darius Cole. But now he was sitting in his car somewhere in the middle of Englewood watching his night coming apart at the seams.

Cole had just come out of the building with two of his men and the woman he kept in the town house.

No Mason.

He said he was bringing Cole back to the restaurant . . . Was that a lie? Because he sure as shit has lied to me before.

Sat across the table from me, told me he didn't know any-thing about a dead cop, or a dead drug dealer, or two dead witnesses . . .

Sandoval watched the foursome get into a black Town Car and pull out onto the street.

If he's not lying, that means something happened to him. So what do I do now? Stay on Cole? Or go save Mason's ass?

Sandoval picked up his radio transmitter, paused a moment, swore, put it back.

I hope you're still alive, Mason, Sandoval thought as he got out of his car and went into the building, *so I can kill you myself.*

DIANA SAT IN THE BACKSEAT of the Town Car with Darius Cole. As she looked over at him, he was staring straight ahead, showing no emotion at all.

"Everyone will be glad to see you," she said. Something safe. Something to get him talking.

In her mind, all she could see was the look on Nick's face as Cole took her away.

"Not everyone," Cole said, staring at her. "Some people didn't mind me being in a prison cell three hundred miles away even if they're pretending to be happy when I get back."

She felt her face flush. Felt his eyes looking right into her.

"Well, I'm happy."

"What about Nick?"

She took a beat, composed her answer. "I'm sure he is, too."

Cole reached forward and touched the shoulder of the man sitting in the front passenger's seat. "You made sure Mr. Winters was invited this evening?"

"Yes, sir," the man said.

"See, there's a man right there," Cole said to Diana. "Mr. Winters will be the first one in line, shaking my hand. Telling me how wonderful it is to see me. I reached an agreement with him before I went away and now that I'm back it'll be interesting to see how happy he really is."

She listened carefully to every word he was saying. Tried to read him. But it was impossible. Always had been. Even for her, the person who was once the closest to him.

"I didn't expect Mr. Winters to put his whole business on hold while I was gone," Cole said. "All I asked was that he live up to our agreement."

He turned to her again. "That sounds reasonable to you?"

"Of course."

He nodded. "That's all I asked for. His loyalty. For him to honor his commitment to me while I was gone."

She wanted to say something, but she couldn't think of one word. As the car slowed to a stop, she looked at her door handle. For just one second. Then she brought herself back.

Nick was right. There was nowhere to run to. Not from Cole.

"I honored my commitment to you," Diana said. "I stayed in that town house, ran the restaurant . . ."

"That doesn't sound like such a bad life," Cole said. "But, then, I spent those same twelve years in a prison cell."

Another long beat, the only sound was the tires on the road and the wind.

"I wasn't questioning your loyalty," he finally said. "But if you really want to go there, answer one question for me . . ."

She waited for it.

"How long did it take?"

He still had the same serene look on his face, his voice calm and seemingly untroubled.

"I don't know what you're talking about, Darius."

"Yes you do. Just tell me when it started, Diana, I'm curious."

She looked down at her hands for a moment, gathering herself. The fear kept rising in her stomach, but she pushed it down. If there was one thing she knew after living with Darius Cole, it was this: *You do not show him fear.*

"You were gone twelve years. Far as I knew, you were going to be gone the rest of your life."

"That's right."

"So what did you expect me to do? Just lock myself away—"

"Like an anchoress."

She looked at him. "What?"

"An anchoress. A woman who locks herself up in a church and never leaves it for the rest of her life. To show her devotion."

"I did that," she said, "you understand? For twelve years, I had no life at all. That's how long my devotion lasted. If you wanted more than that . . ."

"I didn't," he said. "I'm not that cruel. Or that naïve."

"Then why are you . . ."

She stopped herself, looked out the window. Felt an anger coming to her from somewhere she didn't even recognize.

I will not fall apart, she told herself. *I will not let him see that.*

"You know, you collect all these people around you," she said, willing herself to stay strong. "Doing all these things for you. And at some point, they're going to fail.

Or they're going to rebel against you. Because what you ask, Darius, sooner or later is going to be impossible."

He watched her carefully, listening.

"I don't even know if you realize this," she said, "but I think you *want* them to fail you. You *want* them to rebel."

"Is that right . . ."

"You could have put Nick anywhere in the city, Darius. You could have put him back in Canaryville, for God's sake, made him feel at home. But no. You put him fifty feet from my bedroom. What did you honestly think would happen?"

He stayed silent for a long moment, studying her face.

"So congratulations," she said, "you were right. You knew it even before I did."

The look on his face, still composed, still unmoved, but with something new . . . a quiet intensity, touched with something almost like sadness . . . It drained her of all of her anger. The fear came back, suddenly doubled.

Because she'd seen that face before. Had heard the silence that went along with it.

Had seen what always came next.

Another minute passed, the city going by in a blur through the darkened glass. Finally, the car slowed down, made a turn.

Diana closed her eyes as Darius came around and opened the door for her. She stepped onto the pavement, reaching out to take his arm.

She didn't recognize where she was at first. It wasn't Rush Street. They hadn't come to the restaurant.

Another long second passed, then it came to her.

We're at the apartment building.

Nick's secret apartment.

She took a deep breath. "Nick is dead."

"If I was going to kill Nick," he said, "I would have done it myself. But that would displease the people I work for."

She looked at Darius. His face was still unchanged.

"You don't work for anybody," she said.

"We all work for someone."

They started walking toward the front entrance and she moved with him, not even feeling her own body anymore. When they were in the lobby, Darius told the man who'd followed them to wait there.

A strange calm settled over her. *I knew this would happen,* she told herself. *From the moment I met him. From the moment I asked him for vengeance for my father. From the moment I lay in his bed.*

It was always coming to this.

Darius let go of her arm, leaned forward, and pushed the elevator button. When the door opened, she didn't move. She felt his hand on the small of her back, pushing her forward.

The elevator door closed. It was just the two of them in that confined space.

I won't beg, she told herself. *Whatever happens, I will not beg.*

The elevator continued its slow climb. It stopped and the door opened. She looked over at Darius. He still looked untroubled, unmoved.

Diana felt his hand on her back again, felt herself moving down the hallway. Darius pushed open the door to Nick's apartment. Of course it would be unlocked for Darius Cole.

"Come in," he said to her.

She went inside the apartment and Cole closed the door behind them.

* * *

MASON BRACED HIMSELF for the next blow, the wave of pain that would come a half second later.

It didn't come. Instead, Mason heard a voice from somewhere far away. A voice he vaguely recognized.

"Chicago PD, let me see your hands!"

Everyone in the room froze. Mason pushed himself back up to his knees, felt a hand on the back of his shirt pulling him to his feet.

"Stand up," the voice said. "Let's go."

As he stood, Mason saw a gun barrel. Then a silver star. Then Sandoval's face.

Mason wiped the blood from his eyes, saw the door open, the hallway, the elevator. He kept moving, leaning back against the elevator wall when the door closed.

He looked over and saw that Sandoval was breathing almost as hard as he was.

"Cole took Diana," Mason said. "Call it in. Find her."

"What the hell was going on up there?"

"Cole found out about our deal."

"Fuck. I should have grabbed him outside."

"You saw him? Was Diana with him?"

"Yeah, they were—"

"We need to find her. *Now!*"

"If they're headed back to the restaurant," Sandoval said, "I'll call in for help. Have a dozen men set up. We'll take them when they get there."

"If she's in that car—"

"She'll be safe, all right? We got this. I just want to put those cuffs on Cole myself."

That wasn't the plan, Mason said to himself. *But right now, I'll take it.*

As long as Diana is safe.

The elevator hit the bottom floor with a thud.

"You're welcome, by the way," Sandoval said.

"For what?"

The door opened.

"For saving your ass," Sandoval said.

Then the detective's head exploded.

Mason fell backward, everything obliterated by the sudden gun blast. The shock washed over him, the blood and brain matter splattered in a bright red and pink arc across the elevator wall. Mason looked down and saw it was all over his face, all over his chest. He pushed himself to his feet.

Mason watched Sandoval's body slide down slowly into a sitting position, slump over. One eye was gone, the other still open.

He couldn't breathe, couldn't hear anything but the ringing in his ears.

"What the fuck . . ." he said to himself, barely hearing his own words.

He looked up.

Quintero stood there, holding the same Nighthawk Custom 1911 he'd drawn on Mason when he found him at his house.

"You killed him . . ." Mason started to say as his hearing slowly came back.

"Yeah. And I'd kill you, too, if I could," Quintero said. "But those aren't my orders."

Quintero realized his critical mistake almost as soon as the words were out of his mouth, tried to swing the gun at Mason's head, but Mason was already moving forward and slipped easily inside his reach. Desperate to get out, beaten up and numb to any more physical pain, Mason landed three straight punches to Quintero's abdomen, hit him with an uppercut and caught him square on the chin. Quintero grabbed Mason by the neck and tore at his still-bandaged gunshot wound—the wound he had sewn up himself.

Mason swung one arm up over Quintero's wrists and pulled them down in a double lock. He hit Quintero in the face with two more quick lefts, but Quintero didn't let go. Quintero pulled him closer, lining him up for a head-butt. Mason quickly drew back his right arm and brought it forward again just as Quintero's head whipped forward. Mason felt the blow to Quintero's nose all the way up his arm, but he followed through as if trying to drive his elbow clear through to the back of Quintero's skull.

Quintero went down to his knees, a shower of blood erupting from both nostrils. It was nothing like a fair fight at this point, but Mason hit Quintero in the face again. And again. He kept hitting him until his right hand was raw and bleeding. For Diana, for his family, for a dead cop on the floor of the elevator.

For himself.

He took Quintero's gun as he stood up. He took his last look at Frank Sandoval, the man who had arrested him and sent him away. The man who'd pursued him for months and kept him looking over his shoulder. The man who'd just saved him.

Sandoval had a wife and two kids. Whatever was left of Mason's humanity would torture him over that simple human fact. Probably forever. But he didn't have time for it now.

He went out the door to go find Diana.

WHEN COLE STEPPED into the apartment, Diana was already standing at the window, looking out at the lights of the city. Cole came over and stood next to her. He didn't touch her.

"This place is empty," Cole said, looking around. "He finds the one place he can have for himself. And there's nothing here."

A day came back to her, the first day she ever saw him. In her father's old restaurant, torn down and paved over by now. Her father long dead and buried, killed by two men who worked for one of Cole's rivals.

Nobody ever found a trace of either man.

She took a step toward him and put a hand on his chest. "Darius," she said, a note of raw fear finally creeping into her voice, "it's me. It's your Diana. Don't you want to be with me right now? It's been twelve years."

He reached up and brushed her hair aside. "This isn't about you," he said. "This is about Nick. I want you to understand that."

A tear ran down Diana's cheek. Cole wiped it away.

"I have to take something from him," he said.

He leaned closer so that his mouth was right next to her ear.

"I have to hurt him," he said in a whisper. "This is the only way I can."

ALMOST TWENTY YEARS after the city had banned smoking anywhere indoors, the Burke family's corner bar still held the stale smell of an ashtray, mixed with spilled beer and greasy food. As Bruce Harper stepped inside, he felt like he'd gone back in time half a century. There were round wooden tables covered with thin sheets of plastic. Molded plastic chairs. A pool table with faded felt. Barstools repaired with duct tape. Harper hit the light switch and a pair of overhead fixtures mottled with dead flies cast a dim glow that barely reached the corners of the room.

Harper went behind the bar, through the kitchen

door. He looked down at the faded bloodstains on the cracked linoleum floor. There were more bloodstains in the sink, and Harper knew that the police had recovered a butcher knife with both blood and scorch marks.

They heated up the knife on this stove, Harper thought. *Burned his flesh with it. Then cut off the fingers of one hand.*

Put the knife back on the stove to heat it again while they asked their question again. "Where's your cousin?"

Seared more flesh and cut off the fingers from the other hand.

Harper went up to the apartment above the bar. Another step back in time: an honest-to-God tube television, a TV tray, piled high with crumpled fast-food bags, set up next to a beaten-up couch.

Harper stood in the center of the room and asked himself: *Was Sean Burke here?*

He picked up one of the fast-food bags and checked the receipt—over a week old. Then he went into the kitchen, saw the dishes sitting in a sink half full with water, a thin film of green mold floating on the surface.

He went into the bedroom, pulled back the bedspread, and saw sheets that needed washing a few months ago. Dirty clothes all over the floor. The only thing hanging on the wall: a map of Ireland, distinctive because it showed no border separating the counties of Northern Ireland from the rest of the island.

This is where you'd come to hide, Harper thought. *This is the closest thing to a home you have.*

He picked up a single framed photograph from the dresser—three men standing outside the bar, one of them a young Sean Burke—sat on the edge of the bed, and looked into the face of a killer.

Harper replaced the crime scene tape on his way out. *It wasn't a waste of time,* Harper told himself as he drove away. *No matter how tight this neighborhood is, a half million dollars is a hell of a lot of money.*

If the son of a bitch who slaughtered those guards comes home . . .

I'll find him.

SEAN BURKE WATCHED the marshal from the bunker getting into his car, noted the white bandage stretched across his head.

He'd watched the man go up and down the street, giving his card to everyone who answered their doors. Burke had slept in the apartment above the night before, keeping the lights off. Nobody in the neighborhood had seen him, and in a few more hours, he'd be gone again. This time, he'd have no reason to ever come back.

Burke went to the back door of the bar, took the old spare key that had lived on the top edge of the doorjamb for the past forty years. When he was in the kitchen, he stopped one more time, looking down at the stain on the floor. He crossed himself, more out of lifelong habit than belief.

Then he went inside to the bar and settled down to wait.

MASON PARKED THE JAGUAR behind the restaurant and went in through the kitchen. One of Cole's men was standing there—there were probably others at each door. This man had his back to the door and he was talking on his cell phone.

"Don't worry," Mason heard him say. "He won't get in here."

It took five seconds for Mason to prove him wrong as

he grabbed a long iron rotisserie spike and cracked the man in the head before he could finish turning around. The man went down. Mason wiped his face with a kitchen towel, put it down soaked red, ignored the two cooks who were staring at him.

He went to the front of the kitchen, where he could see into the dining room. He scanned through the men in suits, women in dresses, waiters in white shirts, looking for Diana. He didn't see her. He didn't see Cole.

Then the front door to the restaurant opened and Cole walked in with two of his men.

Diana wasn't with him.

Mason watched everyone in the room stand up to applaud Cole's arrival. As Cole came into the center of the room, everyone surrounded him. He was shaking hands, kissing women, and Mason knew this would go on all night. With no good chance to separate him.

Mason's plan had already fallen apart. He didn't have a new one. All he had was pain and pure gut instinct. And a growing fear that he had to keep pushing out of his mind.

She's not dead, he told himself. *Diana is not dead.*

Mason moved quickly through the crowd. Cole looked up in surprise when he saw him, but nobody screamed until Mason already had Quintero's Nighthawk pressed against Cole's head.

"Where is she?" he said into his ear as he wrapped his free arm around Cole's chest from behind.

More screaming. One of Cole's men drew his own gun and pointed it in his direction.

"Everybody relax," Cole said, already recovered from the surprise, his voice strangely calm.

Mason pulled him into the kitchen, Cole going along with every step. Not trying to resist. They went out the back door. Into the car. Cole in the passenger's seat, the gun still aimed at his head as Mason came around and got behind the wheel.

"Where is Diana?" Mason said.

When Cole didn't answer, Mason hit him across the face with the gun.

Cole wiped his mouth and said, "You made a deal with a cop, Nick."

Mason hit him again. His hand was still raw and now swelling, with at least two broken fingers, but he didn't care anymore.

"You're already having a bad night," Cole said. "Think about what you're doing right now."

Mason put the car in gear and started driving. He opened up on the expressway, the Jaguar roaring. When they reached the South Side, he pulled off and drove down the dark streets, the car quiet enough now for Cole to speak.

"First time I heard your name," Cole said, "you were part of that team that hit the harbor. One of your friends gets killed. Another gets away. Never did find the fourth man . . ."

The image of McManus's dead body floating in his pool came to Mason. He brushed it away and kept driving.

"But the only man who does time is you."

"Tell me where she is," Mason said, his eyes on the road. "I don't need a fucking trip down memory lane."

"I'm just trying to understand, Nick. How we got here. We used to walk that fence line every day. You and me, in the yard. Just talking. I could have been selfish and kept you there."

"You're a real prince."

"How many years did you have left on that sentence? Twenty? At a minimum? You'd still be in Cellblock A right now, wondering why your family forgot about you.

Instead . . . look at you. I gave this to you, Nick. *I gave you your life back.*"

"Some fucking life."

"You got to see your family, Nick. What's that worth to you? How about a little appreciation?"

Mason pulled over to the side of the expressway with a screech of tires and a long blare of horns from behind him. Cole rocked forward and back. Mason grabbed him by the collar of his jacket.

"This life you gave me," Mason said, putting his own face close to Cole's, "it's a horror show. And that bunker in New York . . . that was a suicide mission. I was dead walking into that place and you knew it."

"You were doing your job," Cole said, his voice still calm and steady. "When we made our deal, was I not crystal clear on the terms? Did you not know exactly what you were getting into? *Mobility, not freedom*—remember? Answer the phone, do what you're told. That's the deal you agreed to."

"I had no choice. You knew that. I would have done anything to get out. And you used that to turn me into a . . . a fucking monster."

"I didn't turn you into anything, Nick. You're the same man who walked into that place. You're just better at it now."

Mason pulled out the gun, racked it into firing position, and pressed it against Cole's left temple.

"It's over," Mason said. "I'm tearing up the contract. No more phone calls. No more killing."

"Go ahead," Cole said, "blow my brains out. You'll be doing the same thing to your family. Every one of them by the end of the night."

"No," Mason said. "No more threats to my family. That ends, too. I'm calling your bluff this time."

"Let me ask you something, Nick. And listen carefully.

If Quintero doesn't hear from me, he's on his way to Elmhurst. When he gets there, do you want him to do your wife first? While the daughter watches? Or the other way around? It's your choice."

"Quintero's not doing that tonight," Mason said, "Considering that this is his gun I'm holding."

Cole laughed. "So, what, you think you're winning this? You think it's that easy?"

Where have I heard that before? Mason asked himself.

From Quintero. When I dared to suggest we should both get out.

"Go ahead," Cole said. "Pull the trigger."

Mason put the gun down, grabbed the stick shift, and slammed the car into gear.

"I'm not going to kill you," Mason said as he pulled onto the road. "Sandoval's not the only one I made a deal with tonight."

AS HARPER DROVE AWAY FROM Burke's neighborhood, he went over every conversation he'd had with the people who lived on the street, everything he'd seen in the bar and the apartment over it.

Something didn't feel right, but he couldn't figure out what the hell it was.

He tried to slow it all down in his mind, replaying everything he'd done. Everything he'd seen. Every step.

The street. The bar. The apartment.

The bed.

It came to him in an instant, the one thing that didn't belong.

The bed was made.

There was a less than one percent chance that the man who lived in that apartment would actually make his bed and let everything else go to hell. *But a man who spent the last several years in prison?* That's a man who makes his bed the second he gets up every single goddamned morning. It's so automatic, so much a matter of pure muscle memory, for a man who lived by a strict prison regimen, Burke probably didn't even think about it.

Burke was there.

Harper turned his car around and sped back to the bar.

BURKE LOOKED AT HIS WATCH as he heard the car pull in behind the bar. He stayed seated in the corner, in the darkness, as he heard the door pushed open. Nick Mason came into the room, along with another man. A man he hadn't seen in twelve years.

Darius Cole.

"Is this my Garden of Gethsemane?" Cole asked him. "I don't see the Centurions."

That's the moment Burke chose to stand up and hit the switch. He stepped forward into the dim light.

Cole didn't say a word, but Mason could see the change in body language as he shifted on the stool. He folded his arms, protecting his chest. For a man who'd spent years surrounded by some of the worst, most violent felons in the world, this was the first time Mason had ever seen the calm, composed façade start to slip away.

"Mason, you're a man of your word," Burke said. "Rare thing, these days. And Mr. Cole . . ."

He bowed to the man. "It's good to see you out."

"Can't say the same."

"How many men did you send to kill me?" Burke said. "Ten? Twenty?"

"Whatever the number is," Cole said, "it obviously wasn't enough."

"Burke," Mason said, "you don't let him die until he tells me where Diana is."

Cole shifted his gaze from Mason to Burke and back again. "I don't think it's going to matter one way or another, gentlemen."

"There's all manner of ways to kill a man," Burke said. "You should know better than most. So give Mason what he wants."

Cole didn't say anything. He didn't move.

Burke smiled. "I was hoping you'd choose the hard way."

But then Cole drew Mason closer and whispered in his ear: "Are you sure you want to know, Nick?"

Mason swallowed hard. "Tell me."

"Check your apartment."

Mason put his hands on Cole's neck, then felt a sudden, sharp pain as Burke grabbed him by the right biceps.

"Leave him be," Burke said.

Mason opened his mouth but no words came out. The war raged inside him, between staying here, hurting Cole, *killing him*. Or running.

Burke let go of Mason's arm. "Go on now, boyo."

Mason hit the door. A few seconds later, his car was speeding away from the parking lot.

That left Burke and Cole alone together in the quiet near darkness of the bar.

Burke smiled again and picked up his toolbox.

HARPER ROLLED TO A SLOW STOP a block away from the bar, got out, and approached on foot. When he saw the slight glow burning in the windows, he drew his Glock and went to the back door. It was unlocked.

He held the gun in front of him, slowly moving through the dark kitchen. A dim light came from the barroom. As he neared the door, he heard noises from inside. A sharp intake of breath. A muffled gasp. The sound of a man in pain.

He pushed against the door with the barrel of the gun and through the slim opening saw Sean Burke sitting on the edge of the pool table. A man was stretched out on the floor in front of him. Darius Cole, with blood on his face.

Burke was holding a power drill in one hand. A long pointed knife in the other. He was sitting hunched over, looking down at Cole with intense concentration. A serious man doing serious work.

Harper stepped through the door and pointed the gun at Burke's chest. When Burke looked up, he slid off the edge of the table until he was standing on the floor.

"I could have killed you in that bunker," Burke said.

"Maybe you should have."

The two men stood facing each other. There was nothing between them but silence and dust, and the inert body of Darius Cole on the floor.

Burke opened his mouth to say something and Harper squeezed the trigger, putting five quick shots in Burke's chest. Then he raised the sight and put a sixth in the center of Burke's forehead.

Burke's head snapped back, the rest of his body hitting the table and sliding to the floor next to Cole. Harper stepped forward, the gun still extended. Cole looked up at him, his eyes open now and blood coming from his mouth. Otherwise, he didn't look seriously injured. A few minutes later, Harper realized, it would have been a much different story.

And then the second thought hit him:

This is Darius Cole, the man who'd ordered the murder of two witnesses he'd been protecting.

I could shoot him right now. Nobody would know. Few people would care.

Cole seemed to know exactly what Harper was thinking. He looked in Harper's eyes as he sat up.

"You know who I am," Cole said.

"Yes," Harper said.

"Think carefully about what you do next, Marshal."

I can't do it again, he said to himself. *A marshal gets one of these in a lifetime. Any more and he's no better than the men he's hunting.*

Harper put his gun away and said, "I'll call you an ambulance."

MASON WENT UP the stairs two at a time. He couldn't breathe anymore but he kept going, slipping and falling, grabbing for the rail, pulling himself up and taking the next step.

Be alive, he said in his mind over and over again.

Be alive.

When he got to the seventh floor, he stumbled down the hallway, taking out his key. He opened the door and slammed his way inside.

"Diana!" he said, knowing even as he saw her that this was exactly what he had been expecting. Exactly what he had known he would find.

She was lying on the floor as if staring up at the ceiling. Her hands were folded over her stomach as if arranged for a funeral. As if the man who killed her had kept one last measure of respect for her and had composed her this way before leaving.

Mason went down to one knee, saw the red marks around her neck. Saw the lifeless eyes staring at nothing.

He stayed with her for several minutes, not moving. Until his cell phone rang. On the third ring, he looked at it. It was the cell phone he'd given Burke.

He answered it.

"Is he dead?"

"Not yet." That deep, unmistakable voice.

Darius Cole.

"Like I said, Nick . . . Do you really think it's that easy?"

23

MASON STOOD ACROSS THE STREET FROM THE TOWN
house. A home that had never felt like home to him. An
expensive container for the cars, the clothes, the entire
life that someone else had provided.

Now all of those things had been taken back.

And Diana, the woman who lived there with him. The
woman he'd just come to know, after months as intimate
strangers. She had been taken, too.

Even the protection he had worked so hard to provide
for Gina and Adriana, the protection that would come
from an unlikely deal with the cop who had dedicated his
life to sending him back to prison. That cop was gone
now, along with the protection that came with his promises.

What were a man's promises worth in death?

That meant that Mason had nothing else to lose.

Which made him the most dangerous man in the
world.

He took the tablet computer from his back pocket, brought up the application that Eddie had installed on it. The explanation behind it was still a blur to him—wireless signals and secure IP addresses—but it all added up to one thing: using this device, Mason could see the live feed from every surveillance camera in the town house.

He had one other thing: the Nighthawk Custom 1911 he'd taken from Quintero, with nine .45 ACP shells in the clip and a tenth in the chamber. At that moment, Quintero was probably hooked up to an IV somewhere, with serious facial reconstruction in his near future. He wouldn't be shooting anything anytime soon.

Beyond these tools, Mason had one more thing working in his favor: an intimate knowledge of the building. Every room, every angle. And as he looked at each video feed, he was quickly able to count four men standing guard. Two of them had assault rifles, the other two were most likely carrying semiautomatics.

One other important fact he gathered from the last two surveillance shots he brought up: the master bedroom, as painful as it was for Mason to look at the bed that Diana slept in, was empty. Then the office: Cole was sitting behind the desk, staring intently at something on the screen of a laptop.

Five men total, at least four of them armed.

It was time to move.

Mason didn't bother with the front door. He knew the lock had probably been changed. Or, even if it hadn't, the security code on the panel inside would have been reset. That would give him only a matter of seconds before the alarm went off. Instead, he went to the farthest of the three garage doors, just beyond the range of the surveillance camera. He'd already studied the movements of the man who was stationed on the terrace. He leaned over the railing, looking, listening, for someone or something to come out of the darkness. Mason figured he had twenty seconds to get into the building.

Even though the town house had the most expensive digital security system on the market, Mason needed only two things to defeat it, two standbys that had helped him into countless cars during his early career: a small piece of wood and a straightened coat hanger. He jammed the wood into the rubber trim running along the top of the door, then inserted the coat hanger through the small gap he'd just created. The quick-release latch on the drive chain was about two feet away from the top of the door. As soon as he pulled the release with the hook of the coat hanger, the garage door was open. He pushed it up slowly, careful not to make any noise, slipped underneath, and closed it again behind him. Start to finish, the entry took twelve seconds.

He came to one knee and checked the Nighthawk. Rehearsed his movements one more time. He felt that same heightened focus he'd developed more and more with each recent assignment—hunting a man up and down the towering floors of the Aqua, stalking a man through the mountains of Georgia, infiltrating an underground bunker—these were the final steps in the pure distillation of Mason's skills.

The machine was complete.

He closed his eyes for ten seconds, took one deep breath and let it out. Now he was in motion.

Mason opened the door from the garage leading into the downstairs foyer. The first guard was standing at the top of the stairs, exactly as expected. Not just the top but slightly off-center to the right. He had stopped being a man at that point. There was no such thing as innocence anymore. No distinction to make between nonlethal and lethal force. He was now simply a target.

The target had barely looked up when Mason hit him

twice, center mass and head. The target went down and Mason moved up the stairs.

Reaction time, proximity. It was an equation now. Pure mathematics. Second target directly ahead, on the couch with the television on, his gun being tucked into his belt putting him at a disadvantage. Mason was already firing as he emerged from the stairway, moving against the left-hand wall, already setting up the third target like a pool player thinking two shots ahead. Mason put two shots just above the line of the furniture, catching the second target right after his first reaction—standing up— and before his second reaction—diving to the floor.

Movement on the right, the terrace, but first the hall-way, on the left, Mason already pressed against that wall. The third target was outside the office door. Mason listening for the footsteps. Hearing them. Waiting to see the barrel come first—an amateur's mistake, letting the shooter see you a tenth of a second before you see him. Mason had his own weapon ready, holding it perfectly steady with two hands. One beat, two, flash of barrel, fire. Mason already ducking into the hallway as he fired the follow-up shot, ripping through center mass just as the incoming shots from the fourth target riddled the walls around him.

Mason had planned for this. He knew he wasn't going to surprise all four of them.

He watched the office door for a few beats, waiting to see if Cole would come out. No sign of him. He refo-cused on the man who'd been stationed on the terrace and was inside the town house now but didn't pursue him down the hallway. Still in a defensive state of mind, the natural reaction after seeing three other men killed. Mason knew the man's heart was pounding. Adrenaline coursing through his bloodstream. He was carrying an assault rifle and he'd fire off a dozen shots at the slightest movement.

Mason ducked into the billiards room, grabbed the cue ball from the table, and edged his way back down the hallway. He didn't think the fourth target had moved yet—he placed him behind the island in the kitchen, ducked down behind it for cover.

He freed his right hand, inched forward just enough to see half of the kitchen. There was a door on the far side, with an ornate Art Deco window like something out of a Parisian bistro, leading into the pantry and wine cellar. Mason took a step back, kicked forward, and threw the cue ball. The glass shattered, and the first shots came back a tenth of a second later.

Mason stood tall for the best possible angle, cleared the corner edge with the Nighthawk, and focused on the kitchen island. The target had come up just enough and had swung his weapon to ten o'clock. He spotted Mason and was already swinging back, but it was too late. Reaction time plus muscle movement, no match for the speed of a .45 ACP bullet. The target's head snapped back from the impact. No need for a second shot.

Mason immediately swung the barrel back to his rear—he had left himself exposed, and Cole could have come out of the office and killed him. But the door was still closed.

Mason didn't have to check his weapon—he knew that he'd fired exactly seven times. He had three left.

He took out the tablet from his back pocket, checked the live surveillance feed from the office. Cole hadn't moved, was still seated behind the desk. It occurred to Mason that he might already be dead. But then he saw him blink and rub the swelling around his mouth. Both hands looked empty, but Cole was the smartest man Mason had ever known. He wouldn't sit there, defenseless, just waiting for him.

Mason went to the door, paused at the side where the

doorknob was for one second, then quickly switched to the other side. If Cole was going to fire through the wall, that's the side he'd pick. Mason reached across the door, tried the knob, moved it a quarter of an inch. It was unlocked. He turned it all the way and pushed the door open, ducking back out of the doorway.

No shots came.

He got down on one knee, peeked around the doorway from a low angle. Cole would have to come up over the desk to shoot him now. There was no motion. Mason stood quickly, the Nighthawk aimed squarely at Cole's chest.

This time, Mason wasn't just aiming at a target. He was aiming at a man.

"I knew you'd come here," Cole said. Mason could see the red band running along the left side of his jawline. A bruise under his left eye that would look worse the next morning.

But there would be no next morning for Darius Cole.

"Maybe you were right," Mason said. "Maybe you *didn't* change who I am. You just made me better at it."

"Before you do anything else," Cole said, "there's someone here who'd like to speak with you."

Mason froze, waiting for a movement behind him. But Cole simply reached out to the laptop in front of him and turned it around so that it was facing Mason.

There was a face on the screen. A white man in his mid-fifties. Dark hair cut close, with gray on the sides. The face radiated intelligence and self-assurance.

It was the face of a man in charge.

"Mr. Mason," the man said with the careful pronunciation of a man speaking a second language, with a vague yet indiscernible accent. "I've been waiting to meet you."

"Who are you?"

"Your employer."

Mason looked up at Cole. "What's he talking about?"

"Mr. Cole works for me," the man said. "Which means that you work for me, too. You have from the beginning."

Mason stood still, the Nighthawk still pointed at Cole's chest.

"I don't know who the fuck this is," he said, nodding to the screen, "but he's not going to help you."

"Mr. Mason," the man said, irritation creeping into his voice, "I need you to listen very carefully."

Mason looked at the tiny camera lens just above the screen. Wherever this man was, he was watching him. It made Mason want to pick up the laptop and destroy it.

"You compromised our Chicago operations," the man said. "It's going to cost me an enormous sum of money to fix it."

"Bill me," Mason said.

"I will. You're going to be working for me for quite some time repaying that debt. In fact, if we hadn't already invested so much—"

"I'm not doing anything for you."

Mason saw the man bristle at the interruption. He nodded to someone out of view of the camera, and then, in the very next moment, Mason was surprised to see another window appear on the screen. It took him another few seconds to understand what he was seeing: a man and a woman walking through an open house, looking at a vent above a gourmet stove, behind them a young girl entering the frame a beat later.

It was Brad and Gina.

And Adriana.

Mason couldn't speak. He kept staring at the image on the screen as the two people who were most important to him, and the man who had promised to protect them, moved to another room.

"This is the house that Mr. Parks put a down payment on today," the man's voice said. "As you can see, the surveillance cameras are already installed."

"No," Mason said, finally finding his voice.

When the window disappeared, Mason had the urge to reach into the screen to bring the image back so he could warn them, so he could yell to them to run away. The image was replaced by the original: the man sitting calmly in front of a camera. Mason noticed now that there was a large window behind him overlooking office buildings that could have been in any city. But it was daytime now, wherever he was. Somewhere thousands of miles away. Untouchable.

"You will continue to do exactly what I say," the man said. "You will execute the targets I give you. Mr. Cole has the details for your next assignment, along with a passport with your new identity."

Cole opened a desk drawer, took out a large manila envelope, and put it down on the desk in front of Mason.

"You'll be contacted again when you reach your destination. If you deviate from my instructions in any way, your ex-wife, her husband, and your daughter will be taken from their home. For the first twelve hours, they'll be bound and blindfolded on a concrete floor, close enough to hear each other but not to touch. Would you like me to describe the second twelve hours?"

Mason didn't respond.

"Good night, Mr. Mason."

The screen went blank.

Mason kept staring at it, unable to move.

This was the moment. The long silent moment when Nick Mason saw everything at once with a blinding white clarity:

Everything I thought I knew was a lie.

Whoever I thought I was working for.

Whatever I thought it would take to end this.
All of the people around me, the price they paid . . .
Lauren's life ruined.
Sandoval dead.
Diana dead.
Gina, Adriana . . . Maybe gone forever.
Because everything I've done . . .
My whole plan . . .
My whole fucking bullshit plan to finally be free . . .
It was all for nothing.
There was never an exit strategy.
Because there was never a way out.

Cole broke the silence. "This was your final audition," he said, nodding toward the dead bodyguards that littered the rest of the town house. "You passed."

"How big is this organization?"

Cole paused a beat and then said, "You'll never know."

Another beat, then Cole reached forward and closed the laptop. The sound of it clicking shut was a note of finality that hung in the air between them.

Cole got up from the chair behind the desk, came around to stand in front of him. In that moment, they were the only two men left in the world. Englewood and Canaryville. *Daimyo* and *samurai*. Mason looked down into Cole's eyes, the Nighthawk still hanging in his right hand.

"Take the envelope and get out of my city," Cole said. "Now if you'll excuse me, that blood is going to ruin the hardwood."

As Cole turned to leave the room, Mason raised the barrel of his gun. Cole stopped in the doorway.

"Nick," Cole said, still facing away from Mason, "do you really think this a good time to do something stupid?"

Mason didn't respond. Neither man moved.

"You're not going to shoot me in the back," Cole said.

"So turn around."

Cole shook his head, turned slowly to face Mason.

"What will they do to me?" Mason asked. "After everything they've invested . . ."

Mason watched Cole's face as he worked out the equation. Then the curtain came down when he arrived at the answer. For the first time since he'd met him, that day he was brought to his cellblock, Nick Mason saw raw animal fear in Darius Cole's eyes.

"Do you know how many men I killed for you?" Mason asked.

"We're done, Nick. You'll be killing for someone else now."

"You're right," Mason said. "This one's just for me. And Diana."

Mason squeezed the trigger three times, the last slugs in his clip tearing through Cole's body. Cole was driven back against the doorframe, his wide-open eyes staring back at Mason, until he finally slid to the floor.

Mason stood for a full minute, not moving. He waited to feel something, to experience some physical reaction to what he'd just done. But he'd been through too much, had already seen enough blood, to last a lifetime. Mason was immune to it now. He was empty.

Mason put the gun down on the desk, picked up the envelope, and stepped over Cole's body on his way out.

He stopped in the room next to the terrace, the room he'd been sleeping in ever since the day he walked out of that prison. He opened the nightstand drawer and took out the tattered photograph of Gina and Adriana, taken before he went to prison when his daughter was only four years old and life, however imperfect, made sense.

He left everything else behind. None of it really belonged to him, anyway.

Then he walked through the town house, past the

dead bodies and the drying pools of blood, down the stairs to open the front door for the last time and went out into the night.

TWELVE HOURS LATER, a 747 lifted off from O'Hare Airport and climbed into the sky. Its destination was Jakarta, the capital of the Republic of Indonesia. Nick Mason sat in a first-class window seat with everything he owned tucked into a carry-on bag under the seat in front of him.

As he looked out the window, the city of Chicago was spread out below him. It was a perfect clear day, so he could see the buildings of downtown, the seventy-one neighborhoods spreading out in three directions and the endless expanse of Lake Michigan to the east.

It was the only city he had ever loved. The only city he had ever called home.

Now he was leaving it, flying to the other side of the world. He didn't know what he'd be asked to do next. What new horror he'd have to face.

He didn't know who'd be waiting for him when this plane landed. Or if he'd ever come back.

He didn't know who he was anymore.

Or if he'd ever be free.

ACKNOWLEDGMENTS

Once again, this book would not have been possible without Shane Salerno, the one person who helped bring Nick Mason to life—and changed my life in the process. Thanks also to David Koll, Nick Carraro, Don Winslow, and everyone at The Story Factory.

I'm indebted to Joe Fitzpatrick, Assistant U.S. Attorney, Northern District of Illinois, and Chicago Police Detective John Campbell for all of your professional insight. And another big thank-you to Sara Minnich, Ivan Held, and everyone at Putnam.

I found the following books incredibly helpful, and highly recommend them:

The Perfect Kill: 21 Laws for Assassins, by Robert B. Baer

*WITSEC: Inside the Federal Witness Protection
Program*, by Pete Earley and Gerald Shur

*Convictions: A Prosecutor's Battles Against Mafia Killers,
Drug Kingpins, and Enron Thieves*, by John Kroger

Finally, to the people who've been with me since the beginning: Bill Keller and Frank Hayes, Maggie Griffin,

Jan Long, and Nick Childs. And more than ever, my wife, Julia, who keeps everything going, my son, Nicholas, and my daughter, Antonia. I will never be a good enough writer to express how lucky I am to have you as my family.

STEVE
HAMILTON

"Whatever he writes, I'll read. Steve Hamilton's that good."

—LEE CHILD